ANDY MALICE

A
RHAPSODY
INTERLUDE

A Novel

Published By Karnival Kingdom Entertainment Inc. By arrangement with the Author.

A Rhapsody Interlude
Copyright © 2012 Andy Malice

ISBN: 978-0-9879371-4-8

KARNIVAL KINGDOM
ENTERTAINMENT

****

To all of the answers we will always be without

Your
Greatest Nemesis
Will Always Be
Yourself

CHAPTER 1

A violent clap of thunder rattled through the building, waking her to a damp and stuffy room. Outside, a storm was assailing the city with relentless hostility.

There was a funny smell in the room, something like wax, and body odor, and empty bottles of beer. She wasn't sure of where she was, but for the moment, she didn't care. She was simply allowing the world to come into focus on its own terms. She lifted her head to look at the alarm clock by the bed. It was 4:38 a.m. She never could sleep peacefully in other people's beds. She never really could sleep, period.

She stared at the plaster ceiling, letting her thoughts come to order and form a perspective on things.

Last night had been painful.

Eventually, she threw aside the covers and sat on the edge of the bed, repulsed by the sight of the bedroom. It was dark, and dirty.

She closed her eyes and took in a deep breath, held it, then forcibly exhaled it through tightly pursed lips. It was a breathing trick she had learned in Karate class when she was a little girl, along with her younger sister, Katy. Her parents had forced her to enroll in the classes because of her vicious temper. They had hoped that a sense of personal discipline might help her control her ravenous anger. From the beginning, she felt an affinity to the breathing techniques. They helped her focus, but they were hardly a match for her monolithic temper.

She rubbed her chest and stretched out like a cat. Her naked legs swayed gracefully through the air like an angel preparing for flight.

Her name is Jessica Sanders.

She looked around and once again scoffed at the general back alley ambiance of the place. There was filth strewn across the room. Laundry, and beer, and candles, and bongs. She felt sad that she had been born into, what she considered to be, a generation thickly greased with superficial idiots.

She looked at the sleeping body next to her. She didn't know him. She couldn't even remember his name.

"Just another well built yuppy," she thought. "Way to go, Jess. Once again, great job."

She scanned the somber floor searching for her underwear amongst the heaps of crap everywhere. She wondered how long since the various pairs of underwear and socks hanging off the lamp shades were last washed. She wondered who this guy was. Was he funny? Was he charming? Was he, Mr. Right?

She chuckled at the thought of it. Mr. Right. She thought it was nothing more than a Hollywood born fairy tale. Like love forever, or faithful marriages. These days, she prided herself as a realist. She did not feel the need for anything else. Superstitions. Mystics. She thought there were enough problems and questions to deal with without the need to further distort things with guesses.

She soon found herself frustrated with her quest for underwear, and no longer cared either way. She just wanted to leave. She buttoned up her blouse and pulled on her pants. She tied her shoulder length hair into a pony tail and grabbed her chapstick from her tiny purse. Jessica hated purses. She had always kind of wished that she had been born a man. So much easier, she thought. No menstrual cycles. No make up. No pregnancies. No abuse. Not even a need to take care of most normal hygiene practices everyday.

"You're a guy," she'd tell friends. "Quit your bitching and put a hat on."

Her only curse, she thought, was that she had been born a pretty blonde girl with piercing blue eyes, the natural body of a model, and the intelligence of a supercomputer that wouldn't stop even if she tried.

Growing up, she had trouble connecting with boys, mostly

because of her strong, intuitive personality. She hated that most guys were wimps. She hated that most guys would turn into nervous balls of delirium when they tried to speak to her. She silently wished that she was a man, but not in any transvestite sort of way. More wishful thinking than anything else.

Her sister, Katy, wasn't as beautiful, or even as smart, or witty, but everyone always seemed so pleased with cute little Katy. Her sister was the girl with the hopeful outlooks on life. She was sweet, and friendly, and caring. She got the good grades, the teachers' approvals, and the charitable fund-raisers started and finished to the end with impeccable success.

All Jessica ever got were the boys.

"Sure, it sounds good," she'd tell her friends in highschool. "Yeah, it's real good having morons throw dumbass lines at you and pinch your ass while you're trying to focus on doing your job and not stabbing the bastard with his own fork."

They'd giggle, but there was so much truth to it.

Jessica grew up as the black sheep of the family. The odd sibling. She was the one who smoked pot, and enjoyed promiscuity in highschool. The one who went to concerts, and tried as much as possible to be a free spirited, go with the flow kind of kid. But it was always so hard. People didn't understand that she was different. She wasn't a bad person, she only perceived the world differently from most people. Nevertheless, she was the one forced to sit in front of her parents' frowning faces throughout the years, braving their disparaging stares, and their disappointed pupils. She never did care for any of it.

"Yes, I'm sorry I got caught smoking weed with bobby in the library stock room. Can I go now? I need to go smoke crack and sell my body on the internet after I sacrifice a goat to Satan."

Her parents would make the sign of the cross and yell at her disappearing figure.

"You're only sixteen, for Christ sakes! What the hell do you think you're doing? You need a serious change of attitude, missy, or you're going to fuck up your life real quick!"

Little did they know, Jessica had always expected that reaction from them, regardless of her actions.

She wasn't one for religion. She just didn't see the point.

When her parents asked her what she thought would happen after she died, she simply gave them the honest answer that came with thinking like a realist.

"Who cares? You're dead."

Her sister, Katy, was her parents' perfect little cookie cutter offspring. She believed it all with the same intensity as Jessica's rejection. Jessica felt that she could not allow herself to simply ignore what was natural to her. Her feelings. Her thoughts. Her outlook on the world. She couldn't understand the benefits of purposely regressing who she was. Everywhere she looked, she saw her truths. She often wondered how many people in the world had that ability. How many people could see their truths everywhere they looked? She decided that whatever the figure was, it was minuscule indeed.

Jessica had one last look at the drunken fool on the bed and sighed. Most people wondered why she insisted on being with guys who treated her badly, never bothered to call, used her, and dumped her. She never tried explaining it, but that was how she liked her life. She felt rather uncomfortable if a guy called her a week or two after she'd screwed him silly.

In reality, she was using them. She didn't hold any particular attraction to any of them, and was comfortably in the habit of running away at the first sign of anyone caring about her. She liked being single. There was no one to consult, no one to ask permission, no one to bother her.

Her sister would insist that she couldn't keep sleeping with random guys whenever her hormones got the best of her; that one day, she would have to settle down. But all Jessica's realist mind could ever say was, "Katy, this is the twenty first century, and we're pretty girls. We can do anything we want."

Her perception of reality was illusion-free. It was a thing many people said they longed for, but most were never quite brave enough to face. Refusing to be a hypocrite often drew a tough crowd.

"It's life," she would say. "Everything settles down eventually. When it doesn't, then you're dead, and you have nothing left to worry about."

But her sister could not wrap her head around that kind

of idea. Nor could her parents, for that matter. Or friends, or colleagues, or coworkers.

All Jessica could do was shrug and say, "I am who I am. I'll never apologize for it."

Ever since she was old enough to perceive the world on her own terms, she knew exactly who she was, and what she believed in, no matter how many people had tried to change her. She liked being alone in life, and rarely ever felt lonely. She was perfectly happy without the need to have someone else in her life to constantly entertain. She owned no pets, or plants. There had never been a need for any of it. She had her job. She had her books. She had everything she could ever want locked inside of her big brain, just waiting to be let out when the time came.

At twenty-nine years old, Jessica was a homicide detective, and one of the youngest in her department. Her greatest asset was her innate ability to piece things together. She was a master puzzler; a riddle solver. She was a shining star in her field– although–if she were to tell anyone the truth, she often couldn't believe how stupid some of the offenders' mistakes were.

Nevertheless, it was her only true passion in life. Puzzling over multi-dimensional enigmas with minimal clues, watching the pieces fall together, revealing the truth about what had happened. To her, that was what life was all about. It was her purpose.

She walked out of the strange, stinky room, headed down a long hallway, and came into a living room where half-naked people slept on variously sized couches. She still couldn't remember much from last night.

Last night had been painful.

She tugged on the door, but there was some kind of stupid trick she didn't know in order to open it. Some lift left and pull type of shit lazy people come up with instead of just fixing the problem in the first place. She pulled again, a little harder this time, and still, nothing happened.

"Fuck sakes!" she hissed.

She grabbed the knob with both hands and pulled on it with all of her strength; the entire contraption came flying out of the door and she landed on the ground with a loud thump. A few heads popped up in confusion from the living room, and Jessica let them have it.

"Fix your door, you morons! What's wrong with you people?"

She slammed the door hard against the back wall and stomped out of the apartment, fuming with rage. That rage was what her parents had forced her into Karate classes for. The same rage that could transform her into a blind and vicious beast with no mind to be reckoned with. It wasn't her fault. She was born with a big, towering temper.

When she got into the elevator, she found herself suddenly trapped in overwhelming sadness. She hated that her emotions could be so acute. When it was all too much, she smashed the emergency button, stopping the elevator, and melted to the floor in a fit of tears. She gasped, and snorted, and choked. She punched at the walls, and kicked at the doors. She couldn't hold back the pain anymore.

Once she managed to calm down, she resolved to staying on the floor of the elevator, staring at the wall for a long time before finally saying to herself,

"There's nothing you can do about it, you idiot. She's already dead."

CHAPTER 2

She stared at the phone while it rang, puffing on a cigarette. It rang a final time and then stopped. She inhaled a last drag from her cigarette and crushed it in the ashtray. She stretched out in bed with a book still clutched in her hand. She felt tired. She felt dark, and distracted. She wanted to take a bath, but then changed her mind and decided to continue reading.

She knew it was her boss calling, and she was debating whether or not to call him back.

Jessica's boss, Captain Briar, was a man quickly approaching retirement. He treated Jessica like his very own daughter, and immensely admired her professional talents. He was a very intelligent man, and had taken Jessica under his wing from her first day as active detective. Jessica also liked Captain Briar. He was a nice man, but what she truly liked about him, was that he treated her with the same honesty she appreciated in the world. Reality, illusion free, no matter how painful. He was smart enough to pick up on that.

He was a family man with 3 daughters and a growing brood of grand kids. He lived in a nice house, with an ample yard, and a picket fence. He'd been married for over thirty years. Jessica thought he was insane.

But, to each their own, she would say.

She thought about why she hadn't picked up the phone. She had a habit of not answering and calling back with everyone, but not usually for work. The main reason, she thought, was because she didn't want to hear Captain Briar's voice yet. She didn't feel quite ready to face her ugly job again.

As a realist, she perceived most murders with an indifferent understanding. In her opinion, murder was simply something that happened; a side-effect of the primitive human instincts trying to live in a sophisticated society. It was no mystery, and it never bothered her to investigate the limp rag dolls lying mangled on rocks, or gravel, or broken glass. Jessica had a saying to sum all of it up into a nice little package of understanding.

You can take man from the jungle, but the jungle will never leave man.

The setting had changed, what with all of those brick and mortar buildings, cars, people, planes, noise, pollution, social events, and still... Murder. Jessica believed that people were a lot like cats. You can feed one all you want, but the second it gets outside, it's going to kill something. It wasn't in the name of hunger or survival, but instinct. Fun.

The most skilled and ruthless killers made the best pets. Usually, Jessica managed to stay rather indifferent to all of those bodies she investigated night after night, day after day, more murder, more death, more reality. She didn't spend any time thinking about their families or how many children they may have had. She couldn't. Her job was to find killers. People thought she worked with the dead, but the reality was that she worked with the living. She was a hunter. The dead were only clues. Tiny glimpses of identity. The real challenge, the reason she even became a homicide detective, was for the hunt.

It was the thrill of hunting people while deprived of fundamental information. She didn't know what they looked like, where they lived, who their friends were, or who they slept with, but she nevertheless managed to find them. It invigorated her to piece the missing links together. It fascinated her that she could not explain where it all came from; it just sort of happened. A natural talent requiring no real input from her conscious mind.

She often loved things that she could not understand, mostly because it reminded her that there was so much more out there to be discovered. It gave her a purpose, and an understanding of what her situation truly was in the universe. Minimal. The eternal perception that cursed and blessed her all at once.

It was what it was.

She lit another cigarette and thought about Captain Briar's reaction to their newest case. Four gruesome murders had occurred over the last three days, each undoubtably committed by one man. It was evidence of a new serial killer in the vile downtown gutters. There was murder. There was fear. There was panic.

Jessica saw serial killers as flawed beings, betrayed by their own minds. Victims of their obsessions, and compulsions. She'd studied killers extensively in college, fascinated by the psychological machinations of a psychopath. Some were sophisticated, others were just angry, but this new killer, she had never heard of anything quite so–repulsive.

She yawned, closed her eyes, and held the image of Captain Briar's face in her mind. She always could remember things so vividly, so concisely. She was still undecided on whether it was a curse or a blessing.

At the first crime scene, the look on his face had disturbed her. It was the look of a man staring at things he had never conceived of. The savageness of the crime had moved something fundamental within him.

His pupils had dilated in horror, then contracted into tiny black dots, as if his mind was trying to protect itself from the inhuman brutality in front of him. He glanced at Jessica with enough horror to make Satan proud. It was a loss of innocence. Some final, naive assumption about the inherent goodness of human beings coming to the realization that it was completely full of shit. It was possible for people to be so evil. It was right there.

Proof.

A cleaning lady had found the body lying limp on the floor. When Jessica arrived at the scene, she didn't know what to think. Most of the crimes she investigated were–normal–if that word could be applied. A body raped and stabbed. One strangled. Another with a severed head and a chest ripped open. But this scene was different. It felt sinister, as though the killer's emotions were forever imbedded into the walls. As though whoever had done it, or whatever had, was not entirely human.

It was savage. When Jessica walked into the hotel room, the miasma of death instantly fouled her sinuses. Dry blood. Escaping gases. Dying cells.

The room was destroyed; evidence of a violent totalitarian rage. The furniture was obliterated, as if an explosion had gone off in the room, angry shrapnel lay everywhere. Anything that could have been broken, had been. The lamps were smashed, the linens were ripped to shreds, and the walls were half demolished. All of it, covered in dark red blood. She had seen a lot of blood in the past, but never that much.

On first inspection, the crime scene appeared to have some type of artistic meaning. An art so evil, so debauched, that viewing it would certainly become a belligerent nightmare that would never subside for the uninitiated. It was devoid of any sense of humanity, or reason.

The body itself was sprawled out methodically and placed face down without a splinter of debris, or even dirt, for a three foot border around it.

"Amazing," Jessica remarked.
"What's that?" Captain Briar asked.

"There isn't even a speck of dust around the body. It's absolutely clean."

"That... that it is," The Captain squirmed. He was so uncomfortable, yet so desperate to not let it show. She had never seen him so shaken.

"Are you okay, Cap?"
"... Yeah, yeah, Jess. I'm fine, thank you. Um, just ah... Just do your thing," he replied. "All right, everybody out of the room for the detective, please."

The photographers and dusters swiftly followed orders, leaving Jessica and her captain alone.

Tiny shards of glass crunched under her weight when she approached the body. At the victim's feet, she stopped, and allowed her first impression to saturate her mind.

There were no words to describe it.
The victim was female. Age unknown. Hair color... Blood. She was lying face down with her arms and legs spread open like Da Vinci's Vitruvian Man. The immediate area around her was

impeccably devoid of debris, but from there, fragments of broken things stretched away at all angles, giving the illusion that the body was bursting outward.

"This... This is..." Jessica frowned. "This is a living painting." Or rather, a death painting, she thought. She'd learned a long time ago to use the filter to her realist brain.

Captain Briar remained silent, and opted to stand at a distance, staring around the room with a dark pain in his eyes.

From an artistic point of view, the debris placed around the body was perfect. The colors were arranged in eye pleasing patterns, despite the horror. The angles were perfectly set with the edges of the body, so that the entire suspended explosion around her was rather fluent. She noted how intricate all of it truly was. Every piece of it had come from that room, but in the shape of a chair, or a table, or a lamp. Everything had been broken for a reason. It had been needed for, for this artistic massacre.

Jessica then focussed her attention on the woman's skin, already knowing that it was the highlight of the macabre canvas.

The body had been carved. Yes. Sculpted. Every inch of exposed skin had been, in some way, mutilated with what Jessica could only assume was a razor blade, or a scalpel. There was no doubt about it, the victim had been quite literally transformed into a piece of sick art, a painting. There were images cut into her; detailed lines and patterns more intricate than Jessica had ever seen in a tattoo, let alone in a dead woman's skin.

The killer, Jessica assuming only one, had filled each cut with colored charcoal, contrasting the blood red background. The overall image was an abstract mix of long lines arching and turning at odd angles.

Odd angles, yes, but not wrong. She associated it in her mind with musical theory; a symphony dominated by minors and sharps, but carried few majors. Ominous. Some of the lines twisted and merged together, while others spread away from them, meticulously changing colors as they went. Painfully precise.

On her back, the lines met near the shoulders and continued down the arms, down the hands, down the fingers.

From her buttocks, the lines shifted shapes and crawled down her legs like ugly vines with graceful movements. Down her feet. Down her toes. Some cuts seemed purposefully peeled back, and made to stay that way for effects of depth and contrast. It was all beautifully disturbing.

Jessica stayed in the room for nearly two hours after Captain Briar had decided that it was all too much, and politely excused himself. He'd never shown weakness to Jessica before. She felt bad for her Captain.

She stayed and analyzed. She stayed and thought about it. She absorbed it all into her mind.

She could still conjure up a perfect carbon copy of the entire scene in her head at will. She could trace the lines down on paper from memory alone. Sometimes, she hated her memory. Sometimes, she hated her big brain.

Her phone rang again and snapped her out of her thoughts. She merely glanced at it and decided to ignore it again. She knew it was Captain Briar. The good Captain had delivered a lot of bad news to Jessica in the past, it was all part of the job, but she wasn't sure if she wanted to hear any more today.

Last night had been incredibly painful.

She quickly tippy toed to the bathroom, and then returned in similar strides, crawling back under the blankets. She enjoyed the way the blankets instantly wrapped her in comfort. She laid her head down on the pillow and closed her eyes.

CHAPTER 3

The first body left experts grasping for answers. The art consultants were flabbergasted. The psychologists were baffled. The crime scene had no evidence to work with, no prints, no fabrics, no forensics. It was what it was.

The fear was rampant.

The media exploded with reports of a possible new serial killer, and caused widespread panic throughout the city. Inevitably, hundreds of tips poured in from the public, but all leads proved unfounded. Jessica knew she had to stop this killer, but she didn't know where to look for him. She felt frustrated, helpless, knowing there was nothing she could do until another murder happened. And if he didn't make a mistake then, she would have to wait some more. Her mind churned with chagrin at the thought of it. Without even realizing it, she had become the lead investigator in the biggest ongoing murder investigation in the country, and she had nothing to show for it.

People talked about it incessantly. The case was on everyone's tongue, on every corner, and on every news media cover.

The Fleshcrafter is out there!

The Fleshcrafter. That was the name the media had given this fool. This demented artist. Jessica felt repulsed by it. It was nothing more than a grand name to sell advertising spots. A name that caused a vast spectrum of reactions ranging from absolute terror, to irrational methods of defense, to profitable merchandising.

Jessica hated people's misguided obsessions with making

psychopaths famous around the globe. There was always someone willing to smack a killer's face on a T-shirt and sell it for thirty dollars a piece. She often wondered who was sicker, the killer, or the guy peddling memorabilia that had no other purpose than to carry on demented ideas, solidifying infamy. Killers who hadn't done a useful thing in their lives, were suddenly signing million dollar book deals to gloat about how great it was to rape, mutilate, and kill people.

She often found herself wondering why people said they enjoyed filling their lives with happiness. From her vantage point, as a detective of horrible actions, all she saw were people addicted to sorrow, and pain, and suffering. No one read books about how great it was to fall in love with five different people, but chop their heads off with a fire poker, and you've just hit the jackpot. Which actors would you like in the movie?

The Fleshcrafter. Every time she heard the name, something sinister stirred inside of her. Only a day after the first murder, a second body was found.

This scene was no less dramatic, and had caused a darker shade of terror to creep into the good Captain's eyes. He was forced against his will to admit that it was real, that this killer truly was that evil.

The murder occurred in an apartment complex that barely passed safety regulations. The main lobby was missing huge chunks of sheet rock from the walls, and the carpet was either moist, or ruined with ancient vomit stains.

The door to the apartment had been kicked in with enough force to rip the hinges from the frame, but someone had forcibly jammed it back into place. The apartment itself was tamed with so much filth, Jessica wasn't able to tell offhand if anything had been disturbed. It was all too chaotic.

She stepped inside, glanced at the door frame, and joined Captain Briar in the filthy living room.

He said, "The neighbors called in the smell. I don't know, coroner says four, maybe five days. Jesus, it's hot as hell in here. I need some air."

He stepped out, feeling ill, but Jessica immediately got to work. Before heading for the bedroom, where the body was, she scanned the living room intently, looking for evidence of a mistake by the killer. Anything was possible, but nothing stood out to her. The place was a jungle of acrid filth, the slime of degenerate humans. Who could tell?

From the hallway leading to the bedroom, she saw red light ominously dousing the inside of the room. She stood inside the door jamb, and lost her breath at the sight of The Fleshcrafter's blatant lunacy.

The body was another woman. She was found naked, on her back, with extinguished eyes. Unlike the first victim, she had been placed on the bed with her head arched back unnaturally, her arms stretched out on either side, and her legs bent at the knees, the soles of her feet resting on the bed.

She was a tiny thing. Jessica guessed maybe five foot tall, and no more than one hundred pounds. The cause of death matched the last; a punctured throat.

Coup de grace.
A fantastic horror.

As far as Jessica could tell, the girl was meant to look as if she were in a marsh. Splintered sticks stood crudely from every angle around the bed, and the floor was decorated with debris, glued there with blood. Some of the standing sticks were decorated with green fabric, but on the floor between them, the killer had systematically placed lamps and covered them with red pieces of cloth. Everything glowed with a heavy, devastating shade.

A blunt disturbance. A visual shock.
Extreme care had obviously been taken in the placement and direction of everything in the room.

Consistent with the first crime scene, the majority of the room was covered in blood. Some places looked like a paint brush had been used; she did not fully dismissed the possibility.

Jessica approached the body with due diligence, and found herself staring at a scene so haunting, it seemed to press on something primitive in the gallows of her mind. Something dark. Once again, she felt evil pulsating from the walls like an afterglow; killer radiation. She felt like a heavy doom still lingered in the air, poisoning her lungs, infecting her mind.

"Truly are the artist, aren't you, you son of a bitch," she said.

The woman's body was painted white, but the cuts in her skin were not colored, rather, they were shaded gray and black for effect. What an effect. It was artistically appealing, but humanly repulsive.

Jessica couldn't remember a time before when something to crept into her mind and made her feel so disgusted. She couldn't remember a time when–anything–had made her swallow a heavy slab of innate fear she could not really define. But it was there. Some basic fear this monster had evoked.

Captain Briar stuck his head into the room. "You okay in here, Jess?"

Jessica said nothing. She was transfixed in thoughts. Perplexed.

"Jessica?"

"She's a swan," she replied.

"A swan?"

"Yeah," she said. "A goddamn fairy tale. It's a piece meant to be viewed from above. She's coming out of a marsh, transformed like a butterfly, and spreading her wings for the first time."

"What about the cuts?"

She took in a heavy breath and let it escape slowly, exactly like she had learned in Karate class all those long years ago.

"They're feathers," she said, almost indifferently.

Poor old Cap was astounded. He felt the same crawling repulsion as Jessica. She felt it as a little girl growing up with her favorite fairy tales. Captain Briar felt it as a father, as an officer, and as a good man.

"Feathers?" he replied. "Good God, is there no conscience left?"

"I don't think there was any to begin with."

***

She thought about that now while lying in bed. The absence of a personal conscience. Psychopathic behavior. She wondered if this killer was a normal man, carrying on a normal life, with a good job, and a nice little family, indulging in a few good killings on weekends. A failed artist? A successful artist? A disturbed artist.

She remembered the pain in Cap's voice. The underlying fear. There was something especially disturbing about a killer turning the most vicious murder anyone had ever seen into a twisted fairy tale. It was wrong.

She remembered the foul feeling she had once she realized what the scene was. He was trying to tell a story. He was trying to reach out. Somehow.

She felt frustrated by this killer. Every lead was a dead one. Every tip unfounded. No one knew a thing. Not a description. Not even a sound. She thought about the door, wondering how it was possible that no one had heard that kind of violent outburst on an apartment door. Evidently, no one had.

All she had to work with were guesses. She researched history books, trying to find a connection somehow, somewhere. But that was the problem. Where? Would a connection be made through art history or through surgical ability? Would his story suddenly be laid out for her to discover in some ancient text filled with weird traditions and beliefs? Or worse, was he simply making it up as he went?

Jessica already knew the truth, no matter how badly she tried to push it out of her mind. This killer, whoever he or she was, wasn't following any kind of predetermined path. Those scenes were the result of deranged introspection. Intense personal torture. Personal hell.

Her burning urge to hunt this killer was in full force, but she had no concrete direction to turn. The bodies stood out in her mind, but mostly because of the incredible theatrics. She was more enthralled with this killer than anything else. She wondered how much time he had spent organizing those intricate crime scenes. How many hours? Days, maybe? How could someone do that? How could someone stay there?

"Fearless," she decided. "He is fearless."

Fearless indeed.

She went through the details incessantly, trying to find a connection. Trying so hard to get to this person, this killer, but all she could come up with was a sad truth.

Once again, nothing would be clear until more terrible scenes were discovered.

It was what it was.

CHAPTER 4

Jessica's body jerked violently at the sound of her phone. She had fallen asleep while lying in bed and thinking about the case. Confused and weary, she checked the caller I.D.

Captain Briar was calling her again; he'd already left three messages. Still not feeling the urge to answer, she ignored the call and sat up on the edge of her bed, staring at the alarm clock in a stupor. She had only dozed off for about twenty minutes, but the nap had drastically altered her mood. She was feeling irritable now, frustrated with the lack of progress in her investigation.

She sighed, yawned, and then thought about when she was a little girl. Her parents used to take her and her sister camping every July. The whole family would pack up coolers of food, toys, and fishing gear, and take a three hour road trip out of the suburbs and into the woods. They would stay in her grandfather's old cabin, nestled neatly in a swath of tall pines that edged a vast, serene body of water known as Mosquito Lake.

As children, she and her sister used to get so excited about the whole thing, and would spend the week long holiday chasing each other on the beach, fishing from the dock, and roasting marshmallows over the licking flames of the fire pit. Those were some of her happiest childhood memories. Everyone together, happy, and having nothing to worry about aside from the looming last day of the holiday approaching with every minute.

She hated how growing up changed things. Sometimes, she hated how time could alter everything if you waited long enough.

Everything was different now.

She thought about last night. It had been the most emotionally painful night she'd every experienced.

Yesterday afternoon, she received an urgent call from Captain Briar.

"Dear God in heaven!" His tinny voice had panted. "Jessica... Jessica? You need to come to my office, immediately."

"But..."

"Right now, Jess! Please!"

"All right, all right, I'm coming."

When she heard his voice like that, she intrinsically knew that something was very wrong. Something very bad had happened. Fifteen minutes later, she was dressed, and on her way to see the good Captain.

She felt nauseous while she drove, consumed with a horrible, undefined feeling that told her that she was in store for news that was about to change her life forever.

At the precinct, she felt like the hallway leading to Captain Briar's office was somehow longer, darker. She knocked quickly on his door and walked in before he could answer, catching him with his face buried in his hands. All doubt had instantly been removed, she knew the news was personal.

"Jess..."

"What happened?" she demanded.

"Umm. Just have a..."

"Goddamn it, Cap! What's going on?"

Captain Briar remained silent for a short moment, but it had felt like an eternity to Jessica.

"We ah..." He swallowed hard. "Jessica, we have two new bodies."

"Two?" she said quickly. "Still our guy?"

"Yes," he whispered.

She frowned and cocked her head to the side. There was something else he wasn't telling her. Something he was trying to delay.

"What is it, Cap? Just spit it out already!"

Captain Briar inhaled a deep breath and said,

"Jessie... One of the victims, is Katy... Your... Oh, God... Your sister is dead, Jessica. I'm so sorry."

CHAPTER 5

She stared vacantly at the television, trying to turn off her brain. Curled up on the couch, she cuddled a blanket, doing her best to keep her mind from running off with introspective realities. Harsh.

After Captain Briar's phone call had jolted her out of dreams and back into reality, she found herself restless with a racing mind. Now, sitting in her living room in the glare of the television, unable to keep from thinking, she found her mind wandering through memories of her past.

When she was younger, she often resented her parents. She had no rational reason for it, they were good people after all, with good jobs, and good intentions in the world; but they had never truly understood their eldest daughter. They weren't able to wrap their heads around what, or who, Jessica truly was. She was a person full of strength, of passion, with a seething distaste for what people, like her parents, considered normal in the world. They had wanted her to prepare for a good career, meet a nice man, get married, have kids, buy a house, and spend the rest of her life, in Jessica's eyes, tending to the mundanity of suburbia until she loathed her boring husband, her stupid kids, and the hundreds of thousands of dollars she still owed for living in a pile wood with shingles on top.

She found the very idea of it repulsive. Marriage. Family. She carried no interest in planning her life out into infinity. To her, life was a series of chaotic probabilities with the power to swing freely in any direction without the slightest concern for anyone–what kind of idiot was arrogant enough to think that they could plan any of it? She spent no time glorifying the past, or over-estimating the future. She was alive today, aware of the universe today; nothing else mattered.

Because of this, her parents worried about her, and tried to push her in directions she resisted. But they had loved Jessica and her sister nonetheless, no matter how badly Jessica had hurt them. She had never intentionally meant to hurt anyone, she just was who she was. Everyone had the option of either accepting, or rejecting it. Eventually, when it seemed like no one was capable of understanding her, she simply stopped trying to explain.

Sometimes, she still felt badly about that; as though there was a way that she could have been closer with her parents, but she had always failed to find the necessary bridge of understanding.

Jessica's parents had died instantly when their car was flattened by a semi only six short years ago.

Even now, whenever she thought about it, her heart sank terribly. She felt like there was so much that had been left unsaid, undone, and unsettled.

The news of their death had devastated her. It had made her feel like an idiot for all of the times she had lashed out at them for stupid reasons. All they had ever wanted to do was help. She knew that now, but she was too young, and too naive, to know it then. She still didn't feel like that was a reasonable excuse, but it was all she had.

By now she had dealt with it as best as she could, but her sister, Katy, was dealt a mean blow by the news. The chaotic probabilities of her life had pushed her into the clutches of confusion and depression as a result.

Slowly, she regressed from her life, and became a recluse. Hiding from the world. Hiding from reality. When the accident happened, Katy was pregnant, and married to a dentist. Friendly. Bondable. Boring as shit in Jessica's opinion, but it wasn't her life to deal with.

Before long, she miscarried, her marriage dissolved, and all of the life loving passion she was known for dribbled out of her as if she had sprung a leak in her heart. She became a dark, hostile, and bitter being. Jessica always wondered how someone like her sister, so sweet and caring for others, could be faceplanted into the gutters by life itself.

Chaotic probabilities.

It was what it was.

She missed her terribly.

Jessica lit another cigarette and stared vacantly at the smoke rising into the air. She sighed and swallowed a hard slab of emotional pain to the pit of her stomach. She felt helpless, and full of rage. She felt a burning urge for vengeance, for justice. She was now all alone in the world. As a teenager, she had wished for nothing more; now realized, she simply wished there was a way to start over from the beginning.

Yesterday, after receiving the news of her sister's death, she hadn't even asked for details before lunging out of Captain Briar's office. She raced to her car and drove maniacally to her sister's house. The Captain had tried to stop her, tried to explain that she couldn't investigate her own sibling's death, but Jessica hadn't heard a thing.

On her way, her phone rang incessantly. She knew it was Captain Briar. She ignored it anyway.

When she arrived, her heart seized at the sight of countless emergency vehicles parked chaotically in front of the house. Getting out of the car and approaching the house, her phone was still ringing, and she finally answered it.

"I know what I'm doing," she hissed like a snake.

"Goddamn it, Jessica! This is–"

"He is my killer! He's mine, and I am going to catch him!"

"I know that, Jessica. I just think that maybe..."

"I'm smarter than he is! I will catch him!"

She hung up on him, his words lost on some obscure channel.

Defiantly, she stood in front of her sister's house, and made it a point to remember the happy memories first. To remember the good times, and the laughs, and the love, before going inside and once again shifting realities.

She climbed the front stairs with a lowered head, and entered the house.

If Jessica had ever felt any real passion for wanting someone put to death for their actions, this was her first experience with it, and it hurt like hell.

In the foyer, she suddenly felt like she couldn't breathe. Her throat was clamping up, and it made her feel weak, despite the furious adrenaline rushing through her body.

She had loathed it. She had feared it. But she had done it anyway.

Reality was grossly uncaring.

Heading into the kitchen, she savored the common smell of artificial lilac oils. She thought about how humans associated smells with people and events. She thought about how some people said it was the thing they missed most about a lost loved one. She thought about anything, except what she was about to do.

She noticed a puddle of vomit on the hallway floor, but knew it hadn't come from the killer; it had come from some idiot cop who couldn't handle the scenery inside the room.

From the hallway, she ordered everyone out, and braved the stares of those who knew. Those who couldn't believe that she was there. Those who wanted to give condolences, but knew better.

With everyone out, she stood at the door, closed her eyes, and practiced her breathing technique. When she opened her eyes again, something somber came over her. The sight of the room made her skin crawl uncomfortably, despite her firm attempt at not letting it get to her. It was punishing.

She scanned the room with the dedicated eyes of a nocturnal predator. Her killer's work was obvious. The room was decimated–decorated–with shattered furniture, and endless blood, and a horribly mutilated body, and once again, she felt the evil. That same evil had been present at the other scenes. It was embedded into the walls so deep that every one of those buildings would have to be burned to the ground–especially this one.

The killer had placed a strobe light in the far right corner of the room, it was still pulsing slowly, sickeningly highlighting the reality of it all.

Repulsed, and fighting to keep her breathing stable, she decided to investigate The Fleshcrafter's newest work of art.

Her sister.

He had hung her naked body from the wall with a giant spike driven through her chest. She looked like a tattered and torn angel, which Jessica guessed, was the point. Blood had gushed from her chest, and dried to a hard, dark crust. On the wall next to the body, the killer had stabbed jagged sticks at odd angles, giving Jessica the impression that the body was coming at her.

The killer had lifted her arms and rested them onto sticks into an inviting embrace. He'd driven tiny shards of a shattered mirror into her skin, into her eyes, covering her entire body.

More hellish art.

She scrutinized the body repeatedly, methodically, sometimes only seeing her own pain filled eyes being thrown right back at her by the countless mirrored shards. She inspected the lines, the intricacies were still as amazing as ever. So precise. A complete lack of any and all hesitation.

She stared at her toes, and remembered them from when they used to chase each other on the beach all those happy years ago. When she finished with her feet, she stood up to go over her again, when something out of place caught her eye, and Captain Briar entered the room behind her, panting.

"Jessie?"

"Don't, Cap! Just leave me alone."

"Please, Jessica. This isn't healthy, or even ethical."

"Fuck ethics," she said. "You want to help, Cap? Why don't you come here?"

Captain Briar's face turned pale, albino. The personification of terror. He was a man standing at ground zero for everything he'd never thought possible in his life.

"Jesus, God, in heaven," he panted. "What in God's name could..."

"None of the other victims were raped, right?" she asked.

"... Ah, no," he answered, unable to remove his eyes from what was before him, more out of fear that it wouldn't go away anyway.

"Come here and look at this," she said.

Captain Briar approached with slow, timid steps, and stopped at a comfortable distance away from the disaster.

"Wh... What is it?" he asked, obviously captivated by her mirrored eyes. The sadness in his face was eternal. Jessica wondered how many times this poor man would think about his own 3 daughters in rooms like these. The emotional torture crushing.

"Where am I looking?" he asked.

"Look at her crotch."

"Please, Jessica," he immediately protested. "I don't want to look at your sister's..."

"Just look," she demanded. "Near the top. Do you see it? Is that what I think it is?"

"It's... It's a..."

"It's a pubic hair," she said. "And it's not hers."

CHAPTER 6

She rustled around in bed and tried to stop thinking. She wished she could stop. She wished that Captain Briar would stop calling her. She wished that everyone would just leave her alone. But her mind had never cared about what she wanted in the past, why would it start now? She turned onto her side and sunk into the pillow, thinking. Always thinking.

In her sister's bedroom, Jessica was locked into a trance while collecting, bagging, and sealing the pubic hair to get it to the lab. She would not accept the slightest deviation.

No sooner had she bagged the hair, did she demand the address of the fourth victim in a fierce argument with her Captain. Reluctantly, he gave it to her, and before anyone could even say her name again, she was gone.

When she arrived at the second crime scene of the day, the situation outside was nearly identical to the first. The same disheartened people stared blindly around themselves, but could only see what they had inside of the building.

Passing through the chaos of emergency lights, she climbed the stairs to the main door and took the elevator up to the seventeenth floor, alone; only her lunatic thoughts for company.

When she entered the condo, she was shocked. The victim was naked on the living room floor, broken into a fetal position, with her hands together against her chest. Defeated. It was a drastic change from the other scenes. The killer had obviously taken great care in considering which items to break and turn into sadistic art, and which ones to save.

Instinctively, she felt like something fundamental had changed in the pattern, but there was no doubting the killer. On first inspection, the overall tone of the new palette seemed much less sadistic. It all was far less intricate and theatrical, but she couldn't help but feel like the killer had spent far more time with this woman than with any of the others.

There was a severe lack of cuts on the body, but she wasn't able to determine why. Had he been discovered? Scared off? She didn't think he would be frightened by anything. She didn't think he would hesitate for a second on anything, and especially not on something he put his entire soul into. She wondered if there was a word to describe a soul like that. Was it evil, or was it tortured? Was it valid, or was it random lunacy?

It was what it was.

Though the cuts in the victim's skin were simple, they'd still been inflicted with unflinching preciseness. The image itself was of a chain, strewn from her knee, up her thigh, to her hip, where the chain ended with what Jessica was sure was half a heart; the other identical half was on her arm, running down from her shoulder.

"Broken heart?" Jessica whispered. "Did you love this one? I think you loved this one very much. Just look at all the love in here."

Around the body was very little of anything. There were a few shards of broken ceramic placed on the ground, but they seemed to be only for background effect. Nothing about it was as dramatic as the other scenes. She took a deep breath and realized the intended softness of the scene. It was meant to be soft. It was meant to be simple. Pure, if that word could be applied.

Aside from the body's lack of cuts, and the room's lack of excessive debris meticulously organized, there wasn't much more of interest she could see upon first inspection. Although, she was certain this victim had also been raped.

The woman's general position, with her arms bent at the elbows and curled back to her chest, caused Jessica to think of how her sister used to do the same thing when she was overjoyed, or over saddened. She used to hold her hands to her heart. Jessica wondered how sad this woman had been. She wondered who she was. She had never done that before. She wondered why.

Standing over the body, she felt tired, and angry, and confused, and suddenly had the urge to go out for a hard drink. She wanted to get drunk. She wanted to destroy herself.

But before she was able to leave the room, something caught her eye. It was the woman's hands. The way they'd been pressed up to her chest, they seemed... Unnatural. She could see that the seam created by her hands against her chest was glued with blood, but it wasn't from her punctured throat. In fact, there was very little blood overall, almost like the killer had taken the time to clean her.

"Hey, I need forensics in here," she called out. Timidly, two members of the team entered the room and stared at Jessica with broken eyes.

"Hi," she said. "Can you guys come around to the other side here, please? I ah... I need you guys to pull her arms back."

Their faces dropped. They weren't keen on being in there, but neither was she. Her sister had just died. Her sister had just been mounted to a wall like an animal by the same son of a bitch who had broken this woman. Jessica had trouble caring about other people's feelings to begin with, she was hardly sympathetic in that moment.

"Now, come on," she said. "One in front, one on the back, and pull."

They got down to their knees and grabbed hold of the girl's shoulders and arms. They pulled, and, after some resistance, the arms came free and back. The man who'd been pulling on her arms puked, the other left in a fit of tears, but Jessica had stood like a marble statue. She never blinked. She only stared.

"Look at all the love," she finally said once again. When they had pulled her arms back, when they had come free and away from her chest, she was holding her heart. She was literally, holding her heart. The monster had cut it right out of her.

Jessica felt her hands shaking. She hated it. She never shook. She never allowed it. She was unmovable. She was untouchable. She was a cold soul.

But someone far colder than she was out there, and she needed to catch him.

***

She left the condo building feeling far more disturbed than she could ever have imagined possible. She refused to be beaten by her own mind. She refused to let others beat her mind. She refused all of it, but it did nothing to make her feel any less disgusted.

By the time she returned to her car, an ugly storm was moving over the city. She barely paid attention to anything while she drove. She stared forward and drove slowly. She kept to one lane and only turned when it was logistically necessary. She drove around the city for two hours. No destination. No direction. Just thinking. Just letting it all sink in.

When she tired of driving, she pulled into a small, obscure strip mall bar. One of those shady places always lurking in the corners. She went inside and sat at the bar feeling tired, beaten. She hated herself.

She ordered whisky shooters, and the bartender looked at her in slight amusement.

"Rough night?" he asked.

"Oh, no, it's been fantastic," she replied. "I'm just a really big alcoholic."

The bartender chuckled, lined up three shooter glasses, and filled them. She downed them without flinching. This was not her first visit with strong drink.

"Fill 'em up," she told the bartender.

He did. She drank. She demanded more.

It wasn't long before a long trail of horny geeks had formed, but she was in no mood for the riffraff, and in no mood to entertain.

She shut every one of them down in sequence, and then had a shot. Shut 'em down, have a shot.

A few hours later, once happily smashed by healthy amounts of whisky, she simply did what needed to be done. It was what it was. She stumbled into the arms of some unsuspecting yuppy.

"Hi," she said.

"Hi there," he smiled big.

"I'm really drunk," she said.

"Are you now?" he replied. "I'm doing pretty good myself. Are you here alone?"

"That depends," she said. "You want to hang out with me?"

His face blazed with surprise. Jessica liked getting right to the point of things. No need for dancing around the bushes.

He then said, "So ah... Do you want a drink or something?"

To which Jessica answered, "No. I want you to take me to your place."

He told her his name, but she hadn't listened, or cared. She followed him to a taxi, giggling and laughing with him on the way home. They crashed through the door just like one of those stupid Hollywood romance movies and threw their clothes around the room like lust filled beasts.

She couldn't remember much more after that. When a clap of thunder woke her up in his bed, dizzy, and confused, she began feeling the devastation from the loss of her sister. After leaving his apartment, she collapsed to the floor of the elevator, finally allowing the ravaging grief to overtake her. She felt so alone. Eventually, after crying, and clawing, and kicking at the walls, she was able to compose herself, and let the elevator go down to the main floor. She felt ashamed. She felt ugly and sad. She hailed a cab back to her car and drove home, zoned out with emotions.

At home, she showered, crawled into bed, and stared at the wall with her head on her pillow. She had tried reading to focus her mind on less painful things, but then Captain Briar had started calling, and she was sent through another painful reliving of the recent events in her life.

Everything seemed so dark. Every direction, blocked. She wasn't dozing off anymore, but inside, she was tired. Exhausted. She needed to find an answer, but had nothing to work with aside from a pubic hair.

How? Where?

He left no prints, no fabrics, nothing usable. He never cut himself and left a drop of blood. He hadn't raped the first two victims, but she was positive he had the last two. She wondered if he had planted the pubic hair, or if he had finally made his first mistake. She thought that would feel like some kind of cosmic justice at the very least. Her sister being the one holding the key to catching the sick artist.

Romantically sinister.

Still on her couch, staring blankly at the television, her phone rang again. Frustrated, annoyed, she finally picked it up.

"Yeah, Cap, hi. I'm sorry, I was sleeping," she said.

"How are you, Jess?" he asked, his voice delicate, concerned.

"I'm fine," she said. "Thank you."

"Ah... Listen, Jess, you know they'll want you off of this case, but, I know, I know, whether they officially put you on the case or not, you'll still be on the case, won't you?"

"He is my killer," she replied.

"Well," he said. "Listen, there will be some questions coming down about conflicts of interest and ethical grounds, but before you get to hear about any of them, we've got identification on the fourth victim. Nicole White, was her name."

"Okay..." she said, obviously expecting more.

"She was a shrink, Jess. Thought you might want to check out her office before the big hammer comes down."

"I'm on my way now!" she said, and hung up.

CHAPTER 7

Nicole White's office was a twenty minute drive from Jessica's apartment building. She drove there wondering if the killer had been one of her clients. A tantalizing thought.

She held deep hope for this victim, her murder had carried heavy overtones of love. Clients falling in love with their therapists was classic. Broken souls who felt like the first person who seemed to care about them, meant they were meant to be together.

Talk about job hazards.

The waiting room outside of Nicole White's office was what could be expected of a therapist's office. A small space subtly layered with irrelevant magazines, leather couches, faux oak furniture, carpeted floors, the aura of quiet, the psychological library.

Inside the office, where Nicole White met with clients, was about the same. A quiet, safe atmosphere. A simple desk. A long bookshelf built into the wall holding mostly collections of books of the same size and color. Encyclopedias. Reference.

There were two extra wide filing cabinets pushed up against the far wall. Jessica opened the top drawer of one and riffled through client files. Faceless names. Printed nightmares.

From the filing cabinets, she moved to the victim's desk. A simple oak desk with drawers on either side and a computer sitting quietly on top. She went through the drawers looking for anything that might catch her eye. Nothing but a stapler, a box of paper clips, extra printer ink, mindless papers, and...

There was a corner missing from the bottom drawer, and when she slid a finger into it and pulled, it came out, revealing a

Duo-tang underneath.

"Bingo!"

The cover was plain black with intersecting red ribbons, like a dark present from hell. It said nothing except, "My diary."

She quickly glanced around the room. Everything around her would be removed, riffled through, examined, and tampered with. There were processes to follow.

She also thought about what Captain Briar had told her on the phone. They would want to take her off of this case. She could maybe beat it by accepting conditions, but it wouldn't be easy. The thought was unsettling. She would have fought hard for this case even before it had become so personal, but now that it was, she was determined to catch The Fleshcrafter even if it meant that she would be killed in the process.

The thought of all that red tape seemed unnecessary. The diary she held in her hands, she knew, had the potential of being a big deal. There was a very real possibility, although wishful, that it could hold the secret to finding her monster. She knew that...

"Jessica," Captain Briar came waltzing into the room and headed directly for her.

She didn't know why she did it. She didn't understand it, but she felt like she had to. She slipped the diary into her jacket pocket.

"Hi, Cap," she half-smiled. "How's it going?"

Captain Briar gently cupped her face in his hands and gave her a deep, warm stare.

"You doing okay, kiddo?" he asked.

"Yeah," she said.

"Yeah? Do you need anything? You know you can always come to me for..."

"I know, Captain. Thank you very much. I appreciate it."

Captain Briar straightened up and looked around the room.

"Anything evident?" he asked.

"No," she said. "But there's a lot of work ahead of us. Look at all the files; can't wait for the fun."

"You know, Jessie. Why don't you take a holiday?"

"Because I don't need a holiday. I need to catch my killer," she replied.

"All right, all right, just suggesting."

"I'm sorry, Captain. I just need to think."

"Well, don't think too much, poor girl. It causes emotional traps."

"I know, Cap. I know. Have you heard anything from the lab yet?"

"Not yet. You'll be the first to know," he replied.

She directed her attention toward the bookshelf. Aside from encyclopedias, it was mostly filled with books about the mind and the spirit. Self-help. Nice gig.

She pulled out a few books and read the covers, looking in, and behind, and under them. She contained her excitement quite well, she thought. Everytime she moved, she could feel the weight of the diary in her pocket. She was wishfully convinced that something useful was in there. Something... Somewhere.

She continued pulling out books and checking them. Flipping the pages. Having a good look. She put a book back into its slot and pulled the one next to it, when she noticed something falling to the floor with a soft landing on the carpet below. She bent down to look at it.

"Ah... Captain," she said.

"Yeah, Jess?"

"I think he was in here."

"What? Why?"

"See this?" she said, holding it with a pair of tweezers. "That's a shard from a mirror. The son of a bitch was in this room. He was here," she swallowed hard. "Right after he killed Katy."

CHAPTER 8

Early the following morning, Jessica was called in for a meeting with her Captain. She already knew what it was about, and that it would involve the Police Commissioner trying to tell her how to do her job. It was about her sister, and her being the led detective on this case.

She was nervous about the whole thing. No matter what happened, she had to remain on the case. Her inability to view any new crime scenes would be a debilitating blow to her hunt. She needed to see them. Fortunately, at least at the moment, she felt like the odds were stacked in her favor, given that she was the one who had processed, interpreted, and pieced together the first four crime scenes. But she would still need to convince them.

She parked her car and kept to herself while making her way up to Captain Briar's office. Her stomach was tied in nervous knots, but the moment she walked into the office, she suddenly felt like she had a chance at getting away with it; though it wasn't entirely out of arrogance on her part, it was mostly due to the other person in the room, the expected Commissioner, who was already googly eyeing her.

"Hello Detective," Captain Briar said, and stood up along with the other body in the room. "Detective, meet Commissioner Dean. Commissioner, meet Detective Jessica Sanders. The very best I have."

Commissioner Dean smiled big as he shook Jessica's hand. Jessica returned the smile.

"Nice to meet you, Detective," he said.

"Same to you, sir," Jessica replied.

"Please, have a seat."

"Thank you," she said, and sat opposite Captain Briar's desk.

"All right, Detective," Captain Briar began speaking. "Commissioner Dean is here to help assess the current developments of The Fleshcrafter case and, well, we may as well get to the point."

Jessica smiled and made eye contact with Commissioner Dean. He immediately returned the smile. He was an older man, much closer to Captain Briar's age than to her own.

"Well, Detective Sanders," Commissioner Dean said. "I must admit, I've heard nothing but rave reviews about you and your work. A very talented detective, is that right?"

"I do what I can," she replied humbly, and crossed her legs.

"Right," he said. "Well, as everyone is already aware–and I am very sorry to hear–this case is now personal to you, and there are some questions about liabilities and ethics coming up. Before going any further, I just want you to understand that we have a reputation to uphold, no matter the consequences. We must always do what is best for everyone. Do you understand why you are here, Detective?"

"I do."

"Good," he replied. "Now, why don't we begin with the case? Where are we?"

"In a nutshell," Jessica said. "We've got four bodies. He punctures their throats, but never slashes them. A quick kill. Almost like the killing is not the thrilling part for him, it's afterward."

"Yes, all right," Commissioner Dean responded. "Every crime scene was different from the last. This killer is using his murders as art. He is using them to express himself in some way. Every body was a different scene. A different, painting." She didn't really want to use that word, but there were no others in her brain to use. "Some are abstract. Others are offensively obvious."

"And what leads do we have so far?"

"A pubic hair," she quickly replied.

"A pubic hair?" he questioned.

"From my sister's vagina," she said, quite matter of factly.

Commissioner Dean shook his head sharply, probably not believing the nonchalance she had said it with.

"Detective, can I ask how it is, exactly, that you feel about your sister's death?"

"Well," she pondered. "She is dead, and there is nothing I, or anyone else can do about it."

"Aren't you upset?"

"At home."

"At home?"

"Yes," she said. "At home. At work I do my job. At home I live my life."

"Interesting."

"Is it?"

He stared at her strangely.

"Listen," she finally broke the awkward silence. "I know what your and Captain Briar's situation is here. I know that keeping me on this case holds serious repercussions if I fuck it up."

She noted how her swearing had made both men slightly uncomfortable.

"But I am telling you," she continued. "I will catch this man. I will catch him, because I am already engrossed with him. If you gave me a page right now, I could draw you every detail from every crime scene, from memory alone. I understand the kind of ethics involved in keeping me on a case in which my own sister was a victim of, but I am not getting emotionally involved."

"How could you not?" he asked.

"Because I don't need to," she said. "In my head, my sister died in a car accident. She died in a plane crash. She had a heart attack. When I went over her body, that body was not my sister's. It was a naked woman I had never met before. I didn't know her family, I didn't know what she did for a living, nor did I care. I was there to find the clues and catch a killer. That's it. I went directly to the second crime scene afterward. I have the ability to disconnect. I can record every scene in my head, and I already know this killer better than anyone else ever will. You can't go back anymore to see for yourself."

Commissioner Dean never took his eyes off of her. "Is that correct, Captain?" he asked.

"Yes, sir," Captain Briar replied.

"I can do it," Jessica reinforced, feeling a wave of frustration tickling her sleeping rage in response to the Superintendant's undertones of doubt.

"And how instrumental is she to this case, exactly, Captain?"

"I found the hair while everyone else couldn't even step foot inside the room without gagging and puking."

He stared at her for a moment again.

"Yes. Captain Briar has informed me of your, let's say, indifferent virtues."

"How do you mean?" she asked, frowning.

"Your ability to walk into a room and stay there no matter how morbid or repulsive. You can deal with it all," he replied.

"Yes, I can."

"You have quite the natural talents, Detective," he said. "I admire that in people. Strength. But strength will not be enough to keep you on this case."

"He is my killer," she finally said.

"I'm sorry?"

"He's mine," she said, a little more casually this time. "I know him. I know how he thinks already. I know that there is a story behind every one of his heinous crimes, and I also know that none of his stories come from any religious texts, or traditional sacrifices. They come from his mind, from his pain, from his torture. The last victim, the shrink, he knew her. He loved her."

"He what?" he questioned, raising his eyebrows.

"He loved her," she said. "Have you seen the pictures? It's love. She denied him. She made him feel rejected, when that's probably the precise reason he started killing. Alienation. Rejection. Darkness. She broke his heart, and he literally cut hers out. I know that he spent more time with this woman even though the scene was much less complex than any of the others. We've searched her office. We've got her files. His name is in there somewhere. It's in there because he was one of her patients."

"How could you possibly know that, Detective?" he questioned. "Is this your idea of piecing things together? You're guessing?"

"Not guessing," she said, straightening up in her chair. "I found a shard of mirror in her office, near the bookshelf."

"And?"

"That shard came from my sister's crime scene. You'll see it in the report in a day or two, the lab will match it there. He was in her office, and I'm betting he was in there after he killed my sister, but before he killed Nicole White."

"Really," he said. "Why?"

"I don't know yet," she replied. "That's why I have to remain on this case. I'll find him, and I will catch him, but it will be done as a professional detective, not a vengeful human being. I can separate myself. That's why I'm so good at what I do, sir. Because I can turn off the caring."

Commissioner Dean took a deep breath and glanced at Captain Briar for a moment. He was thinking about what she'd said.

"What do you think, Captain?" he asked.

"I think we'd be foolish not to have someone like Jessica on a case like this. This man, this killer, you haven't seen his wrath first hand, sir. It is ungodly. It is inhuman, and Jessica is instrumental in catching him."

"And what about the conflict of interest?" he asked.

Captain Briar looked at Jessica and then back to Commissioner Dean. He was about to speak again when Jessica pipped up.

"Make Captain Briar my baby-sitter," she said.

"You know," Commissioner Dean said. "Smart girl, indeed."

Jessica smiled shyly.

"Here's what I propose," he said. "And this is strictly until further notice. You, Detective, are forbidden to go anywhere that is related to this case without Captain Briar physically being there to supervise you. You do not enter a room, take a note, or even arrive on the property of any new crime scenes without his friendly smiling face standing right there next to you. Do you understand?"

"Yes," she answered.

"I don't care if you have to pee, you ask him permission. You do not do your own thing and make him cover for you. The man is nearly retired, for Christ sakes, don't push him too hard."

"I understand, sir," she said again.

"Good. And please, understand right now, before anything else happens. The moment you break the rules, you are done. There are no second chances. There is no room for mistakes on this one. This guy has to be caught, and he has to be caught soon, before the goddamn media hangs us out to dry."

"Yes, sir," she said.

"Captain Briar, do you fully understand the new terms?"

"Yes, sir," he answered.

"Good then," he said. "I will be watching closely from this point on. One slip, and it's all over. Don't forget it."

"I won't, sir," she said. "Thank you, sir."

"You're welcome. Now go and catch this psycho before he kills more innocent people. Make us proud, Detective. And please, do not make me regret this decision."

"I won't, sir. I promise," she said, and stood up fumbling with her blouse. "Thank you, sir." She smiled and presented him her hand. He shook it.

"You're dismissed, Detective. Thank you for your time."

"Thanks again, Commissioner Dean," she said. "Captain."

"Goodbye Detective," Captain Briar said.

And just like that, Jessica was allowed to stay on the case, at least until further notice, and as long as she didn't screw anything up, she would remain exactly where she was. Poised to catch her killer.

She was ecstatic about the decision. She was proud of herself. She was happy, and now, she was heading to the lab to demand an explanation for why she still had not received any results on the pubic hair, or the mirror shard. Now, she would get this monster in the name of her sister.

The media had named him The Fleshcrafter, but Jessica called him The Katy Killer.

CHAPTER 9

The short lady at the lab said they were still working on the matches, but Jessica demanded a time line.

"Tomorrow morning," the lady promised, with a touch of pity in her eyes.

"All right," Jessica replied, sighing resolutely. "Thank you."

The elation of what had just happened in Captain Briar's office was steadily withering away, leaving her tired, and feeling the cold reality of her life like chilled spiders embalming her spine. Raw. She really wasn't in the mood for work. She really, just, missed her sister. She decided, to the satisfied encouragement of Captain Briar, to go home and rest. She urged Captain Briar to promise that he would call her immediately if anything came up. He agreed, of course, wanting her to rest her mind and begin the grieving process she was so vehemently denying. Jessica thanked him once again for defending her with Commissioner Dean.

"No problem, kiddo," he said. "Just catch the bastard." She drove home without the radio on. No noise. A quiet reflection. At home, she had a shower and sat on the bottom of the tub, thinking it all over once more. She eventually turned the water off, dried herself, and brushed her knotted hair with only one thing on her mind.

The diary.
Perhaps it held the key she needed to complete the puzzle. Perhaps it didn't. Either way, she felt that it might prove to be an interesting read. A distraction, at the very least.

She lay down on her bed and stared at the cover. "Okay,"

she said, and took a deep breath before opening it to its first page.

She had automatically assumed that the book was Nicole White's diary. She had found it hiding below the false bottom of her drawer, but on the very first page, it was obvious that this was not her diary at all.

The title read: The Story of Brian Hotz.
"Brian Hotz?" she said, quickly flipping through the pages. The book was nearly complete with scribbly handwriting on almost every page. She couldn't see any other clues to help define who the owner of the book was. Only "The Story of Brian Hotz."

She reached for her night stand and lit a cigarette. The words on the first page went like this:

The Story of Brian Hotz

Hello. My name is Brian Hotz, employee number 6698. Just another number. Just another regular face. Just another pawn in a giant corporation that doesn't care about you. Healthy or sick. Tired and beaten. Nobody cares.

My life is a string of nearly indefinable actions. A numbing experience, really. Shallow in existence.

My days begin at 6:00 a.m. with the screeching wail of my alarm clock. After lying there for a while, trying to muster up the will to actually let my feet hit the ground, I finally do, and that's when the real fun begins.

I brush my teeth, have a cup of coffee, eat my perfectly bronzed peanut butter toast. I watch the news and wonder how all of it could be real? Are these wars real? Are these problems real? Are any of these people, real people?

I get dressed in one of two standard uniforms I wear to work. My perfectly pressed light blue shirt with blue and yellow striped tie, or my plain white dress shirt with red wine colored tie. Never wear the same thing twice in a row, people may notice.

I brush what's left of my hopelessly receding hair line, and momentarily wonder if any of those miracle cures truly work. The spray paint crap. The neat looking follicle stimulating brushes you see on the shopping channel. Electromagnetic shock therapy. Hair plug surgery. The mystical wizard potions. Would any of it matter?

Probably not.

I live in a semi dilapidated apartment building in a rather rough part of town. Fourth floor with screaming foreign couples on either side of me and a violent drunkard above. There's nothing quite like being sprung out of bed at two in the morning during one of your neighbor's drug fueled paranoid rages because, "The goddamn roaches are coming through the ceiling!"

It's all very exciting!

The hallways are filled with a generally debauched ambience. Ancient to recent blood stains and crusted over vomit, all commingled with a vast array of offensive stenches, and the occasional drunk on the floor with piss stained pants. It all serves to skyrocket a man's pride.

My apartment itself is a luxurious entity with its off-white sterile illusioned walls, off-white ceilings, and off-white floor tiles. A bland dwelling for a bland man, I suppose. The painful cracking of ancient water heater pipes. The infinitely leaking faucets. The impenetrable bathtub stains from who knows when. Do they sell them pre-stained?

The cold wood framed windows. The filthy carpets. The demeaning light bulbs. The outside is peeling stucco and multicolored graffiti. People's underwear hanging from balconies. The plastic plants. The fake comfort that we are all healthy, happy, normal beings.

I wish it were only an illusion, but the filth really is creeping through the walls.

At night, I try to sleep against the steady drone of screaming voices, breaking glass, angry sirens, and the occasional gunshot. The stray cats searching for scraps. Some woman's screaming orgasm.

Every day, I drive to work in my very fashionable 1999 Toyota Camry with its black smoke from the tailpipe and the driver side back door locked tightly with a mess of fraying bungee cords. I obey the rules. I stop for yellow lights. I never speed.

I check my mirrors and always give the right of way to the next guy. I ignore the Cadillacs with the stunning wives in the passenger seats, the BMWs with 30 year old drivers, the laughing, babbling cell phones, and I tell myself, I am happy. I am comfortable with myself. I love myself.

I tell myself, but I've yet to listen.

I park in lot 87, my designated eight foot space of asphalt, far away from the luxury sedans and not even on the same side of the street as the building I work in. I cross the street with the same beaten, silent ants sipping on $4 expressos and sucking back Marlboro cigarettes, probably trying to match their lungs to the same black, molasses-like consistency of their souls.

I walk through the expensive looking glass doors with polished brass handles, pass over the marble tiled floors, and enter the steel box filled with bleak faces. Masks. Pain. I'm usually bursting with feel good zeal by this point.

Fourth floor, I hate irony. I stare at endless rows of perfectly separated half wall cubicles just buzzing with mindless chitter chatter, ringing phones, and clapping keyboards. I nod hellos, but I only get blank stares in return.

That girl over there, Lisa Willows with the big boobs and the perfect ass, she would sleep with a monkey with Down's Syndrome if it could lie on its back for long enough, but God forbid she would flash a smile my way. Christ, she even sucked off Bill Hunter in the bathroom at last year's Christmas party! That Dilbert-looking overweight guy with the extra thick glasses and who, for unknown reasons, always seems to have mustard stains on his chin, but never quite in the same spot.

I walk down the eternal half-hallway until I get to my very own feeble, gut wrenching work space. Jesus, it's smaller than my parking spot.

I sit in my dilapidated swivel chair with the shifted foam lining that cuts off circulation in my left leg. I stare at the overflowing mess of paper, and usually, I'm fighting back the urge to cry. I wonder why God made us so graceful? If we are made in his image, what does that say about him?

I turn my computer on and sigh horribly for the entire twenty minutes it takes to load its own goddamned operating system. Yes, the hype was correct. Technology has completely revolutionized our world. More aggravation than ever. New swear words. More paper than has ever been used in the history of mankind. To those marketing geniuses I say thank you for making my life so much more efficient.

I cringe at the voice of my supervisor barking away in disdain as he hands me my daily list of clients. He asks me if it would kill me to smile once in a while. He asks me if I have my reports ready from yesterday. He asks me if I like my job. I tell him I had a great night. Almost beat level 18 of Tetris.

He scoffs and I wonder why I'm the uptight one.
I stare at the list of names my zestful supervisor hands me. These are the names I must meet with today. These faceless names. These nameless faces. This is the highlight of my morning.

I tear through the list and see names like David Flake, William Bent, Ashley Doomore, and I wonder who these people are. What kind of shallow existence do they lead? What kind of wild excuses will they present me with? I wonder if they have families, people who care about them, friends to hang out with. I wonder if they are real at all.

And then it comes on like a raging tsunami. The room swells and spins and my face blows up with lava-like blood. My heart races, and suddenly, I can't breathe. I can't... I can't breathe! I feel the walls closing in, the people staring, the snickers, the whispers. Everything gets far away and I watch my numb hand slam against my desk frantically as the piles of papers crash and swirl around me like a whirlwind of doom. My fingers grab at the pill bottle, but I can't... I can't feel it!

The tremors. The chills. The panic.
Suddenly, I watch the lid fly off into oblivion and I dump a few yellows into my mouth. I force them down. I try to breathe. I try to keep it together, and suddenly... I do!

My vision focuses. My heart slows. The tremors calm. Artificial peace is restored. My shirt is soaked. People stare.

"I choked," I fakely chuckle. "I'm fine, thank you."
Nobody cares.

I go through the motions. Fill out the forms. Respond to the emails. Make generic phone calls.

"Good morning Ms... Vaunt? This is Brian Hotz calling from the Dufferin Collection Agency.... Hello?"

Story of my life.

"Hi there! This is Brian Hotz calling from... What do I want? Ah... well this is rather import... Hello?"

After those disasters beat me further into submission, I wobble over into a packed cafeteria filled with static creating plastic chairs and rectangular tables covered with vinyl. I ignore the big wigs, the cheerful laughter, the friends eating together. I sit alone near the back, near the big window overlooking the park, where I watch couples holding hands and dogs being walked. I wonder if I'd like being a dog? A simple life. Eat, shit, sleep. People like dogs. I like dogs.

At least 3 times a week, while I'm sitting here observing the lemmings below, I cringe at the sight of an approaching beast with even lower standards of life than my own. His name is Norman. Norman likes me, unfortunately. I see him smile big the way children do when they see Santa at the local mall, only... I'm Santa, and by this point I'm trying to shove as much food down my throat before he actually makes it to my table.

His sweating bald head and bulldog-like cheeks. His short stubby legs. His jiggling stomach flap that hangs way too low beyond his belt buckle. That thing is creepy as hell, the way it swings and sways as he walks like a timeless pendulum. I wonder if he plays with it at home? I wonder if he buys shirts three times his actual size? I wonder when the last time he actually saw his penis was? Does he lift it at urinals? I suppose he has no other option.

Lunch itself is a tasteless mishmash of some type of processed meat stacked on top of processed cheese in between two slices of processed bread. If everything else is processed, what does that make us?

Afternoons are appointments with all kinds of riffraff coming through the doors. Sometimes, while a client is talking, I can't help but wonder what kind of degenerate DNA is at work inside of them.

"I forgot," "My ex stole my money," "I got a really great deal on a flute."

These are the stories of people's lives. The blunders. The mistakes. The failures. That's the only side of lives I ever get to see. The losers. The fights. The pain. I suppose we all have our own ways of dealing with life.

I pop a few Advils for my throbbing headache. Every day around this time. Seems I've had a runny nose for years now. Seems I'm susceptible to rashes. Seems I should start drinking.

I drive home and ignore the same distractions from the morning. I eat my microwaved TV dinner with a side of anti-depressants and a glass of processed, homogenized milk. I take a shower and notice more hair in the drain, more wrinkles and sags appearing, more age leaving its ugly scars.

I wonder if my penis still works? I forget what a woman feels like. I forget that I've forgotten.

I crawl into my cold bed and read a book. I like books that help me see a different time, a different place, a different life.

I hate biographies, I always feel envy.
I swallow a Valium and wait for the darkness to overtake me.

CHAPTER 10

Jessica's first impression was, "What a wimp."
She didn't understand why, but once her initial surprise
dissipated over what was inside of the diary, she was feeling
rather repulsed by this Brian Hotz character.

"A wimp," she had decided.
She wondered if it was an actual diary or just a manuscript, a
story Nicole White had been working on. She didn't think it was
irrational that she would have hidden it in the bottom of a drawer,
some passions were worth more than anything else in life.

She continued reading.

The Story of Brian Hotz

The stethoscope feels ice cold on my back. The deep breaths...
shallow, the exhales restricted. I feel sweat on my forehead. I feel
my palms clammy and ice cold at the same time.

"So what do you think, doc?" I ask with a crackling voice.
"Is everything okay?"

The Doctor sighs loudly.
This man is my only true friend.

"Brian," he says, and stares into my face. "You're fine.
Everything is fine. Just like last week, and the week before that.
Please Brian, you need to relax. How's work lately?"

"It's the same," I reply. "Everyday. Same day."
"Maybe you should start walking a little after dinner, huh? Get
some exercise. Maybe clear your mind a little."

I stare at the floor while slightly kicking my feet off the
side of the table. "You look tired, Brian. How have you been

sleeping?"

"Well... I haven't really, since, you know, I noticed that mole on my back," I say.

"Brian, I've been your doctor for ten years, and that mole, it's been right there for ten years. You need to lighten up."

This room, this place, it's the only real comfort I know. The sterilized walls and floor tiles. The steel examination table with the thin white paper strewn across the top of it. All the medical grade instruments, the stainless steel tools, the cotton balls, the syringes, the popsicle sticks.

All of it somehow... feels safe.

When the robe comes on, nothing can touch me. When a pill slides down my throat, I feel healed. I am a glowing ball of health.

Sometimes, I wonder how I became such a wimp. I can't even remember the last time I had a cold, but on the same note, I also cannot remember when my nose didn't leak. I wonder if there is such a thing as balance? I wonder if I've fallen?

"I try," I sound so desperate. "But you know... It's hard sometimes."

I hate the way his smile looks. His perfect teeth. His glowing face. His long crows feet running away from his eyes. Proof of a lifetime of laughter. Happiness. Completeness.

"Brian, you need to speak to someone. Have you called Dr. Miller? She can help you, you know?"

I feel tightness in my chest. "I ah... no, I didn't." I reply. "Well why not?" he asks nonchalantly. "Aren't you tired of feeling so beaten down all the time?"

When the pressure's on, all I want is to ask for Barbiturates. Amphetamines for depression. Steroids for self-confidence.

"Yeah, I guess," I reply.

"You guess? Jesus, Brian, I don't want to sound judgmental here, and this is coming from a friend, not a doctor, but you're a goddamn mess. I'm worried about you."

"Can I just have some more pills? You know, more yellows, or blues maybe? Maybe some reds?" I plead.

"Brian, you cannot deal with life through drugs. You have

to face reality. It'll make you a better person."

Professional feel-good opinions like these fill me with enthusiasm! Thanks, Doc! I love myself again!

I say nothing.

"Listen," he begins. "Call Dr. Miller. She knows her stuff. I promise you, you won't regret it. Aside from my suggestion, there isn't much more I can do for you, Brian. I'm sorry."

You're sorry? I don't even know if I can take this robe off and walk out of here! The door knobs are infected with human filth. The air is rampant with viruses. The sun causes cancer!

When the public surrounds me, I can see the bugs crawling. The centipede bacteria. The fecal worms. The semen viruses.

I wonder if I need new glasses?

"Brian?" he asks, his voice filled with concern. "Are you all right?"

I realize my momentary catatonia, my saliva spider paranoia.

"Huh? Oh... Yeah. Of course. I'm, I'm fine, doc. Thanks." His suspicious eyes. His frowning forehead. This is the way my mother used to look at me. This is the way everyone looks at me.

"Right," he says. "Well, Brian, I apologize, but I have a very busy schedule today. I better get going."

"Yeah," I say. "No problem at all."

"Oh!" He stops at the door. "And please, Brian, do yourself a favor and call Dr. Miller, okay?"

"Yeah," I say with too much fake enthusiasm. "First thing when I get home. Thanks, doc."

Squinting eyes again.

"All right, well... You're welcome. Now go and have a nice day; and get some rest, will you, you'll catch a bug."

I feel a whirlwind of magma swirl through my stomach. A heart stopping shock. Volcanic ulcers.

When the doctor leaves, I bask in the sterilized silence. The bland walls. The bright lights. I take a deep, invigorating breath and imagine how clean it all is. I look around with wide, admiring eyes, and wonder; do I come here to see the doctor, or the room? Is this what heaven feels like? Is this place... Real?

I take the robe off and wonder if I should take it with me. Will it serve me well? Does it carry this type of peace with it no matter where it is? This blissful abyss.

In the waiting room, the pretty blonde behind the counter asks if I would like to book an appointment for next week. I think I feel a tickle in my penis. I wonder if it's contagious? A rash?

I know I shouldn't. I know better. This week, I will do something different. I will take control of my life. Exercise. Eat healthy. Sleep great. I will be healthy. Strong. Attractive. I will finally stop being so weak. I will stop being afraid. I will...

"Sure," I say. "Thank you."

She doesn't look up and jots something down.

"I'm sorry," she says. "What was your name again?"

I've been coming here for ten years. She's been here for six.

"Hotz," I reply. "Brian Hotz."

"Okay," she says and turns her attention back to her computer screen while I stand there like an asshole.

"Okay then," I say.

I stare at the door and wonder how clean the knob is. Does it have telescopic sized infectants? Creepy crawling brain parasites? Urethra eating sloths? I wonder if there's any disinfectant around? The air suddenly feels ill. The coughs. The sneezes. The floating disease.

I feel panic slowly creeping up the edges of my spine. Is that panic? Or life? Is this living on the edge?

Somehow, purely fueled by instinct, I get to my car. I feel dirty. I feel... I feel nothing.

Sometimes when I lie in bed, I wonder if life is predetermined. Sometimes I wonder if I could be different. Sometimes... I wonder what's wrong with me.

I feel the Valium slide down the back of my throat, and I think no more. Is that what peace means, the absence of thought?

Yeah, that's what I feel. Peace.

Jessica put the book down and tippy toed to the bathroom, and then back to her bed, burying her face in the book.

The Story of Brian Hotz

5:58 a.m. My alarm hasn't gone off yet, but the problem with pills is... They give you horrible gut rot. You know the feeling. That grinding, torture spiked ball smashing against the sensitive lining of your stomach. Like you're being eaten from the inside.

Do people really get off on pain? Are orgasms truly attained through torture? I think I'm going to be sick!

This is a regular occurrence in the exciting life of me. Sometimes, I think it's the only thing that reminds me that I am still alive. I am a living, breathing, physical being. I do occupy a notch on the space-time continuum! The proof is right there in the toilet bowl.

Some people hate vomit. I qualify myself with it. I like to think that it's only my body rejecting the fakeness of life. An excessive concoction of fake meals. I've gotten used to it over the years. With great pain comes understanding. Well... At least that's what the saying is. The reality is so much more brutal.

The stomach does not take lightly to heavy intakes of pharmaceutical chemicals mixing and mashing together like a healing orchestra. The sleeping pills, the anxiety pills, the ones for depression, for pain, for headaches, for cholesterol.

I stare into my medicine cabinet and I think... I should change careers. I should be a pharmacist. Schooling would be a breeze!

Viagra for your broken penis? No problem, sir, only one dose before the big event. No heart problems? No history of diabetes? All right then, have a great erection!

Laxatives for your impacted bowels, Ma'am? No problem. Aisle 4, and Lubricants are in aisle 8. Have a great day!

Yes, sir! Thorazine for those evil bunnies and screaming voices? Here you go. Ipods are by the checkout counter.

I am a living, breathing encyclopedia of pharmacology. I am sustained by it.

When the rotting holes open up and the bleeding ulcers fire on all pistons, there isn't much time. Dash toward the porcelain! Marvel at how far projectile vomit really can, well, project. Feel the powerful fear flash up the back of your neck as you realize that at least half of it is blood. Feel the sweat. The pounding heart. The spinning room. Try to breathe. Try to breathe! Swallow a yellow, it's only the ulcers! It's only the ulcers! Not cancer. Not tape worms. Not flesh eating parasites. Relax. It's only... the... ulcers.

Swallow a ginger tablet, and then a handful. Wash 'em down with processed milk. Shove a few pieces of processed bread down your throat. The enzymes will help calm the angry acids raging through your stomach. Avoid coffee. No juices. Only water, or milk. Take a shower. Watch the news. Swallow your cholesterol pills. Your antidepressants. Your muscle relaxants. Have another glass of....

Shit! Empty carton. Already I can feel my palms sweating. My legs twitching and stiffening. My mind recoiling in horror at the thought of it.

I have to go to the grocery store!
When I pull into the parking lot, I stare in disdain. It's not that I don't like shopping so much as I know that through those doors is a raging cesspool orgy of disease. A rancid filth bed of free flowing decay.

Where's my disinfectant?
I walk down the aisles and wonder how clean the shelves are, how clean the food is. What kind of preservatives infected the edibles? How many chemicals are on those bananas? Herbicides? Spermicides? Varsol with a touch of methyl-hydrate? Impossible to know. I pass the processed bread, the powdered eggs, the endless rows of pre-diced cans of every possible fruit and vegetable you could ever think of. I pass the steroid inflated beef, the antibiotic filled pork, the lab grown chicken, and I think, what ever happened to reality? If I ate virgin meat, would I die?

I turn the corner toward the next aisle and stop dead in my tracks!

Right there, perhaps 30 feet away, some hacking hag is spewing her filth all across the goddamn place! I feel the sweat beading. My heart racing. My lungs seizing. This is why I never use a cart. I'd rather lick a public toilet seat.

I panic. I feel the swoon coming. I can almost see the

spreading wave of disease floating outward like a stone thrown into a pond. I feel rabid anger flare through my body.

Instantly, I turn and nearly run back down the aisle I just came from, cursing the filthy harlot on the way.

"All I want is some fucking milk!" I say.
I speed walk through and turn the corner. Avoid the snot riddled little fiend trying to catch up to his mother, there is nothing worse. Careen around the shabby old hobo, just get to the goddamn milk!

My chest tightens. My vision gets hazy. I can feel the oncoming delirium. This isn't worth it!

When I get to the glass doors, the whole place is spinning wildly, and I can't see what I want. Only colors and indistinguishable shapes. 1%, 2%, Homogenized, breast milk, Jesus Christ! What's wrong with me?

I blindly claw at cartons and spill a few to the ground. I whimper out loud. People stare. Children cry. Where are my fucking pills?

I pop the cap and swallow a few. Steadily, reality returns. A horrible, nightmarish reality. The confused stares. The tears. The snickers. The security.

I secretly try to escape. This is not real. It's a dream! The alarm clock will go off in a few minutes. Anytime now, and my mundane existence will return. I am a healthy, normal man. People like me. God likes me. I am a strong man with strong dreams. I am not the man sitting in a pool of fermenting milk in the middle of the grocery store while people huddle around him either laughing or asking if they should call for an ambulance. I am not that guy!

Oh, God... No... Am I crying? Please tell me I'm not crying!

When no one pays attention, you crave nothing more. But once they do, you want nothing more than for them to stop. It's funny how the mind works. It's fucking hilarious.

The black uniforms in front of me babble things like, "Are you okay?" and "Do you need an ambulance?"

I don't remember standing up. I don't remember the crescendoing laughter at the expense of my milk soiled pants,

or the child I apparently sent flying into the potato chip stand. I
don't remember driving home, or crashing through my apartment
door like a raging bull.

I only know that I'm home now. In the shower, sitting,
hugging my knees and wondering what time it is. Wondering... If
it actually happened. Had I gone to the grocery store? Did I have
gut rot? Am I out of milk?

I turn the water off and brush my receding hair line. I
wonder about hair products, I eat my toasts, I watch the news,
and then I drive to work and park in lot 87. Safe now. Sane now.
Tomorrow, I'll check the refrigerator for the milk situation, but
not today. Today is a regular, mundane series of actions no one
pays any attention to. Today is the same long day as the rest of
my life.

I am Brian Hotz. Employee number 6698. Just another
number. Just another face. Just another shadow creeping up the
walls of society's backwoods. I am so full of life right now, I
think I'm about to burst!

As much as I'd love them, there are no alternate realities.
No wormholes to crawl through. No strings to vibrate us all into
a parallel universe. And as far as I know, there is no God. If there
is one, well, not only does he not care about me, I think it's fair
to say, he hates me. No caring deity would create such a being. If
I am made in his image, I apologize to the rest of you.

I cross the street with the ants. I pass through the brass
handled doors. I enter the steel box, destination, irony. I walk
down the half hallway. I am the center of my universe.

My computer is taking extra long this morning. I wonder if
it's sick? Digital viruses. Electronic worms. Is there anything out
there that cannot die?

I pop an Advil for my headache. I wash my hands with my
trusty gallon of disinfectant. I wonder why my nose is always
leaking? Maybe I should stop thinking so much.

"Brian!" The bark is from behind me. My morning jewel is
up with my list of marvelous personalities who, and this is daily,
fill me with a pure, unadulterated zeal for life.

"Yes, sir?" I say.

"Brian, does the name Amy Hill mean anything to you?"

I turn to face him. His demeaning little eyes. His bloated beer belly. His cheap smelling cologne.

"Amy Hill?" I question. "Not really. Ah... Why?"
"Why, Brian?" he says, and the tone of his voice clamps my throat shut. My heart rate rises. My lungs are empty.

"I'll tell you why, Brian," he says. "Miss Hill, here, says that you asked her out to dinner yesterday. A client, Brian. Do you remember the rules about having social contact with clients?"

I can't breathe! I feel the hot blood flush my face. Oh, God! I'm starting to spin!

"Do you remember the consequences, Brian? Do you? It's called, TERMINATION!"

The word echoes through the air. Suspended. Shock. Termination? What now? Overdose? Loss of consciousness? Crying? Did I cry this morning? Was that real?

"Are these allegations correct, Brian?" My lungs are shot. "Did you ask her out?"

Tremors. Chills. Nausea.
"Well? What do you have to say for yourself?"

And then I hear it. A scream. Wild anger. Frustration. Madness. Defeat. I hear it bouncing off the walls. I hear the telephones ringing for too long. I hear the keyboards halt. The conversations stop.

Suddenly, I can feel it roaring from the pit of my stomach, and I realize... It's coming from me!

I should be losing consciousness right about now. I should be panicking. I should be... I should be anything but watching this frightened manager's face transform itself into absolute astonishment.

I can hear my voice ripping through the place and obviously, I'm not the only one shocked by it.

"Fuck!" I scream, and astonishment turns to heavy fear. "Brian!" he says.

"Fuck you!" I snap, and hear the sound of breaking glass. I smell the acrid stench of an electrical fire and notice my computer monitor smashed on the ground. Nothing but pure terror on his demeaning little face now.

"Jesus Christ, Brian!" his voice cracks with uncertain fear. "What are you doing? It was only a joke, man! I was just fucking with you a little."

I see things fly from my desk and over the cubicle cell I waste my life in. My stapler, my telephone, my keyboard, all hurled into space. Terrified faces duck like threatened groundhogs.

"You small cocked fuck!"

Why did I say that?

"You ego-whore bitch!"

What's happening to me? Is this it? The final wave before the annihilation? The single shred of life before death?

I see faces everywhere staring back at a wrathful beast. Pure horror. Pure astonishment. But through it all, no one is more astonished than I am!

By this point, I should have shoved half a bottle of yellows down my throat. I should have fought to stay conscious, to breathe, to stop the spinning. I should have been soaked in sweat, trying to convince myself that it never really did happen at all. No one noticed. No one cared. Losing yet another piece of self-respect. Self-esteem.

But none of that was happening. I didn't feel choked by incredible fears. I didn't feel myself clawing at the floor, trying to avoid being swallowed up by some mystically dark abyss.

What I felt was... Was... Powerful!

Was this it? The bottom? The final crack in the constantly thinning ice? My hands and arms tingle with awesome strength. My chest feels enormous. My mind, though caught in shock, is astonishingly clear. I think I'm getting an erection!

The squatting little shit begins to speak again and I lose it on him.

"Goddamn it, Brian!"

"Shut the fuck up!" I scream into his pale, sweaty face. "Shut your fucking mouth! Shut up!"

I suddenly love the sound of my voice.

"All of you... Demeaning little shits! You laugh at me! You talk about me! You all think I'm some big fucking joke! Well laugh now, assholes! Go ahead! You're all better than me! Stronger!

Smarter! Go ahead and laugh!"

I throw a stack of photocopying paper and watch every page flutter through the air like butterflies in a hurricane. I throw my pen holder. I throw my chair and my gallon of disinfectant. I revel in the way people duck in fear. I am the sleeping dragon that has been poked by one too many sticks. I am the angry beast exacting his revenge. I am God!

I rip off my shirt and throw it on the industrially abrasive rug.

"Screw it!" I scream. "Screw it all!"

I kick the cubicle wall and set off a slight domino effect. I begin to storm out and step on my supervisor's hands. I love the pain in his voice. That is my pain! I, and I alone have total control over it!

I walk down the remaining half-hallway toward the steel box. No shirt. A smile as big as a god. Life radiating from my every pore.

I love how people quickly stow away from me as I walk. I am Moses parting the fools.

I am finally a rock star!

As I approach the elevators, a figure suddenly jumps in front of me, angry as hell. It's the big boss, Mr. Lieberman, screaming gibberish that doesn't even register in my enlightened ears. I say nothing and simply grab his entire face in the palm of my hand and shove him off to the side. He hits the ground in his $900 suit. I don't even blink. I am the smoldering star of my life.

When I get to the main lobby, I snap my head back and walk with the accumulated confidence of every goddamn lion in Africa. I walk passed the guards, the young professionals with satchels and expensive phones. I walk passed the snickers and stunned stares aimed toward a shirtless man prancing through the lobby like he just won the lottery.

I smile big.

"Fuck you all!" I pronounce. "Every single one of you!"

I kick the brass handles and the doors smash open like a king is arriving. I cross the street. I take a cigarette right out of some woman's hand and begin smoking it. I cough. I have another puff and inhale as deeply as I can.

When I get to my car, I'm filled with pure energy. Ecstasy. I get in, turn on the ignition, and suddenly, I feel my abdomen contract. I can feel it tighten and convulse. An alien feeling. And then... I laugh!

I laugh so hard that tears stream down my face and I can't catch my breath. I laugh and slap my steering wheel. I hold my stomach. I feel my face infused with hot red blood. I wonder when the last time I had truly laughed was. I can't remember.

I put the car in reverse and slam on the accelerator. I feel the rubber squirm on the asphalt. I'm still laughing. I put it in drive and floor it. I see the parking attendant's concerned face inside the booth as he realizes that the car isn't going to stop today. I see him duck for cover.

When splinters of wood fly up and over my windshield, I feel liberated! I laugh even harder! I feel like a lunatic! A blissfully unhinged lunatic!

I speed. I run a red light. I don't stop for pedestrians. I cut off a cadillac and give him the finger. I blow a kiss to a pretty girl. I wonder if I've completely lost my mind.

When I get home, I run up the stairs to my apartment. I get naked and have a shower. I am still half-laughing!
I feel tired so I go to bed feeling unbelievable. Feeling like a lightning bolt. I wonder when the last time I felt anything remotely like this was? Probably before I was ever born.

I stop thinking. I fall asleep. A deep, calm, peaceful sleep. No pills. No panic. No pain.

If Brian Hotz was a real person, she would know in a day or two by going through Nicole's files.

Of course, she couldn't speak to anyone about the book. She had stolen evidence from an on-going investigation. She had broken the Commissioner's rules before the man was able to set them down.

It was what it was.
She was getting tired of thinking so much, tired of trying to piece together an impossible puzzle. She wondered if anything would come from the pubic hair, and if the mirror shard would be matched to her sister's murder. She wondered, she wondered a

lot of things.

Mostly, she wondered about Brian Hotz. She wondered what it was like to live a life dominated by fear and anxiety. Jessica was never one for fear. Everything just was what it was. She could not see the logic in worrying about the inevitable. If things could not be changed, then where was the good in worrying about them? In the same vein, if things could be changed, then why didn't people change for themselves?

She wondered if that was why she felt so repulsed by Brian Hotz. This character, this unknown man, he seemed to be her direct antonym when it came to perspectives on life. She was rather fearless, and he was sustained by fear.

She jotted down the Dufferin Credit Agency in her mind, right underneath the name Brian Hotz. If it was a real place, she would be a mile ahead in the search for Brian Hotz.

CHAPTER 11

The Story Of Brian Hotz

"Hi! Hello?... Hi! Dr... Dr. Miller?... Yes, hi... I, I, I need your help! I, I need some help!... I, I, I, I don't know! Just please!.... Yes, ok! Thank, thank you."

This morning, when I opened my eyes, when I saw my alarm clock telling me it was 11:00 am, I puked my brains out. I filled my bed with stomach blood. I got the tremors. I got the spins. I got the fear.

"Oh... Ah God.... Ah Shit... What the... What the fuck?" Pure panic as I pace quickly through my bland living room. Absolute terror. Anguish.

"What's happening to me?... Ah man!" My eyes can't focus. I rapidly scan the off white walls, the fake paintings, the empty pill bottles, the babbling television. I see them all, but none of them make any difference.

When you're caught in a panic, everything is so far away. Depression does the same. So do countless other diseases. Nothing seems real. You know it's there, you can feel it, smell it, hear it, and yet, it seems so distant. As though you're looking at the world through a thick, not so transparent ectoplasmic cocoon. Wrapped in the overwhelming emotion. Trapped in the horror. You are dead to the world. Not happy. Not sad. Just existing. I wonder if I have a brain tumor?

Mosquitoes spawn in water and grow to transport diseases from one species to another. Did God do that?

I pace frantically, nervously trying to remember what the hell happened yesterday.

I try to remember. I try so desperately, but I get nothing but... flashes and grim emotions. The smell of an electrical fire. The breeze against my bare chest. The tingling zeal of manic power.

All I get are glimpses. What happened to me? Was I poisoned? Was I drugged? A bad allergic reaction to conflicting pharmaceuticals? But, why now? Oh, God, have I lost it? Has my mind finally cracked under the massive pressure?

Where are my yellows?

I feel hung over. I wonder if I've ever been hung over. I wonder if it was all just a dream, but strangely, I know it wasn't. I don't know what happened, but heavy weights sit on my shoulders. I know it was bad.

This morning, after the puke and the frantic swallowing of all kinds of multicolored pills, after the breathlessness, the tremors, the giant black hole opening up at my feet, I went outside and stared at my car for a good hour. I could see the nasty dents and the yellow paint, and I just stood there, letting the fear numb my face, wondering just what in the hell had happened. Then the flashes started. Quick and brutal like rabid lightning. I opened my eyes and stared at the blue sky. The back of my head throbbing like a squashed melon against the asphalt behind it.

That's when I called the doctor. Out of terror more than concern. Panic more than willingness. She agreed to see me immediately. I curse myself for calling. I don't want to go. I don't want help. All I want is to crawl into bed and slowly sink into decay.

***

A doctor's office is supposed to be a place for the sick to reunite in a sterile environment. Breathe in, breathe out, lift your arms, say ah, feel the safety, the peace, the healing. Nothing can hurt you here.

But not this doctor.

The walls are beige. The lights are dimmed. This chair I'm sitting in, it's not stainless steel, it's expensive padded leather.

There are no instruments here. No blood pressure gauges.

No weight scales. No syringes. The air is stagnant, the floor is covered with plush carpet. There is nothing safe about this place!

And then there's the doctor! My doctor is Jewish with a pelican nose and Dumbo ears. He wears a lab coat with numerous pens packed into his breast pocket. He's a balding 68 year old man who wears latex gloves and warns you that the following may feel a little awkward.

But not this doctor. This doctor is a woman. A gorgeous, stunning blonde with luscious blue eyes and a body to envy. That body, safely tucked away behind a pin striped business suit is something like a work of art crudely veiled by a professional facade.

Some butterflies have wings that look like a face in order to fend off predators.

I can smell her strong, nearly emasculating perfume. Her hairspray. Her make up and deodorant. I wonder what she looks like naked.

"How are you, Brian?" she asks. I shift in my seat.
"Ah... I ah.... I don't know, really," I say. "I'm ah... I'm strange."

I watch her entire face frown. Girls in high school used to give me this exact same look. Girls at work now give me this look.

"Okay," she says. "How do you mean?"
"I ah..." I can feel my blood pressure rising. "I... think I quit my job... I don't know what's happening to me. I... I can't remember!"

She peers at me intently.
"You... can't remember?"
"No!" I lash out. More out of terror than anger. "I don't know what I did! Oh, man! I... I think I'm losing my fucking mind!"

I grab my hair, soaked and matted with sweat. I feel the spins. I pop some yellows.

The doctor sits silently, simply observing me. I wonder what she's thinking? I wonder if I seem attractive?

"Okay," she says. "Let's ah, just calm down here for a minute, okay? I don't want to get ahead of ourselves. Let's ah, just start with some basic questions, okay? If they make you feel uncomfortable, or you begin to feel tense, just let me know and we'll switch subjects. Okay? Sound good to you?"

Her voice is soft. Sweet. She seems caring. Interested. I don't trust her at all.

The devil has the face of an angel.
I nod yes and wring my sweaty hands. I cross my legs. I feel tighter than a tourniquet. I wonder when the last time I relaxed was?

"All right, um... Let's just start at the beginning. Can you tell me your full name?"

Her eyes are seductive. Her face glowing. I want to leave!

"Ah... Brian," I say. I sound like such a pussy. "Brian Mark Hotz."

She smiles.
"Well, it is very nice to meet you, Brian Mark Hotz. I'm Denise Evelyn Miller."

I shuffle in my padded leather chair. I feel the collecting sweat soaking through my shirt across my back. I flash my teeth but say nothing.

"Okay, um... Where do you work Brian?"
I wait for a moment. Debating the question.

"Ah... The Dufferin Collection Agency," I reply.
"Oh," she says. "As a collections agent?"

I nod yes.
"And how long have you worked there for?"

I shrug. "Thirteen years."
"Wow," she smiles again. She feels repulsive. "Do you like it there?"

"I think I quit yesterday!" I snap impatiently.
"Yeah," she says, unaffected by my emotions. "You said that. You can't remember anything at all?"

I shake my head no.
"Do you often forget things, Brian?"

"I try to," I say.
Her perfectly trimmed eyebrows drop low on her angelic face. "How do you mean?"

I shrug again. I can't look at her in the face. She makes me nervous. My hands tremble.

"Just... You know... Some things are just... Better, if you

forget all about them."

"I see," she replies professionally. "So... Is that what happened yesterday, Brian?"

"No," I reply quickly. "I ah... I don't know what... What happened! I just... Oh, God! I..."

Pure panic again.

"Okay. It's okay," she says. "You're safe here, Brian. It's okay. Let's ah... Let's talk about something else, okay?"

I say nothing and try to breathe. I try to focus on a single stationary point. I wonder why people drink?

"Okay, ah... Let's see. What kind of hobbies do you have?"

"Hobbies?" I question.

"Yeah, you know. Ah... Do you like to read, or write maybe? I don't know... Maybe build models, or draw?"

"No," I say.

"Really? No? You don't like to read at all?"

I do. At night. To help me forget.

"No," I say.

"Um... Okay. How about TV? Do you have a favorite TV show?"

"No."

I still feel the panic bubbling inside of me like a volcano ready to burst. Just smoldering. Smoking. I quickly fumble in my pocket and hang on to the pill bottle, ready to shoot into defense mode.

"Ah... Brian? Are you all right?"

"I'm fine, thank you."

"Is there anything you would like to talk about?"

I squirm against the thick leather again.

"Yes," I say.

"Okay. What would you like to talk about?"

"I ah... I don't think I can."

"Why not?" she asks. "It's okay, Brian. Nothing can hurt you here. I am here to listen and to help. Not to judge. I want you to feel free to tell me anything you want."

"I ah... ah..."

I let my eyes travel aimlessly about the room. The volcano is erupting. The big bang has arrived. I feel my eyes begin to roll back into my head. I panic and drop the pill bottle on the floor. I try to get them but fall to my knees. I hear a female voice in the distance. Gibberish. Garbage. I try so desperately to get to the goddamn pills. The darkness is closing in. Not much time now!

And suddenly, it begins to recede. It begins to... to go away. And I realize that I'm on the floor, on my back, staring at the ceiling. And then her face is high above mine, looking down at me with a mask of frantic panic.

Her mouth is moving and, slowly, I begin to hear the words.

I am melting in incredible embarrassment.
"Brian? Are you okay? Are you all right? Do you need anything?"

"Ah," I mutter. "No... No... I'm ah, I'm fine."
I attempt to sit up but the disorientation is heavy.

"Take your time," she says. "It's okay. It's all right. Just relax."

I look around and see the mess of pills. I am the discovered drug addict. I am the sunless life of the universe.

I wonder if God ever gets lonely?
"I ah... Ah... I have to go," I exclaim.

"No, Brian. Please just, ah, just take a moment and relax. Please, I have to make sure that you're okay before..."

"I'm fine!" I snap in panic and frantically pick the pills off the floor. "Happens all the time. But I have to go. I'm sorry. Thank you for your time, Dr. Miller."

I walk away in desperate strides toward the giant oak doors of her office.

"But, Brian, wait!" I hear her behind me. "How often does this..."

The doors slam shut behind me and suddenly, I'm running like a frightened antelope from the lions. I pass the elevators and run down the stairs to the main level like a crazy person, straight out of the doors and into the parking lot.

The lot is loaded with strangers. All kinds of irritating, smiling faces. Telling jokes. Enjoying the weather. Why are they looking at me? Ah, God, my head is going to explode.

I once again wonder if this is the rapture. The final assault from an exhausted organ. The last crack.

I stumble to my car like a drunken fool with a sudden mission, but when I get there, everything just gets worse.

There are too many people around. Too many minuscule anal roaches and mosquito viruses. Too many kids. Too much air exhausted. Too much... fucking noise!

I frantically try to rush past a lady, but accidentally knock her flat to the ground. "I'm sorry!" I pant. "So sorry." But her husband would not have it. He shoves me against my car and the world slows by five thousand frames. His face forever suspended in the twilight of non-existence.

I feel ugly and black inside. I feel that concentrated low level emptiness no one should ever be aware of. Everything suddenly goes dark and I find myself hopelessly lost in limbo. Forever forgotten in time.

When I crawl back to consciousness, I'm speeding through an intersection at eighty miles an hour, eyes crazy with panic. I'm covered in blood. Is it mine? Am I dead? Please... Please tell me I'm dead. I can't do it anymore. I can't...

I search my pockets with vicious determination. Where the fuck are my pills? I can hear pills banging against each other when I move, but where, goddamn it? My hands, lush with half dried blood, stick horribly to the insides of my pockets. The aggravation worse than the panic. Worse than all the pain in my brain. Worse than the sum total of my existence.

I struggle and scream in fury.
"Goddamn piece of fucking shit!" I rip my pants and begin punching the dashboard, more out of confusion than real anger. Out of pure desperation.

I realize that I am still driving with my foot pressed tightly against the rusting floor boards. I look up and see nothing but darkness. Not even blur. Not even close to substance. And then I feel the rush as my brain releases endless amounts of chemicals, shocked by reality, and I am nowhere to be found.

I don't know what's happening. I don't know anything. I feel stunningly numb. Elegantly wrecked.

I smell the faint odor of a fire far away. No sound. No flashes. Only the smell. I feel like convulsing, but I have no body. No containment for this forsaken soul. No chance of ever putting a real notch on the tree.

And out of the absolute darkness, a point appears. No color. No reality. But it's there. Staring at me. Staring through me. I can't look at it. I can't look away. I can't react. I let it happen. I let it grow. I let it blind me and burn me.

And just like that. Everything is gone.

"Good God," Jessica said. She was having trouble deciding if she should feel bad for Brian Hotz. She usually never felt bad for people when it was their own fault. She wondered if it was his fault. Had he chosen to become such a scared little pill popping fiend, or was he simply insane? She couldn't decide right then.

If she were telling the truth, Brian Hotz disgusted her. There was no doubt about it. The unfolding story in the diary was one of failure. One of doubt and weakness. One of questions on things she considered irrelevant to question. The story was one that went against everything Jessica. It made her uncomfortable to feel like she was there with him, like she was him.

She thought she felt both for him. She did feel bad for him, and at the same time, she didn't feel bad for him at all.

CHAPTER 12

It was late in the afternoon before Jessica put the book down and got out of bed to eat something. She fixed some eggs, had a cup of coffee, watched some television, and then returned to her bed, picking up the book once again.

The Story Of Brian Hotz

I wake up blind. Pure white stabbing me in the eyes like daggers, sending unyielding, echoing pain through my skull. My brain smashed.

Where am I? What happened? What the... What the hell just happened to me?

The eternal questions. The endless voids. The constant lack of any answer what-so-ever. Man is a being of hopeless direction.

Forms begin taking shape in my field of vision. Blurry colors and obstructed shadows. I give up questioning the reality of it. Reality. Consciousness. All of it means nothing to anyone. It is nothing more than a glimpse of something possibly solid on the horizon of the sea... but no one knows for sure.

I soon realize I'm lying on a solid bed, in a solid white room, with solid sounds and an all around solid appearance. This is what we believe is reality.

My mind flashes incessant scenes of horror. That moment, the one when I realized that I was driving at top speed in unknown directions, the one when I noticed that I was entirely covered in blood, I swore I felt something inside of me snap; like a breached emotional barrage.

I wonder where the blood had come from? Was that part

even real? Am I... dead? Is this my hell? This eternal limbo of blinding lights and distant pain that feels physical, but could very well be psychological.

I think about pills. So many pills. Inside of those variously sized and fun colored tablets, so much inner peace is encapsulated. So many weak and feeble safeties provided by the illusion. So many truths to be found in the misery of it all. The truth, that none of it ever matters.

They should make a pill for that.
That feeling. It's ugly. It's... It's so empty. So null, and void.

I am suddenly aware of my new, slowly forming reality. This place, this room... This is heaven. These aggressive overtones of sterility. These harmless, yet overly bright light bulbs. The distant coughs and laments. The never ending beeps. The never ending hope.

I stare around me for some time, quite emotionless about the whole thing. I am comfortable here. I am happy and complete. I am safe.

I stare at the woolen blankets other people have undoubtably died in. I stare at the very distant, very unconnected sight of the tiny television hanging silently in the far corner. I stare at the tubes, and the digital displays, and all of the subtle reminders that help us forget what we truly are.

Scared.
Perhaps terrified is a better word to use. Everyone terrified. Every minute. Every day. Every direction we dare take a stab at.

I can see only blue through the tiny window by the side of my bed. The occasional bird flying by almost in mockery of my situation. That kind of freedom was never ours to have.

I stare at my own shape bunching up the blankets from underneath. I feel nothing. This containment is only temporary, I'm sure. This body, this machine, it won't last forever. Anyone who has ever had trauma knows that. How is anyone to deal with a trauma when their very own body feels like it's someone else's? Something else that is simultaneously connected and disconnected from your being.

Oh, the troubles with consciousness.
Leeches will slither into your body and suck out your blood.

How did that fit into God's image? Sometimes I wonder if we are nothing more than leeches. Sometimes I wonder if there even is an image. Sometimes, I wonder why God hates me so much.

I stare at my hands, my knuckles are raw and covered with hard dry blood. Even the mere shape of my hands don't register as mine. They are as alien as if I were staring at yours. Useless stumps. Dead digits.

I follow the flooded veins that nurture my hands. The way they sort of twist and turn around each other, a testament really to the supreme engineering intelligence that none of us will ever know or even begin to understand. It is all far too advanced. Or perhaps so simple that we refuse to accept it.

I feel something cold around my left wrist, and I immediately realize why. There are handcuffs around it, the other end clasped to the bed. I'm... I'm... Trapped like a savage. I'm... I'm...

Instantly, I feel that grotesque rush of ugly wash through me with incredible speed. The illusion has been shattered.

A beaver will chew through its limbs in order to survive and will continue to do so until no limbs remain.

I can hear the scream more than I can feel it. Panic. Pure and absolute and obliterate. My mind's a concocted mess of horrors. The thoughts assaulting my very core.

What if there's a fire? Oh, God. Please don't let me die chained to a bed. What if terrorists take over and begin shooting completely at random? I would have nowhere to hide! I would be wasted! What if some tuberculosis infected motherfucker comes hacking by my door? What then? Oh, God! I can see the microbes swimming through the air like graceful angels with the sting of rotting death. I can feel the infection already! I can feel my lungs beginning to rot, beginning to soften and then harden. Restricting. Constricting. Fucking...

Something is jabbed into my arm but I never stop. Those goddamn diseases wouldn't, and neither would I! The room swells and contracts around me. The cold sweat bursts from my pores. The eyes wild. Pupils savage. The smell of shit.

I watch as various objects fly high into the room's stratosphere and then crash back to the ground. I can hear screams. I can hear fear. Chaos. Madness.

"Stop him!" I hear. "Just give it to him now!"
Frantic figures rush from all angles around me as I twist and
lash out like a savage beast being pushed into a corner. I foam. I
scream. I am lost in confusion.

My tongue suddenly feels awfully thick. Numb.
Featureless. I try to scream against the oncoming darkness.
Against the horrors. The ghoulish, haunting nightmares. But it's
no use. I can't think, let alone move.

I suddenly feel an unwanted, internal submission overtake
me. That quiet, universal resolve that only comes out in the end
when no other questions remain and it is all over.

The big joke.
I was about to giggle.

But I can't remember why.

Jessica didn't want to read the story anymore. She didn't
like it. She hated it, actually. It said things that she said in real
life, but with a different meaning, a different context. She put the
book on her night stand and lit a cigarette. She wrapped herself
in soft blankets, and propped her back up against the headboard,
thinking about the possibilities of the diary being related to her
case in some way. Could she have been so lucky? The more she
read, the more likely she felt like the story was a work of fiction.
Perhaps Nicole's; perhaps not. But the probability of it belonging
to the man she was looking for, well, she was unconvinced.

In a way, she enjoyed that possibility. The one that the
book was nothing of importance, because she would never have
to risk anyone finding out about it. But if the other possibility
was correct, and this book was in some way related to her
sickening case, what then? She supposed it would depend on
what kind of information she would discover. A name was easy
to get away with. Specific details that could not otherwise be
known, that was another story.

She put out her cigarette, and stretched her arms up high in
the air, yawning. Her eyes were heavy, and welling up with tears
of fatigue. She turned her lamp off and slid onto her back.

Jessica was no longer thinking.

CHAPTER 13

Her phone woke her up. She had been dreaming of something happy, but she couldn't remember what it was. She sat up frantically at the sudden sound. She hated being woken up like that. Loud noises. Jolting panics. She looked at the phone and realized it was Captain Briar calling her. It was 12:48 a.m.

She already knew there was another victim. Another piece of art for people to gasp and gag at. Another nightmare that people would never get out of their heads.

Reality shifted again. Some things could not be undone. "Hello," she said.

"Jessie?" Captain Briar also sounded half-asleep. "Yeah, Cap, hi."

"Hi, Jess. I just got the call. They've found another one." "Where?"

"South end of the city," he said. "Where do I meet you?"

"Meet me at the office first," he replied. "And Jessie?" "Yeah, Cap?"

"They already warned us; this one is especially bad." "How so?"

"They said..." He hesitated for a moment. "They said you'd have to see it to believe it. Dear God, what kind of monster is this man?"

"A real one, Cap," she said. "We need to stop this, Jessica."

"I know," she replied. "We will." "I can only hope to God," he said.

"I'll see you in twenty minutes," she said.

"All right, Jessie. See you there."

Out of bed, she quickly brushed her hair, got dressed, and left her apartment.

When she pulled into the parking lot, Captain Briar was already standing outside waiting for her, smiling warmly when he saw her. A sweet man, she thought.

"Hi, Cap," she said. "Get in."

"Sure," Captain Briar said, and climbed into the passenger side.

"So?" he asked. "How have you been holding up, kiddo?"

"I'm fine," she said. "How about you?"

"Oh, well, an old man like myself has no other choice, does he? Ha. Ha. Either fine or dead."

Jessica chuckled.

"So I should be getting my matches by tomorrow morning," she said. "Hopefully it'll give us something to work with."

"Yeah..." The Captain trailed off, but Jessica sensed that he was keeping something from her.

"Yeah?–Are you all right, Captain?"

"I'm ah, I'm fine, yes. I'm... Well, Jessica, I won't lie to you, because I don't think I can, but I don't know if I can actually handle this case anymore. I mean, nothing has ever shaken me in thirty two years. And now, on the home stretch to retirement, this bastard comes out of nowhere and infects everyone's minds with ghoulish nightmares and irrational fears. I, I'm sorry, I don't want to bore you with..."

"It's okay, Captain. I'm listening just as much as you would do for me."

She was correct in that statement. Jessica and Captain Briar had a special relationship that extended beyond their professional affiliations. He cared for her as though she was one of his own daughters. She cared for him as though he were her father. She could always go to Captain Briar to talk about anything, and he would never judge her, or belittle her. He gave her the truth, which was all she ever wanted. Just the truth.

"Yes, well, I appreciate it, my young girl," he replied.

"Have you been sleeping, Cap?"

"I have. I've been having trouble with nightmares, but I am falling asleep. Ha," he chuckled. "All those years and now something gets me. The worst part is, I don't think I will ever see anything more grotesque in my life. Nothing will ever top this type of manic psychosis."

"Yeah," Jessica said. "He's a real piece of work, isn't he? I bet he's afraid of us. If not, well, he should be."

"They should all be afraid," he said. "But they rarely are, my dear. They rarely are."

It was true. The people Jessica had hunted and brought to justice since she'd started working with Captain Briar, had all been fearless. Fearless, yes. Psychotic, yes. But none of them had ever succeeded in being so blatantly evil. So perverse. So haunting.

"So what did they tell you about this?" Jessica asked. "Only what I told you on the phone. They said it was especially bad. I'm not exactly sure what that means. I'm not sure I even want to go inside of that room."

"I'll be there, Cap."

"Yeah," he said. "I admire the confidence you hold in yourself in order to do what needs to be done. In some ways," he chuckled. "You're more of a man than I am."

Jessica laughed. Her Captain was a humble man. He was kind and caring, and she also didn't think that he should enter those rooms anymore if they were bothering him so much. She had learned a long time ago that most people were not like her. Most people could not consciously choose which parts of their personality to turn on, and which ones to turn off. Most people, she thought, had very little control over themselves.

She didn't feel bad for those people.

"Well, Cap," she said. "You're the only man I really do need in my life. If you can't make it inside of the room, don't. I've got it."

"I know you do," he replied. "It just doesn't seem fair." "Please," she said. "It's my decision. My fault. My consequences."

"Your parents must have had a tough time with such a free mind."

She grinned a little. "You have no idea."

They finally arrived on the scene, where a whirlwind of

emergency vehicles and curious onlookers clogged the street. The murder had taken place inside of a house, centered in what seemed like an otherwise quiet neighborhood. A school across the street. A daycare. A playground.

She and Captain Briar made their way through the assembling crowd of curious bodies and entered the house. Once inside, standing at the precipice of the bedroom, Jessica immediately stopped everything.

"Everybody out of the house, now," she ordered. "Not in the kitchen, not in the living room, everyone outside."

Tired, beaten eyes stared back at her, and then complied without objection.

"You can stay here if you want, Cap," she said. "Don't do anything you don't need to. You're too old." She chuckled.

Captain Briar tried to chuckle, but just standing inside of the house took the ability away from him. Jessica wondered if he could also feel the evil embedded into the walls.

They had not lied. The people who had called Captain Briar were fully correct in what they had told him. You'll have to see it to believe it. But, even though she could look at it, didn't mean that she believed it.

The victim was another woman. Same general age, about mid-twenties. Same general body type. She had been stripped naked like the rest of them, but it hardly mattered. She was barely recognizable as a human being.

This time, the killer had outdone himself. She was sprawled out on the floor, on her back, with her legs spread open. He had nailed her feet to the floor. Her arms had been stretched over her head, and also nailed down. He had painted her yellow. Jessica knew that she was supposed to be a star.

He had smashed everything in the room, as per his usual ceremony. The perfectly laid out debris was present, radiating away from her, but he had also systematically placed and burnt dozens of candles around her. A literal star, it seemed.

Deep, precise lines were cut into her flesh, all driving away from her core. Most of them were simple, and straight. The illusion was artistically correct, but what confused Jessica most, was her face. The killer had made a mockery of it. He had beaten her to a pulp, leaving evidence of a savage, beast like rage. He had done no such thing to any of the other victims.

He had sliced her cheeks open, leaving dead teeth glaring, and cut tribal-like lines over her entire neck. Jessica immediately thought of the first victim. The abstract scene with the tribal cuts.

She studied the cuts closely, but then noticed something odd from in between her teeth. The tip of her tongue seemed to be sticking out. She wasn't certain at first, but once she got closer, there was no denying it. There were cuts on her tongue, too.

She quickly fumbled in her pockets for a pair of latex gloves and her tweezers. She put the gloves on, and stared at the tongue again, sticking out from a macabre face. A broken mouth. There was definitely a visible cut on it.

She tried to open her jaw as delicately as she could, but it was impossibly seized shut by rigor mortis. She grabbed a hold of the woman's tongue with the tweezers and pulled. They kept slipping off, but little by little, it was coming out. When Jessica thought she could probably grab it with her fingers, she did, and pulled.

The tongue came out, and Jessica dropped her tweezers to the floor and sharply stepped back, knocking over some of the debris. She was speechless. She was panicked. She had, for the first time ever, scoffed involuntarily in pure horror.

Cut into the woman's tongue, Jessica could very clearly see a word.

Her tongue said:

Sister

CHAPTER 14

"This ends now!" Jessica said.

After the woman's tongue, after she had felt embarrassed by her initial shock, and after she had demanded that the team get back into the house and comb through every inch of the place twice, she told Captain Briar to get in the car.

"Where are we going?"

"We're going through Nicole White's files ourselves, and right now."

The Captain clearly didn't understand, he stared dumbly at her.

"This one is a fresh kill," she said.

"Right, okay?"

"He knows who I am, Captain. He knows he's killed my sister. He knows who I am, and now I'm going to know who he is."

"Easy, kiddo. Easy. How do you know?"

"Captain... He left me a note."

"A note?" he was astonished.

"Sister," she said. "The sick bastard carved the word sister into her tongue."

Captain Briar momentarily needed to lean his head against the headrest. It was all becoming too much. She noticed how his eyes went blank, and terror obviously flashed through his mind. That was the worst kind of terror, she thought. The type without direction. It just comes from all angles, yet still lacks any real definition. It's a haunting terror.

On the way back to the office, Jessica thought about Brian Hotz. She was positive that if Brian Hotz was a real person, she would find him in Nicole White's files. She was going to find him, and she was going to hunt him. She'd had enough of being made a fool of by The Fleshcrafter.

Jessica and her Captain, along with a few other helpers, sifted meticulously through Nicole White's files. Jessica's brain mulched through the information. She caught every name, every note, everything she needed to know, and stored it deep in her mind. She was looking at the names and simultaneously, wishfully, thinking that the next file on deck would be titled Brian Hotz. Although she did not entirely believe that Brian Hotz was, in fact, a real person, the last murder scene had been enough to make her push every available lead to extinction. Every option, every possibility, explored.

"He's in here somewhere," she said to Captain Briar. "I... I don't know how we are to distinguish anyone from..."

"I'll know, Cap. Just look for anything that stands out. Anything at all, even if you don't understand why it caught your eye, just put it aside."

She was feeling incredibly frustrated. There was an overbearing sense of urgency coming down on her. She was slashing through names with unflinching determinism. Name, description, next. Name, description, next. She was looking for side notes. She was looking for anything that Nicole White might have left for her to discover. A direction. A sense of direction. A scribble. An odd word. Brian Hotz.

When she was suitably frustrated, she went outside and lit a cigarette. She thought about the woman's tongue. She thought that if the killer knew who she was, maybe she should use herself as bait to lure him in. Even if she did die in the process, at least the principle would still hold true. He would never get away with doing anything more to anyone after she had dealt with him. Dead or alive, she would make damn sure of that. Somehow.

She puffed on her cigarette and thought about Brian Hotz again. That disgusting little character. That pill popping little fiend. That freak. She thought about her sister. She thought about all of the other victims. She thought... She thought that she was stuck, and there was little more she hated than being stuck.

She extinguished her cigarette and went back inside to

riffle through more boxes of files. It felt like reinforcing the reality that it would take an eternity to sift through every folder; that the possibility of actually finding a name just sitting there with a neon sign around it was quickly disappearing. It wasn't going to happen, and it definitely wasn't going to happen in one night.

Eventually, once the sun was up and people started pouring in for work, Jessica found herself with heavy eyes.

At 9:00 a.m. exhausted, she rushed to the elevator, heading down to the lab. She walked in and the short lady immediately smiled.

"Good morning, Detective Sanders. I've got some good news for you."

Jessica felt something happy rupture inside of her. She thought it felt like relief. She thought... She thought it felt like hope.

"You've got a match?" she asked excitedly.
"Well, it's actually bitter sweet," the short lady said. "The mirror shard was from the third victim's home which... I'm sorry to hear, Detective."

"Thank you," she said. "And what about the pubic hair?"
"It's male," she said.

"What about a name?"
"That's the bitter part," the short lady replied. "He's unknown. No matches in the system."

"No matches at all?"
The lady shook her head disparagingly. "I'm sorry, Detective."

"That's all right," Jessica replied.
The short lady's eyes were full of pity. Jessica didn't really know her, but she genuinely felt sorry for the loss of her sister. So much so, that it was making her quite uncomfortable.

"Thank you," Jessica said. "I'll be back with anything else I find."

She walked away with a sense of defeat on one hand, and a sense of progress on the other. Sure, she didn't have a name or an address for a door to kick down, but at least she now had a reference point. At least, if she did find a suspect, she was now able to conclusively prove his guilt or innocence, without having to fight for a confession. She had all the confession she needed.

She thought about the mirror shard. She had already known it was the same killer who had committed all of the crimes, that much was blatantly obvious, but obvious never held up in court. Now she knew it, without a shadow of a doubt.

In her mind, she pictured her sister's body with those uncountable shards of mirror pushed into her skin, turning her into some psychotic's idea of art–of a joke. She remembered her sister's violated eyes reflecting her own face right back to herself. She remembered the pubic hair that had finally caught her eye. It felt like hope, no matter how feeble. It felt like progress. A break, and one she'd nearly missed.

She wondered, momentarily, that if no one noticed something, did that still make it real? She wondered why she had let Brian Hotz's thinking into her head. She hated that book. She hated the story–yet–she couldn't bring herself to stop thinking about it. For all of its obscene repulsion, she'd had a difficult time putting it down and focussing her mind on something else. The book was in her big brain, and it was lurking around in there behind every other thought she had. She couldn't simply forget about it.

She went back into the office, where the exhausted bodies of those who'd volunteered to help were still huddled over endless amounts of files in unnatural postures. Their wasted eyes reminded Jessica of stoners at a highschool party.

"Okay everyone," she said. "Just take a break. You can all go home for now. Get some rest. Calm your eyes, and I'll get another team working on this while we're out."

The team hardly hesitated before heading out of the doors like panicked animals, nearly running across the parking lot toward their vehicles.

She told Captain Briar about the pubic hair and the mirror. It was conclusive, they now had a reference point, and although it wasn't much, for the first time since the bodies started appearing, they had something concrete.

He was happy about the news, but he was worried about Jessica burning herself out, and asked her if she was also going home to rest. He was urging her with his eyes. Reluctantly, she agreed, and moments later, left the building.

While she drove through the busy morning streets, she thought the silence was unbearable. There was a somber stillness pressing hard against her temples. It made her feel eerie. She turned on the radio, but it did very little to stop the silence. That silence was one of internal struggle. That silence was making her crazy with unfocussed thoughts.

When she walked into her apartment, she stripped, and jumped into the shower. She sat on the bottom of the tub and thought of her sister once again. She thought of her parents. She thought about how devastated they would have been by all of this. She thought about all the victims, and all of the demented art. She hated how clearly she could see them all. There was no way of toning them down; no process to make them any less clearer than crystal clear. She thought about the latest victim and her tongue. She thought the killer knew who she was. She thought Captain Briar would end up losing his mind. She thought... She thought she was going to cry.

She felt a choking helplessness race up her spine like cold shivers. She felt the gasping her body was doing, her convulsing diaphragm, her shoulders bouncing up and down with every sob.

Never in her life had she been shaken with such brute force.

She thought about how she had always believed that it was impossible for anyone to do this to her, much less anyone she didn't even know. She hated it. She hated being human in times like these. She hated her emotions, and her weakness. She liked being a machine. Strong, unmovable, untouchable. She hated that a bigger machine than she was out there, and that machine had managed to shake her violently. She hated that she already knew that the bigger machine would never stop killing innocent women until she stopped him.

She hated, that she still felt so alone. She hated that this monster had made her feel so lonely. That he had actually made her fear him. She hated that she couldn't make the connection yet and blow his mangled little head off.

Jessica thought that if she could help it, there would never be a trial for this demon. She would do everything in her power to end it right then and there, wherever she'd manage to find him.

She thought about the fact that he probably already knew where she lived. It wouldn't have been very difficult to find out. Not for him, or for anyone else interested. It was all over the media. Every headline seemed to begin with, "More developments on The Fleshcrafter case tonight. Another body was found..."

She took a deep breath and told herself that she wasn't afraid of him. She didn't feel the need to sleep with her gun on her night stand, or tucked neatly underneath her pillow like a silent guardian.

She turned off the water in the shower and dried herself. She stopped crying and focussed her mind to a comfortable, stable mood while she brushed her hair. She was unmovable. Untouchable. It was early in the morning, and she was fully exhausted, but her mind would not cease. She sat around and vacantly watched television for a while, waiting for the fatigue to build, waiting for her mind to calm.

It was 4 p.m. before she finally flopped herself onto the bed, nestled inside the blankets, sunk her head into the pillow, and closed her eyes.

"I miss you, Katy," she whispered before falling asleep. It was what it was.

CHAPTER 15

The Story Of Brian Hotz

"Do you remember anything at all, Mr. Hotz?"
This guy smells like leather. He also blinks too much, which does
nothing to help stow my own terminal nervousness. His teeth
are stained from too much caffeine. His face creases up when he
speaks, as though he were an intricate origami caricature sprung
to life in my very own special nightmare.

I can hear him breathing. I can see the billions of microbes
spewing from his mouth. I don't trust him at all. It's his eyes. He
seems... Genuinely concerned.

I must get out of here!
"Anything at all, Brian?" he reiterates.

He told me his name when he first came into the room
while I sat on this cold steel chair feeling like my body was about
to burst open in anxiety. The sweating hasn't stopped. Neither
have the tremors, or the nausea. He told me his name, but I was
thinking about my leaking nose. That eternal faucet that's never
quite closed. Sometimes, I wonder if it's my brain slowly losing
substance. Quietly escaping until there is nothing left for anyone
but an empty carcass to be shoved into the ground forever.

"What's going on?" I mumble. My voice sounds even
weaker to me. I sound like even more of a goddamned wimp. If a
space heater came on in this room, I doubt I'd even hear myself.
I wonder if it's contagious? I wonder if I'm dying?

"Well, Brian, first I would like to see what you can tell
me."

"I don't remember anything, all right!" I snap. "I don't...

I don't know what the fuck is happening to me! I think I'm... I think..."

I burst into tears, and suddenly, I can feel my sense of doom clearer than ever in my life. This decaying existence. This microscope stuck on one spot, one emotion, and never deviates.

Some people think crying is a good thing. Those people have never truly cried.

"All right," he says calmly. "It's all right, Brian. Nothing in this room can hurt you."

Prostate worms. Testicular eels. Ear dwelling parasites. I pant, trying to regain my composure, but I feel overly exhausted. I feel like a train hit me at high speed and never bothered to stop. I feel like... I feel like these walls are going to burst open in a massive explosion and make shrapnel of us all.

I pray for it.

"Brian, would you like some water?"

I nod yes, but when he gives me the cup, I see nothing but menace. Has it been filtered? Disinfected? Treated? Is this processed water? What would happen if I drank unprocessed water? What kind of evil devils would I host then?

I drink the water anyway, trying to ignore it all.

"All right, Brian. Now, we are..."

"Where am I?" I cut him off.

"Well... You are in Saint Joseph's Mental Health Hospital."

My heart stops. I can already feel the restraining jackets. The syringes of unknown wonders in my arms. The drool. The boredom. The hell.

"Wh.. What?" I ask again.

"Brian, you've been involved in a little... Situation, let's say. Now, I am only here for an assessment of how you are doing."

"Situation?" I frown. "What... What kind of situation? When?"

"Three days ago." He replies.

"Three... Three days?" I question as the waves of empty memories come crashing in. I can remember feelings. Always, just the feelings, but nothing of the actual reality. I remember the panic. I remember the crescendoing swoons. I remember the blood.

Three days is a long time without memory. Three days is a long time without anything. Had I been sleeping? Had I been awake? Was I awake now?

It took Jesus three days to die, go to hell, and resurrect. I wonder why it took him so long? I wonder if he remembered any of it? I wonder how upset he is these days?

"Please... Uh... Dr.?"

"Dr. Bill Harper. But you can call me Bill if you'd like." He smiles. There is nothing to smile back about.

"Bill..." I crackle. "Bill, um... What... What exactly happened to me? How did I get here? How did... How did... Um... Where are my pills? I could really use some yellows right about now, doc."

This man said he was a doctor. He spoke like a doctor. He stared like a doctor. But he looked nothing like my doctor. This wasn't even a doctor's room. It seemed more like an interrogation room. Void of any discerning detail aside from a large Formica table and three chairs. The rest was dim, quiet, and psychologically abrasive at best.

Then again, that woman with the padded leather chair had also said she was a doctor. This had all started with her. Her angelic face. The face of Satan.

"Do you take many pills?" He asks.

"What? Um... I guess."

"Can you tell me what kinds?"

"Hmm, take your pick." I sound so desperate.

"Do you take anti-depressants?"

"Anti-depressants, anti-nausea, anti-headaches, anti-ulcers, anti-acids, anti-gas, anti-life, anti-existence, anti-Me!" I scream. "Anti–fucking–everything. Always. Always anti-fucking me!"

He remained silent for a moment. Gauging me. Judging me.

There has never been a shred of evidence to show that an ostrich buries its head in the sand.

"Do you always feel like you are not a part of anything, Brian?"

I stare for a moment, my eyes screaming, "Are you fucking kidding me?!" My forehead is soaked with sweat. In fact, my entire body is soaked. My back, my legs, my useless testicles sticking against my thigh.

I say nothing.

"All right, Brian, I need you to tell me what the last thing you remember is. Is there anything in particular that you remember? It would make this all a little quicker if you helped me out a little."

I browse through the cast of memories stored in my twisted mind. Flashes and attacks of all kinds. Some real. Some not. Most unknown.

"I ah... Ah... I remember blood," I whimper.

"Blood. Okay, that's a start. So blood. What else do you remember?"

"Ah... I... Can I just get some pills, doc? Please! I'm about to crack here!"

"In a minute, Brian. In a minute, I promise. Please, what else do you remember?"

"I ah... I... Remember white light."

"White light?"

"Like I was dying," I say. "Have... Have I died?" I question it, and instantly, I feel a mute, deadpan fear of the answer. But at least it was an answer.

"No, Brian, you are quite alive. Quite alive indeed." The way his glasses sit on his nose, the way his eyebrows move to accentuate his words, it all makes me want to punch him in the face. I want to punch him. I want to kill him. I want to kill me.

"Great," I reply. I feel pure depression.

"Yes, quite great, Brian." He quickly agrees with a pursed, professional smile. "Now what else? What else comes to mind?"

"Ah..." I pant. I can feel the rush coming on again. It's like every tendon in my body contracts, sealing my lungs. "Ah... I.... I remember the sterile room. I... I remember the voices. The panic in them. The sound of things falling to the floor. The... The handcuffs!"

I stop at the realization. The handcuffs!

"Was... Was I arrested? What did I do? Ah, God... Did... Did I hurt someone? Did I screw up? Did I... Did I hurt anyone?"

"Okay, okay, it's all right. Let's just slow down here, okay,

Brian? One thing at a time."

"Did I kill someone or not?" I snap, and for a moment, my voice sounds exactly like it had in the office. A spontaneous memory. So clear now. The God-like tone of it. The monstrous confidence. The dream.

"No, Brian, you didn't kill anyone."

I remember the man's face, the one who shoved me against my car after I'd knocked his wife to the ground. I can't remember a conclusion. I can't... I can't remember anything else.

"I... I didn't?"

"No, you didn't. But you did hurt someone."

"What?"

Again the rush. The room swells fifteen sizes, and suddenly, everything is suspended.

"I... I hurt someone? Oh, God, who? Where? How... What the hell happened?"

"Okay, Brian. It's okay. It's okay. We'll figure this out together. I will explain to you what is happening, I just need you to..."

"I'm so fucking scared!" I exclaim, and burst into tears again, the pain unbearable. The possibilities negatively endless. The crack, where was the goddamn fault line to all of this? Where did the end lie?

"What are you afraid of, Brian?"

I say nothing and try to calm the tremors. My heart feels like it's ruptured. I wonder about my cholesterol.

"Brian?... Are you all right? Are you okay?"

I still say nothing.

"What is it that you're afraid of, Brian? What's scaring you?"

"I ah..." I clamp up again. Too many fast flying visions swirling though my head. Too little control.

"Brian, please. What are you afraid of?"

I then hear it coming out of me without any conscious consent on my part.

"Myself."

***

It was 8:14 p.m. when Jessica woke up; only four short hours after falling asleep. It was 8:36 p.m. now, and she had just finished going through her first chapter of Brian Hotz's disgusting little story for the night.

She truly did miss her sister, and thought that her sharp sense of loneliness was the culprit disturbing her dreams. The subconscious always has plans of its own, regardless of the conscious intent.

Jessica and her sister hadn't been very close when she was still alive. Of course, when they were innocent little girls, they got along quite well, but once their respective layers of innocence began flaking away in the face of reality, things inevitably changed.

She and her sister had been born opposites. Jessica had always been driven by a raw need to remain human, with all of its faults intact. She naturally carried an astute perspective of reality, and always, for one reason or another, tended to gravitate toward the darker side of life. She enjoyed the dark side. She thought that there was much more truth to be found through the darkness than through the sugar coated plastic that covered most people's scars and bleeding personality warts.

It was what it was.

Her sister, on the other hand, had truly believed that society was a thing fully capable of change, and all it really took was someone to take charge. She believed that with a little effort, all of the world's persistent problems could be eradicated. War, famine, genocide, all of it. She believed that there was a plan in God's eyes. She believed in God. She prayed to God.

Jessica hardly agreed. War could never be eradicated. Peace could never be established. Famine could not be stopped, and neither could genocide. She believed that her sister's thought process conveniently left out one factor that would always stand in the way of all of those goals.

People and their opinions.

She had tried to explain this to her sister only once, but Katy had immediately shut her mind to it. She didn't want to hear that the real problem was that whether in science, or religion, or war, or politics, or peace, or famine, or love, or hate, they were all matters of opinion, and only a true fool believed that everyone would unanimously agree on anything.

Jessica understood that humans tended to not change unless they had no other option, and even then, everyone had an opinion that others would not like, and would kill for, establish religions in the name of, segregate because of, hate, love, and define things all based on their own personal opinion of what was undoubtably correct, and why everyone else were idiots.

It was as real and as simple as anything else in Jessica's brain. All of it was a giant pipe dream filled with desperate opinions and hateful resistance. Humans would never make it to the end of time on their own. Not without the help of evolution to produce more intelligent, less opinioned beings, with far less concentrated lusts for satisfied egos.

Jessica saw it as a joke. Humanity's problem was its existence. It was plagued with so many mysteries and contradictions, that if looked at from far enough away, it was suddenly hilarious.

To have the awareness of the problem, but helpless to do anything about it. Hilarious indeed.

Jessica thought that for all of his disgust and repulsion, Brian Hotz was a person of hilarity. Trapped in eternal questions that would never be answered. Looking for answers to completely unfounded questions. Dealing with it all with pills, and fear, and confusion. She realized that Brian Hotz was even more opposite from her than her sister had been, yet, somehow, he was even more alike. The thought of it was unsettling.

She wondered for a moment on the intricate connection of all living things. She did believe that people were connected on some basic level. That people would evolve to be, at the very least, fundamentally alike, no matter what their personal situations were as children. She wondered how it was that a man like Brian Hotz could ask the same questions, and think the same things as she and most everyone else, and yet, no one was even close to being the same. No one anywhere was a duplicate.

She rustled around in bed feeling disparaged. Feeling... Feeling beaten. The sad reality was that the case still wasn't

going anywhere until more horrible art was unveiled. As evil as
evil gets.

She lit a cigarette and sat up against her headboard with
the book again.

The Story Of Brian Hotz

They gave me some ungodly pharmaceutical that's making
my eyes dry, and my mouth unbearably watery. Some cause the
opposite. Some also cause various locations of the body to leak,
swell, and hemorrhage. But almost all of them cause the peace.

Some say we're trying to play God. I think we are trying
to beat him. Feverishly aiming for peace no matter how artificial,
and regardless of consequences. Reality is hardly what matters.

One day, I think we may solve the universe riddle... And
will undoubtably deem to have found things wrong with it. If that
isn't offensive, I don't know what is.

Apparently humans know best.
While I sat in that room with that doctor, trying to keep my very
last finger nail of a grip on reality, the untrustable doctor told me
great tales of weird things and savage confusions.

His eyebrows raised up high when he tried to snap me
out of hopeless catatonia and keep my attention on the reality at
hand.

"The reality is," he said. "That you seem to be having an
increasingly difficult time keeping your awareness in reality." He
said, "You have trouble knowing the difference between what is
actually happening, and what is not." He said, "Do you tend to
masturbate constantly, or never at all?"

His eyebrows dropped low on his creased face pretty
much anytime I spoke. Something went flying through the room.
Seemed to flutter and smash. I wasn't sure.

A nurse came in and delivered a fantastic shot of heaven
directly in the bicep. I instantly felt the peace. The healthy
tranquility. The nirvana in my head.

The room settled, became still again, and my vision went
from a bad, to a good level of blur. A comfortable numbness. A
happy place.

I then sat quietly while the doctor continued with his frustrated stares. I wondered if I had a snot hanging. I wondered if he was staring at a new mole. I wondered why I was still able to think rather clearly through such a blissful abyss.

He told me about the man, the husband I remembered, the woman I'd pushed, the panic that had torn me apart. He told me about the husband's injuries. He told me about the broken glass I had driven into his face by smashing it repeatedly into my car's windshield. He told me about the broken arm. He told me about her shattered nose, and the accident, and the fire. My car had caught fire. I had lit my car on fire by smashing it at top speed into a parked vehicle. I had aimed directly for it. He told me that they couldn't understand how I was still alive. He told me I was losing it again. He told me... He told me that my survival without so much as a scratch was nothing short of a miracle.

I felt my heart stop again. I felt my lungs squeeze. I felt... I felt fear again.

I wanted to speak, to say something, but I was beyond lost. Trapped in a heaven that was trapped in a hell.

He told me the couple were going to be fine. He told me they were initially pressing charges, but the lady had persuaded her husband to drop them on account of my current mental state. He told me I had to stay here for three weeks on court order. He told me I had no choice, but it might do me so good.

Then they shoved me into this wheelchair and crammed me in front of some obscure window. Lost to the outside by 30 something other stories.

Story of my life.

I've never been on the outside looking in; always on the inside looking out. At least I wasn't on the fourth floor. That kind of irony would probably be too much to handle right now.

Outside, it's raining in the dark. Inside, I am completely sedated. Stoned into conformity. Drugged into the system.

The rain is collecting but I'm not really paying attention. I'm silently wondering how any of this could be real. Do I still have a job? Am I actually in this place? Am I still out of milk?

I think of my hairline. I think of my apartment. I think of my puke. When was the last time I had puked? The last time I had qualified myself.

I think about the couple. I try to remember something, anything. How could I forget driving a man's face through a windshield? I've never lifted a weight in my life. I cower like a little girl in the face of the most minuscule form of confrontation. How could I have done something like that?

I think about the accident. The speed. The apparent deadlocked suicide attempt. I aimed for it? I would never have the balls. I am that much of a coward. Trapped in a fiery blaze? Not a scratch?

A miracle?

That word makes me more uncomfortable than any other in existence. Miracle. It implies care. It implies... Meaning, and, and God. God. God cares? Why would God care about anyone, let alone me? If I am made in God's image, I do not want him to care. I do not want any help. I do not want anything from anyone.

As I sit here, silently baked out of my skull on incredibly debilitating pharmaceuticals, debating the meaning of such things, I can't, for some reason, get the image of the girl's face out of my head. The beautiful doctor. The lady who smelled like heaven and made me recoil in horror. The hot embarrassment on my face like a highschool kid who'd just dropped his bag of weed in front of his parents. The mess of pills around me. The incomprehensible look on her face. The confusion. The impression.

I wonder if she still thought about me? I wonder what she thought about it all? I wonder if she'd seen what happened in the parking lot? I still wonder what she looks like naked.

I think that I really miss my series of meaningless, mundane activities that allow me to live in the darkest shadows, where I may not necessarily be happy, but at least I feel safe.

Or do I?

Jessica put her cigarette out and continued reading.

I think I'm beginning to learn it. The peace, I mean. These drugs, flowing so gracefully through my beaten veins, I think they're beginning to teach me something. A feeling. A place.

Perhaps I've had too big of a dose, but for the moment, I can do anything.

My stay at the Holy Joseph's Hospital for Mental Health has been rather easy, seeing as the charges against me were dropped. I am here on court order alone in order to determine my mental stability, my ability to successfully reintegrate myself as an adjusted individual into society once again, and of course, to make sure I'm not going to blow my head off the second I walk out of here.

Of course, they keep me armed to the teeth with fantastic concoctions of opiates, and barbiturates, and all kinds of wonderful chemicals that mask what's really happening. And what's really happening on any scale, no one has an answer for.

The various doctors here shuffled me through aptitude tests, and memory tests, and psychological tests. They tested my body, my mind, my soul. They pressed me with questions and probed deep into things that had never happened in the past.

No, my father was not abusive. No, I was not molested as a child. No, my mother was not a vindictive frying pan wielding maniac. No, I didn't have any siblings. Yes, my father died when I was young. No, we were not poor.

In fact, my father had been a successful small business man. He manufactured car parts to fill aftermarket needs. He'd had over 60 employees. My mother was a housewife. My grandparents visited almost every weekend. My cousins slept over. I used to have a best friend. I used to be normal. I used to be happy. I used to... I used to be a child. I used to be oblivious.

No, there was no trauma or dramatic event that set anything off. No, I do not remember feeling this way when I was a child. No, I was never really good with people. I like the background. It's safe. I like the mundanity, no matter how soul wrenching. It's safe. I like the pills. The pills... The pills make it all tolerable.

Do I think I may have a drug problem?
Of course not. I don't think I know anyone who does not take a pill for one reason or another. It's what people do. A bad heart, a constant pain, a blistering headache, a soft dick, anything remotely resembling being human, take a pill for it.

Yes, I grew up playing video games and chatting on computers. Yes, I remember those years rather well. Yes, I was always kind of a loser; girlfriends were definitely scarce events.

No, I do not know why I am who I am. What kind of question is that? I do not know why any of this is happening. I do not know anything. Nothing at all. I don't even know what I want to happen next. No goal. No direction. No concrete thing whatsoever.

The doctors here advised the court that I had in fact completed all necessary prerequisites in order to leave the facility. They also advised the court that they felt it would be very helpful for me to be forced to see a psychiatrist on a weekly basis. The judge asked me what I thought. Nobody ever asks me what I think.

I asked for the doctor with Satan's face, to which the judge agreed. So, for the next year, I would have to see doctor smell good devil face every single week.

I have been thinking a lot about the pretty doctor lately. Wondering what she is thinking about. Wondering if she remembers everything vividly. Hoping that she would not.

I thought about her at night. If I could feel anything, I might do something about it, but the drugs do fine for now.

Especially since right now, they are doing a fantastic job of keeping me distant while I sit in this circle of broken souls. They are keeping me calm around these people who have no lives to identify with, no emotional roots to base themselves on–these people–these people are just like me. Sad. Depressed. Batshit insane. We sit here every second day and talk about what we are thinking about.

Ah, to be a comedian.
Some of this stuff, even to a broken little wimp like myself, well, it's hard not to take notice. Evelyn, over there, she's been thinking about taking a tampon out for the first time in weeks. Something about bugs. And I was delusional? Although, I could see her point.

Fucking germs.
Dave over here has been thinking about some comet or other that is supposed to pick him up on the way by, and all I can think of

is, if you're right, I'm coming with you.

Mary, right here next to me, has been thinking about penises. She hates penises. Mostly because penises were jabbed into her when she was a young girl while her back was used as an ashtray. Maybe, maybe she knows something I don't.

My entire life, my entire long sequence of meaningless actions, has always seemed like one long day. Same day. Same reality. Same safety. I don't even think in terms of days anymore. It's all more of a rhapsody. It never ends. It never begins. It never happened.

The counsellor is wrapping up the session for today on account of Henry losing his mind and throwing a chair clear across the room right after Mary's penis freakout. Perhaps he too was jabbed as a boy. Despite his sheer violence, from my standpoint, he is still better off than I am.

Less pain in his eyes.

I think about the doctor again. The way she smelled would bring a beast to its knees. The way she smelled caused your heart to skip. The way, the way she smelled made you want to take her.

I now only have two days left in this horrid place filled with crazy screams and overwhelmingly powerful drugs. Three weeks here already, but I don't think it's helped. I don't think it's done anything except turn me into an honorary junkie. A "Legal Junkie" as they like to call people being pumped full of poisons by their government. This entire time I've been trying to feel something. Anything. But I have nothing. I am a fried brain. I am an exiled soul. I am dead.

And then what? What after this? Back to the dilapidating shit hole I call home? That wonderful place where so many times the walls have closed in on me, the ceiling collapsed, the muted screams echoed against the rubble as the floor opened wide to swallow me into oblivion. Where so many times the very fabric of reality seemed to rip open right before my eyes and crash me into panic, into pain, into regression, into... Into... What?

Into what, indeed.

I no longer have a job. I no longer have a car. I no longer have anything. How can people who have nothing still lose? Is that what life is about? Is that part of God's image? Is all of this somehow entwined into a universal connection?

Well... I still can't hear anything out there. And nothing is always much worse than anything.

Despite the drugs, and the sessions, and the doctors, and the confusion, and the fear, and the loss of reality, despite it all, I still feel the same. I still feel nothing but fear's monstrous grip wrapped around my throat; I'm perpetually trapped in the squeeze.

I feel like I need to break out, but I've given up trying all those years ago. I've tried to deal with it. I've tried to stow it, and take control of my emotions, and be in control of myself, but that's the funny thing about control, no one ever has it to begin with. No one controls anything.

But I feel like I'm quickly approaching the breaking point, and I'm terrified. I, like all conscious beings, am completely terrified of being lost forever in the great annals of nothingness. Although, lost is something you can deal with, forgotten is not.

When you feel your skin tighten like it's about to burst, and your heart swell up like a watermelon, and your brain shake in horror, eventually you start to think that you might need some help. You also begin to think about the meaning of it all; about how you matter, how you make a difference in this savage jungle. How will anyone possibly remember me? How does any of this serve a purpose without an obvious goal, and without a way of qualifying it all?

This is fear.
You think I'm afraid of God? How could I be? I've already resolved that he hates me. I think that part is quite obvious.

My father would be so disappointed if he could see me now. This little wimp. This little insignificant speck of dust merely floating through the everyday grinds, always in the background, always a piece of furniture, always a painting on the wall looking out.

He would laugh at the frail frame of my body, and curse my lack of faith in God almighty. He would ridicule my apartment, and tell me not to give up on myself. He would tell me not to lower myself like I have been doing my entire life, and the reality of it all is, I don't know any other way.

The grass is never green on the other side when you look out in the dark.

He would tell me to man up, to make a mark on the world, to learn something useful, to become the best at anything I do, to save my money, invest my savings, retire young, and have the ability to choose to work instead of not having another option.

He would tell me all those things and more with a straight face, and taking himself with absolute seriousness, and to me, it would be like watching television. My entire life, I've just been watching television. I see what comes through. All of these shows and plays and movies and important expressions of art and literature and dance... And none of it includes me. Not even for a frame. Not even for background.

I am no one.

The nurse just gave me another pill. I don't even know what I'm taking anymore. I am taking peace. That is all I know. She wheels me into my room where my suitcase is, still packed from when I arrived. No use in making another horrible place like home. No need for these walls to come crashing down on me the second someone sneezes, or coughs, or farts, or run their fingers through their hair.

No need for any of it. No need for me.

I lie in my cold bed and shut my eyes. My jaw still clenches tighter than a pit bull's when I sleep. My hands form involuntary fists. My body does not lay perfectly straight or still for any extended period of time.

And suddenly, I'm standing on top of a mountain. The view is incredible. The sky is as clear and blue as an upended ocean. The air... The air is so fresh, so... Pure.

Below me are endless valleys crudely carved into the earth's surface. A thousand feet below me, infinite streams of water flow to the tune of something we have all lost touch with. The great winds of time. The master architect unleashing his science project.

I stare at a bald eagle carving gracefully through the perfect sky with its perfect wings and its perfect strength. This is perfection, and in one moment, it will be gone forever.

The bird suddenly seems to be looking directly at me. He...

He seems to be turning and twisting himself toward me. He's coming straight for me!

I marvel at what's happening. There are no tremors. I am not afraid of this beast of a bird. I'm usually afraid of microscopic rodents, but not this bird. I know it carries untold diseases. I know it eats raw meat. I know that it could kill me like the swiftest assassin ever created.

But I am still not afraid, and I cannot understand why. I should have panicked by now. I should have been screaming like a crazy person and end up killing myself in a panic stricken jump instead of being eviscerated by this hauntingly beautiful bird.

I never blink. The bird lands right next to me. The rush of air created by its wings is intimidating. It's sheer power. The thing stares at me with its finely tuned, savage eyes. There is nothing in them. There is nothing in me. There is suddenly nothing around us. Only the bird and I, perpetually suspended in some invisible fabric.

I stare back in complete silence, and I don't feel anything either way, until the bird cocks its head to the side and opens its beak.

He says:

"I am afraid of you."

CHAPTER 16

When Jessica woke up, she was violently ill. She felt nauseous and weak. She ran to the bathroom and puked, gasping and heaving.

She felt fine when she'd inexplicably awoken only four hours after falling asleep, but now, she felt like crawling death.

She rinsed her mouth and crawled back into bed after calling Captain Briar to say that she would be staying in for at least the morning. No problems at all.

She closed her eyes, and fell asleep.

***

She'd slept three hours, but she could instantly tell that she wasn't feeling any better. She wondered what it was. A flu? Was she pregnant? She had never really worried about getting pregnant, but now, she thought that perhaps a baby would bring a welcomed change in her life for once. Of course, the thought of marrying a child's father had never even crossed her mind for a–she rushed to the toilet and puked again. She hated being sick, and especially now, since the unwanted arrival of Brian Hotz in her mind. She had a hot shower and stared at the water escaping into the drain.

Eventually, she returned to bed and lay on her back for a long time, staring at the ceiling, and letting her guts process whatever it was having so much trouble processing. The human machine has a way of grabbing attention when it wants it. It wasn't long before Jessica fell asleep again.

***

It was 1:08 p.m. when she woke up again. Her stomach was still tied in painful knots, but her temperature was returning back to normal. She felt tired, but was sure that she could handle her body a little better now.

She got up, brushed her hair, and then fixed something to eat. She sat on the couch and turned on the television. She stared at it, but she was really thinking about Brian Hotz again. She was thinking about the last chapter she'd read; about the bird in Brian Hotz's dream–or–psychotic episode.

"I'm afraid of you?" she whispered to herself.
She wondered what that meant. When she was a little girl, she remembered how disappointed she'd felt when she'd realized that there were no explanations for dreams. She had thought it was rather banal that after thousands of years of experience, no one had a clue. It was ironic to her that humans were already exploring space and distant worlds, when they couldn't even understand half the mechanics of their own bodies, or the planet, or the oceans. They couldn't help diseases, but they could definitely land on Mars, and observe impossibly distant worlds.

Psychology was still the greatest, most obscure mystery of all.

She finished eating and then fetched the book again, returning to the couch. She wrapped herself in a blanket and continued reading.

The Story Of Brian Hotz

The padded leather chair still makes me uncomfortable. The smell in the air is repulsively good. Disgustingly delicious. The room is still called safe, but nothing ever is. There is no such thing as safe.

This is my first visit with Dr. Satan face since my release from the incredible drug hospital only a few short days ago. Since then, I've been having some trouble.

"I don't think I'm sleeping," I say.
"Okay," her angelic eyebrows lower again. I wish I'd never been made aware of this exact look. This is the look that qualifies my

life in society. That, "What the fuck?" look.

"How do you mean you're not sure?"

"Well," I shift against the leather. No person has ever made me feel so uncomfortable before. I hate her interest. I hate her soft, soothing voice. I hate her perfect body.

I love her.

"I'm, ah... Well, I'm not exactly sure," I say again. "I, ah, I go to bed. I take my pills..."

I stop and feel the hot embarrassment flush my face at the mention of pills. I remember her face so vividly, so completely transfixed in my mind. So clear and concise. So... Real. Yeah, so real it disturbs me.

"Are you all right?" she asks, watching me obviously wrestle with some inner thoughts.

"What? Yeah," I say. "I'm... I'm sorry. I, ah... I want to talk about something else."

"Okay. What would you like to talk about?"

She uncrosses her legs and recrosses them the opposite. There is no telling what I would give to hold her in my arms.

It's a funny thing to be infatuated and repulsed by the exact same thing. Once again, it's fucking hilarious.

"Um..." I hesitate. "Well... I... Ah..."

"It's all right, Brian. This is a safe place. I am here to help you. I am here to listen and try to guide you toward finding a better awareness of yourself to live with."

I nod, not really knowing what else to do.

"Ah..." I pant again and shift against the leather. My back is soaked with sweat. My eyebrows feel like they're pulling more gravity than the rest of me. I feel sad.

"I, ah... Wanted to talk about ah, about last time," I say. Her face remains constant. No deviations. No reactions.

"All right, well, that's good. This would all be much more comfortable if we just got the elephant out of the room."

Elephants are said to remember everything. What a goddamn curse. And with the word elephant, I instantly see elephant infectants. Tusk disease. Trunk cancer.

"Ah... Yeah... Well. I don't... I don't really know...."

"Would you like to know what I am thinking about it all, Brian?

Is that what you would like to know?"

I timidly nod yes. I still can't make eye-contact. I never have been able to, much less with a stunning goddess.

"All right, well," she begins. "I don't really know what happened, to be honest. You lost consciousness in my office and then panicked and ran. Would you like to tell me how you feel about it?"

"Did you see what happened outside?" I ask.
"Did you?" she replies.

"I, ah... I..." That question throws me off. What did she mean? Does she hate me? Does she think I'm psychotic? How could she not? I think I'm psychotic.

"Do you remember anything from that day?" she asks again.

"I do," I tell her. "I remember... I remember the pills, and the panic. I remember the woman outside and her husband. I remember the black and the empty. I, ah... I remember... Your... Your face."

"My face?" Her eyebrows frown again. "My face when?"
"Ah..." I no longer want to talk about this. It's making me itchy. It's making me feel the edge that I will always unwillingly go over. I feel something burning at the back of my throat. I think that maybe I'm getting hemorrhoids. "I, ah... Can... Can we change subjects?"

"It wouldn't make anything any better," she responds.
"Ah..." Aimless words rush through my head. Which ones to use? What do I say? What if she rejects me because of it? Resents me? What then? Who would listen then?

"When I fell," I say. "Your face above me."
"And why do you think you remember it so clearly?"

"Ah... I ah..."
"How did it make you feel?"

I let at least a minute pass before answering, searching for the most honest answer I can find. I have never been completely honest, mostly, because there was never a need for me to be either honest or dishonest. People just sort of leave me alone.

"Ugly," I say.
"Ugly?" she reiterates, and her entire facial mask drops. Oh,

God! I messed up again. Now she's going to hate me. She's going to recommend that I see some musk smelling fat guy who's just counting the minutes until it's all over and he can go back to living his happy existence while I rot in mine.

"Why would you say ugly?"
The room begins to throb ever so lightly, just enough for me to take notice, and I instinctively fall into preparations for the defense attack.

"I... I don't mean that you are..."
"I know, Brian. It didn't sound literal. But why ugly?"

"Ah... Your eyes," I say.
She says nothing and merely allows the silence insinuate everything that needs to be said. Carry on.

"They... They were the same," I say.
"The same?"

"As everyone else. My whole life, those eyes. I see the concern. I see the questions and the inability to understand. I see the judgements and the indifference. I see me... I see me in a way I can't stand for much longer."

"Are you having any suicidal thoughts, Brian?"
"Do I look like I'd have the balls to do it?"

"You drove your car directly into another."
"I don't remember that."

"I know," she says. "Sometimes a traumatic event causes the brain to block out all memories of it. It's a defense mechanism."

"It wasn't the trauma," I say.
"I didn't necessarily think that it was."

What did that mean? She thinks I'm crazy. She thinks I'm ugly. Why does she care? Her care is unbearable. My heart is starting to skip every few beats.

"Wh... What?"
"What I mean is, during our last visit, you told me that you purposely forgot things."

"I'm a defense mechanism with legs," I say.
"Maybe," she answers. "But just the awareness of it is a huge step toward dealing with whatever it is you need to deal with."

I stare at her for a moment. I like her breasts. They are

perky and inviting. They are tight and young and succulent. They probably smell like the rest of her. They probably feel better than any pill I could ever take.

She is the type of woman I will never experience.

"Do you think I have a lot of issues to work through?" I ask.

"Do you think so?"

I feel rabid frustration. These shrinks and their goddamned questions. These shrinks are like religions. No answers. Only more questions.

"I, ah... I don't know. I guess so. Shit, I can't even stand myself on a good day."

"What constitutes a good day for you, Brian?"

"Simple," I say.

"Simple?"

"Simple. Easy. Safe."

"Do you believe that you need pills in order to carry on with your life?"

"I'd never get out of bed," I say.

"Do you take sleeping pills, Brian?"

"I take pills for everything," I say. "To sleep, to eat, to shit, to... To fuck." Even I'm surprised.

"When was the last time you dated a woman?"

"Long time."

"More than a year?"

"More than five," I say.

"Do you masturbate, Brian?"

"What?... Ah..." I'm blushing again. Sweats again. Tremors again. Swoons again. "I ah... No."

"Never?" She questions again.

"Never," I say.

"Do you like women, Brian?"

"Yes."

"Do you enjoy sex?"

"I... I guess."

"Do you ever watch pornography?"

"No."

"Never?"

"Never."

All I see in porno are Venereal Disease and E.Coli attacks. I see microbe hot beds being licked and penetrated and I imagine those people going home and dying from horrible bugs that ate them from the inside out. It's like a nun being into snuff films. A porno is my idea of a horror movie.

"Any fetishes?"

"Aside from pills?"

"Yes," she smiles warmly. I want to hug her. I want to fuck her. "Aside from pills."

"No."

"What about your interests? What kinds of things do you like?"

"I've... I've never really thought about it."

"Really?"

"Yeah," I say kind of sadly. "I'm always just... Trying to get a grip on things."

"Do you struggle a lot?"

"With what?"

"Everything."

"What do you think? I can't even make it to a grocery store without a massive ceremony of disinfecting vaccinations."

"Are you afraid of dying, Brian?"

"I... I... I, ah..." The shakes are coming. My stomach twists violently and then seizes like a blown engine. "I... Don't think so. What is death? What does any of it mean?"

"Well, it means to you whatever it means to you. It's not the same for everyone."

"Death..." I think about death. I think about disease. I think about suffering. The human condition. "Death is... I don't know. It's not death."

"So you're not afraid of death?"

"I... I think I'm afraid of life."

"Are you?"

"I usually can't masturbate even if I want to."

"Why is that? What kinds of feelings does it bring up?"

"... Ugly."

"Ugly," she repeats with the exact tone.

"Yeah..." I sigh. "Ugly."

"What else are you afraid of, Brian?"

"I... I don't know. I don't know what I'm afraid of. I'm not afraid of anything. I'm afraid of everything. I... I... Ah, God. I... I'm just... Fucking... I'm fucked!"

"Okay, okay. It's all right. It's okay. Umm... Let's try the question in a different way. Are you afraid of suffering?"

That word I loath almost as much as miracle. Suffering. What is suffering? Does physical suffering mean anything when it's mental suffering that will crush you like you never thought possible? Wasn't I, wasn't this... Suffering?

They say Jesus suffered. Sometimes, I wonder how scared he was. Sometimes, I wonder if my father is up there with him, watching me. Are they laughing? Do they feel shame? Do they feel pity? Do they care?

"Brian?"

"Ah..." I think of suffering. I feel infections inside of me. I feel dying cells and malignant foreign bodies attacking healthy ones. I see death, and rot, and empty, and decayed fragments of my existence. I see nothing. I see everything. I see me. I see nothing.

"...Yes," I finally pant. "Yeah... I... I think I'm afraid of suffering."

"Do you feel like you sometimes make yourself suffer?"

"I... I don't know. Maybe. Do you ever make yourself suffer?"

"It's a matter of opinion, I suppose. What's your opinion?"

That question always sets me back. Why do you care what I think?

"I... Guess in a way... I guess we all in some way make ourselves suffer," I answer.

"Do you think that maybe sometimes you are... Let's say, comforted though suffering?"

"Comforted?"

"Yeah, you know... Like in sadness. There is a certain comfort in sadness that some people sometimes enjoy, no matter how sad they feel."

"Suffering?" I say.

"Yes. Suffering."

"I, ah... I..." I didn't know. "I like to puke."

"You like to puke? Why?"

"I... I don't know. It's like... It's like it's... It's as real as it gets, you know? It's real. It's concrete, and it's there, and it comes out of me. Ah... Substance. Realness."

She remains quiet and jots another line down in her duo tang. I wonder what she's writing? I wonder if she finds me slightly more attractive now? I wonder if, deep down, she really does care? I wonder... I wonder... I wonder.

"Okay..." She smiles again. "Do you vomit often, Brian?"

"I try not to."

"So you don't do it on purpose?"

"No... No," I say. "It's not one of those eating disorder things. Everything we eat is fake. It's ah... It's the ah... The pills do it."

"Which ones?"

"I don't know. Maybe one of them. Maybe all."

"And how often does this happen?"

"I don't know... Once or twice a week."

"Do you ever vomit blood?"

"Ah... Every time. Ulcers."

"When's the last time you saw a doctor?"

"I see your colleague, Dr. Manilek, every week."

"You see a doctor every week?"

"Yes."

"Are you afraid of disease, Brian?"

"Ah..." I actually let a small chuckle out. "Ah... Terrified."

"Terrified? Really? Do you think you sometimes worry too much about disease?"

"I probably worry too much about everything," I say. "Do you think your fear causes you to do, and think in certain ways that bring on symptoms of diseases?"

"Why would I do that?"

"Because it makes it feel real. Perhaps deep down, it may even feel safe."

I'm flabbergasted. I don't like this thought. I don't like the thought of responsibility. I am not responsible for anything. My life is simple. It's boring, and it's safe. It's quiet and frantic. It's... It's beyond anything I could ever understand.

I am the extinguished light at the end of no tunnel.

Birds will chew food and regurgitate it to feed their young. Is that their idea of processed? Is that their idea of safe?

Safety is a comfortable illusion.

Perhaps it even feels safe? Safe. The real definitions of the words safe and happy are not made by the human brain. They are the same thing. There is no happiness without safety, no safety without happiness, and from there, a seamless piling of more illusions none of us are ever aware of. The system, it seems, is quite perfect.

"Are you all right, Brian?"

I stare at the floor, completely confused.

"Brian?"

"I... I... I don't know what to say."

"To what?"

"To... To feeling safe."

"Do you feel safe?"

"No."

"Why not?"

"Because it's not real."

"But you can feel it, can't you? At some point in time, you've felt safe? You've felt secure and strong?"

"But..."

"What is it?"

"That would mean that reality is only as real as you feel it is?"

I feel a heavy weight on my chest. I feel my head pound. I feel my eardrums go numb and leave me with nothing but white noise. That soundless tone that is only real to you.

She ponders on it for a moment, her staring pensively at the floor now.

"Well..." She perks up. " I suppose you're right."

And right then, I realize that her legs are covered in blood. Shock binds her face awkwardly, seizing her eyes in impossible coldness. She isn't breathing. She isn't moving. She is staring at me with a look that cannot possibly be described with words. It isn't fear; it isn't... It isn't anything.

It is nothingness staring back at me. Pure shock.

I feel my head explode against the side of her desk. A massive thump that doesn't really matter. It's too far away already.

I wonder if it's possible for a man to turn into a black hole?

She wondered if Brian Hotz had a connection to her case, or if she was simply trapped in wishful thinking. She knew that Nicole White could have authored the story just as well as any other person she happened to cross on the streets. It was a story, and the reality of stories was that they were always exaggerated. In this case, Jessica hoped for both. She hoped it was all real, and simultaneously hoped it wasn't.

She continued reading.

The Story Of Brian Hotz

It's 3:39 a.m. and I'm staring at the ceiling. I am in my bed. I am home. Safe, as they say.

Sometimes, I wonder what the consequences would be if all of this actually had any meaning. What if what's happening to me truly does have a meaning, only, the meaning is far too complex for anyone to wrap their heads around, so they throw you into a straight jacket and make a sanitarium your new home.

Who knows?

The answer is always no one.

What if, I don't know, what if all of this is something like that Kurt Vonnegut book, the one where the main character becomes unstuck in time. What if that were the truth? What then? What if, what we call hallucinations are simply glimpses of some other dimensions? Where do dreams take place? Where does anything spiritual take place? Is it reality? No. But is it real?

Absolutely.

Does it affect reality? In fact, I believe it partly makes reality. A person who believes they have been touched by God may be inclined to change his or her entire life based on that belief. The very environment around him or her is therefore affected, and shifted accordingly.

Does that mean we ultimately have control over everything? I think it's a little bit of yes, and a lot of no.

Seems to me, lying here at... 3:42 a.m. trapped in the grip of multicolored capsules of peace, well... I'm deathly afraid that my horrible vantage point might just be correct. That I am not alone in this hell. That this, all of this, is one of those universal things that everyone is somehow aware of, at least on some subconscious level. It's instinctive. Innate.

The real truth.

The truth that we have nothing but grey areas. Nothing but guesses. Nothing but traditions and expired ancient beliefs. Nothing but questions. Nothing but darkness surrounding our little bubble in the middle of an infinite landscape of nothingness. We are all here, and we all have nothing.

Hilarious.

All of these people, living, and dying for things no one knows anything about; for things they consciously chose, force, to make real. For things that have altered countless other realities directly, and indirectly. And in the end, no one knows for sure.

People say they feel it, they say they feel God, but how can anyone possibly be sure? The exact same spiritual connection is experienced in incredibly vivid form on pretty much any hallucinogenic drug. Is that real?

Why not?

Some use it specifically for that purpose. What are we seeing? Truth, lies, or grey areas?

A man could think of such things for eternity. A man's brain is simply nowhere near advanced enough yet to be conclusive in any way. All directions lead to the same questions.

But these are not the only things stirring inside of me tonight while these extra doses of useless sleeping pills run their course. There are a few other thoughts I am having. The first is about sleeping. I think I feel better when I sleep less. I think sleeping helps nothing when it comes to emotions. I think... I think that I think too much.

I am also thinking about Dr. Satan face. For a moment there, right before I smashed my head on the side of her desk, right before I gasped in shock and awe in the face of the pure terror captivating her eyes, I thought I had killed her.

I didn't know how, or even why. I watched her body tense up in a sort of crippled mess. An uncomfortable flinch. I watched her eyes glass over and turn cold. I watched her disappear and leave her body behind.

I felt something... Primitive there.

It was the blood. The blood was what had sent her into cold shock. It was what had sent me into a convulsing mess on the floor with a concussion, and the embarrassment level of Superman having his ass handed right back to him by a 5 year old little girl.

I felt amazing.

Even when I lose consciousness... I never lose the panic. It keeps going. It doesn't care if I'm there for it or not. On some level... On every level... I feel it.

My brain had shorted out, sending flashes of chaotic light in my vision. I felt my chest open up and tear to pieces. I felt my arms go numb and become dead limbs. I felt the darkness. What had I done? Why had I done it? Why could I not remember? Why goddamn it? Why?

I then heard her voice. She was calling my name. She was... She was patting me on the cheek. She was alive! She was alive!

She was... Alive?

She rolled me onto my back and helped me sit up. The delirium was so heavy I couldn't even sit straight. All I could see was blood. Was it mine, then? Had I killed myself? There was panic in her voice. I hadn't killed myself.

When the room settled again, I started crying right there on the floor while one half of my head swelled to inhuman proportions. Crying like a baby, covered in puke. I had puked all over the poor doctor. If she did like me beforehand, I think it's the first time I see something "Safe to say" in a very long time. She no longer did.

The blood was from my stomach rejecting the fakeness of life. The ulcer volcanoes erupting. The blood plumes ejecting. I had produced the most embarrassing mess I could ever have thought of, in front of the prettiest woman who has talked to me in... Forever.

Forever is another comfortable illusion.

Projectile vomit. Pure red. Pure death. Pure panic.

This little event bothered me for the rest of the day. I couldn't shake it. I was afraid. I was ashamed. I was... I was being me. Weak. Little. Small. Uninspired. I was worried about the doctor. I liked her no matter how repulsively infatuating she was to me. I wanted her. I wanted her to be a part of me. Part of this.

It bothered me right up until I swallowed all those pills and closed my eyes. I fell asleep. I woke up. It was 3:04 a.m. I panicked. I had reason to panic. I had fear pressing tightly around my throat, and squeezing my scrotum so tight I thought my testicles were about to burst.

I'm not afraid anymore. No, I do not know why. I didn't take anything. I didn't really do anything. I just laid down, and started thinking; like an old dog too tired to chase off a rodent from the lawn. Too old and tired to care.

This is what I had been trying to convey to the good doctor long before I covered her in my blood puke. This is what I meant by, I don't think I've been sleeping. She asked me why, and I couldn't explain any of it.

The truth is, I am sleeping. I am losing consciousness. I am floating away into dreams, or dimensions, or whatever we choose to call them. I feel regularly rested when I wake. I feel the usual pain, and the heart stopping loneliness. I feel the headache. My leaking nose.

But something has been going on. Yes, something indeed. You see, the problem here is that I was under the impression of possessing zero artistic talents. None at all. I have never been able to write a poem, or paint a naked woman, or even draw a stick man to proportion. Which worries me. It never had before, but things were different then. Things are different now.

I am sitting on my bed, looking over this intricate mishmash on the floor. My apartment is never out of order. Never. But that's not really the worrisome part, that part has to do with the intricate detail with which all of this seems to have been laid out.

I think it's a building. It's been built out of little pieces of broken items from around my apartment. Little pieces of colored glass and chunks of wood, all either sharpened or formed, and assembled into some kind of structure. There is some kind of pattern to it. It's not complete, yet, but it's enough to send my mind recoiling.

Vases broken, pieces shaped, assembled, built. The old evolving into the new. The patterns of life itself. Destroy and create.

Tiny windows affixed to the crude walls. A tiny door. A family home, perhaps, with a chimney, and love pressing up against the walls. Or maybe a prison. Or maybe nothing. Nothing at all. I stare at this thing, and it is actually quite serene in its rawness. Its beauty resides in the raw, the crude, the violent. Art.

But none of this is the problem. Not this building. Not this mess. Not all of these meaningless broken materials.

The real problem here, is who the hell built it?

"Holy Shit!" Jessica screamed. "It's him! It's him!" She pounced like a startled cat, frantic to get the hell out of her apartment and find Brian Hotz. The proof was right there in the book. Right there, smashing things and making art. She shuddered at the thought of it.

"Good God," she thought. "He's real. I can't believe he's real!"

She fumbled with her underwear, ripping her thong with her foot. "Shit!" she said. She fumbled for a minute more, and in no time, she was dressed and rushing down the hallway like a panicked mother heading to the hospital. She took the elevator down to the parkade, started her car, and squealed the tires on her way out.

She was elated on one hand, and disturbed on the other. She was simultaneously smiling one second, and quite serious the next. If she were telling the truth, she didn't really know how she was feeling. It was all too unexpected.

"It's real," she said again. "How could I have been so lucky?"

Jessica cruised through the streets with the accumulated skills of her professional training. Weaving in and out of traffic, she arrived at her parking spot in only 15 minutes. She hit the ground running, heading directly toward the boardroom where all the files were still being examined.

When she crashed through the door, she startled a few

people, most notably Captain Briar, who was wondering what she was doing there.

"I feel fine," she panted, out of breath. "I just... I need to go through these."

"Jessie," Captain said. "Please, Jessie, go home. Take a break, this isn't healthy. Not for you, or for anyone else. We need you to be at the top of your game."

"I'm on top of it, Cap," she said. "I'm always on top of it." Instantly, she began digging through boxes like a psychotic in her own right, having only one name in her mind, Brian Hotz. She didn't believe that was his real name, so she was also looking for relevant details that could somehow connect one of the files to the diary. She was now quite certain that Nicole White had not penned the manuscript herself.

Name after name flashed by her eyes, her brain recorded them all. People she would never meet. People who would live out their lives completely unaffected by any of this, except for perhaps the need to find a new therapist.

She asked the young brunette responsible for categorizing the files into a spread sheet for all of the names that began with a B. The girl twirled her laptop around, and Jessica immediately scrutinized the list.

"Bob, Billy, Bailey, Baxter, Bill, Brian?... No, Brian Stahl, shit..." she whispered to herself.

"What is it, Detective?" Captain Briar asked.
"Ah... I just... I got a hunch." She replied.

"A hunch?"
"Maybe unfounded," she said. "Maybe not. It came to me in a dream... For some reason. I think his name may start with a B."

Captain Briar gave her an odd look, thinking that Jessica knew something he obviously did not.

"Detective Sanders, we've been through almost all of the files, and there isn't much there," the young brunette with the computer said.

"How many files are left?" Jessica asked.
"About two and a half boxes," she replied. "Over there, underneath the table."

"Okay," she said. "Could you pull all of those B files for

me please? Thanks."

She scurried over to the boxes and pulled out the closest one to her. She began scanning the files, taking the time to read through them all. Descriptions. Diagnosis. Deranged thoughts.

She was looking for anything out of the ordinary. Any mention of art, or debris, or suicidal thoughts, or savage confusion, or women, or murder, or anything that could possibly give her a glimpse into who this killer was. She knew he was in there. She could feel it deep inside of her bones. This killer had known Nicole White. He had raped and killed her. He had killed five women in total, so far, and he was still out there, free, but she instinctively felt like he was trapped in one of the boxes around her.

She was determined to find Brian Hotz, no matter what his real name was. She would find him, and she would hunt him down like a rabid dog.

***

After a few hours of digging, the names began to lose their meaning on her. She quickly realized that simply searching through names would do nothing to advance her case. She felt as though she had a good understanding of who Brian Hotz was based on the personality in the diary alone. She could only hope that Nicole White had taken the time to write down the perfect words. What those words were, exactly, she didn't quite know, but she firmly believed that she would once they crossed her dedicated eyes. Some type of parallel to the disgusting little story she had been reading at home. Something that would grab her attention, force her to analyze deeper, and realize that she was reading the same words as the book's, no matter who had written them.

The process was grueling, but Jessica had already resolved that she would not move from that room until she had either found him, or physical limitations demanded that she could no longer continue without rest.

The names were meaningless. While some of the descriptions appeared vague, others seemed almost intrusive on certain patients' privacy. The only true constant remained the total lack of content that would cause her mind to reel wildly with a rabid type of hope.

She suddenly realized that she hadn't felt her stomach grumble with menace for hours, but once she did, she was forced to run to the washroom down the hall like a half-insane person attempting to escape the voices. She crashed through the door and startled a few women conversing by the bathroom sinks. She couldn't hold it. She burst into a stall and puked. It was all very brutal. She hated how illness proved your true weakness. It proved that not only were you human, but you were also as weak, uncertain, scared, and vulnerable, as any other person anywhere.

Jessica heard the snickering whispers from the other women by the sinks. What did she care? She was sick. She was desperate. Desperate to find a killer. Desperate to end this case once and for all.

She took a wad of toilet paper and wiped her mouth. She hated vomit, and now, she hated Brian Hotz so much that she actually chuckled right there on her knees with her head in a community toilet.

"Qualify yourself with puke?" she said. "You sad, little, insignificant monster."

She stood up and fumbled with her skirt and blouse, realigning them. She took a deep breath and opened the stall door. To her relief, she found herself alone in the bathroom. She rinsed her face in the sink, and fixed her wired looking hair. Once she felt presentable again, she straightened out her posture and walked out of the door, only to find herself face to face with Captain Briar, who had apparently been waiting for her in the hallway.

"You okay, kiddo?" he asked, obviously concerned.

"I'm... I'm fine," she replied.

"Don't lie to me, Jessie," he said. "You can't do it to me anymore than I can do it to you."

She immediately thought of the diary.

"I'm, ah... I'm okay, Cap. I just need to get back to work."

"Oh no you don't," Captain Briar said. "You, young lady, are going home to bed. To get some rest, and recharge. You'll be no good to the case like this. You need to slow down and take a breather. Take the time you need."

"Captain I really don't think that..."

"Right now," he cut her off. "It's an order. Go home and go to bed, and don't come back here until you're fully recovered. Okay? Please, Jessie, do this for yourself. Do it for me, and for the case. You need rest. Go rest."

Jessica didn't want to go home. She wanted back into the room with the files. She wanted to find Brian Hotz–now–right now, but Captain Briar wouldn't have it. He was simultaneously telling and asking her, both as a boss and a friend, to go home and sleep. Her hands, it seemed, were tied.

Jessica sighed.

"All right," she said. " Okay, maybe you're right."

"Home," he said. "Sleep. Don't worry about anything. By the time you return, all those files will be better organized for you to plow through anyway."

Jessica gave him a sly smile.

"Okay," she finally said. "Fine. I'll call you when I feel better."

"Good," he said. "And rest, okay? Relax. Try to forget about the case for a little while. Sometimes, distancing yourself makes subtle details seem obvious when you come back to look at them."

She knew what he meant. She still didn't want to go.

"All right, all right, Captain," she said. "You win. I'm out of here."

He smiled and gently rubbed her shoulder with his hand. "You take care of yourself, kiddo. I'll see you when I see you."

"Bye, Cap."

She walked slowly through the halls, her guts continuing their violent churning and painful convulsions. She wondered what she had eaten. Nothing she could think of would have caused such an adverse reaction. She once again wondered if she was pregnant. She realized that she had never seriously thought about it twice in her life. She thought that maybe Captain Briar was correct after all. Maybe she did need some rest. Maybe her brain just needed to tap out for a day or two and simply do nothing.

When she got to her car, she lit a cigarette and pulled out

of the parking lot. Traffic was sparse in the downtown streets. Phantom pedestrians. She thought it was going to rain again. She thought that sometimes, she also thought too much. But there was something else egging at her while she made her way home. She wondered if perhaps she had shot from the hip. She wondered if maybe she had been wrong; that she had acted much too quickly without continuing the story.

"But it was right there," she tried assuring herself. Brian Hotz's little debris building. It was all too close not to be the killer. It was too similar. Too unbelievably parallel. He had written that various things in his apartment had been smashed. He had called it art. Art! It was too close, and yet, it still meant nothing. Nothing in the files. Nothing anywhere for her to find.

She was almost certain that The Fleshcrafter had written that journal. She could feel it, but she could also feel nothing but frustration when she was faced with those mountains of worthless files, and a completely idiotic story that apparently had some kind of bearing in real life, yet had no bearing whatsoever. Brian Hotz did not exist. The man did, she was certain of that, but the name did not. That name was meaningless. It was hopeless. It was wrong.

She pulled her car into the parkade, and walked toward the elevator, taking it all the way up to her apartment floor. The doors slid open, and she instantly felt something odd, but couldn't quite tell what it was.

She walked her tired and beaten body past door after door, until finally reaching her own, where she suddenly knew what was odd.

Her apartment door was ajar. She would never have left the door opened. Never.

She pulled her gun from its holster and felt her hands clam up. If anyone was in there, it would take something drastic to keep her from shooting them. She would, after all, be expecting her monster.

She took a deep breath and peered in through the crack in between the jamb and the door. She couldn't see anything. Slowly, methodically, she crept the door open slightly, eternally listening, forever scanning.

Still nothing.

She kicked the door open with brute force, and stood frozen in the hallway.

When the door flew open, the gun fell out of her hand and hit the floor with a loud thump.

That was the second time in so many weeks that something had involuntarily fallen from her hands.

CHAPTER 17

"Captain?" she said into her phone.

"Yeah, Jessie? Is everything all right?"

"Well, you know that team of ours?"

"Yes."

"I need you to send them over."

"Send them over?" he questioned. "To where?"

"To my apartment," she said, and they were suddenly trapped in an awkward silence. "Captain—he was here. The son of a bitch was in my apartment."

"I'm coming over right away!" his voice was filled with panic. "Are you all right?!"

"I'm fine. I never even saw him. But he was here."

"We'll see you in 20 minutes, kiddo. Hang tight."

She hung up the phone and took a deep breath. She was standing in the middle of her living room, in the middle of an incredible mess. Everything had been smashed. Everything had been riffled through, and turned over, and looked at by unwelcomed eyes.

Jessica already knew that it was him. The Fleshcrafter. The Katy killer. She wondered why he had come. She thought it was an awfully stupid thing to do. She must have expected that a young woman at the head of investigating such gruesome crimes would probably be sleeping very closely to her government issued handgun. He had to have expected to be killed the second he kicked the door open. Intruding, and being met with a bullet to the head.

She decided not to waste anytime. She returned to the hallway and began knocking on neighboring doors.

"Hi there, I'm Detective Jessica Sanders. I live right over there, in that apartment. I'm just wondering if you happened to hear or see anything odd out in the hall this evening?... Nothing at all? Okay, thank you for your time."

"Hi there. I'm Detective Jessica Sanders..."
She went to every door. She spoke to every neighbor. She was still left with nothing but doubts. No answers. No sounds. No witnesses.

By the time she was disappointingly assured that no one had anything useful for her, Captain Briar and the team had arrived at her building.

"Hi," she said to Captain Briar as he came out of the elevator holding a sickening concern in his eyes. He was terrified.

"Jessica," he said. "What happened?"
She led them to her apartment and crept the door open to let them in, but at the sight of it, Captain Briar let out a gasp of desperation–of imagined horrors.

"Good God," he said. "Oh, Jessica. This is not good. This is not good at all."

His eyes scanned the room, and she could tell that he was imagining what the killer had wanted to happen in her apartment. She could tell that his heart would not take much more of this. Not so close to home. Not with having 3 daughters of his own. Not... Not with this killer.

Jessica's apartment had been ravaged as badly as any of the other crime scenes they'd seen. Everything was broken. Walls demolished. Glass broken. Shattered fragments of her existence. Every book had been ripped open. Every container opened. And yet, when she had first walked in, the first thing she'd thought of was the journal. Was that what he had been after? To kill her and steal his diary back, therefore annihilating any and all connections? But how could he possibly have known that she had it? He couldn't have. Her own Captain had no idea.

Searching frantically, she had been surprised at finding the book pretty much where she had left it. It was lying where her night stand would have stood, before it was decimated. The diary had seemed untouched.

If she ever caught the man, she would have to make it seem like some grand miracle of perception had connected the puzzle together. She would have to lie.

Once she'd found the journal, she stuffed it into her pocket even before calling Captain Briar.

Looking around, she didn't even feel violated. She didn't really care who went through her things. To her, stuff was just stuff. She had never really cared much for any material thing in her life, but this had been beyond that. She had been too stunned to think about her stuff. She couldn't understand. Why had he left the journal behind? It made no sense.

Captain Briar was still standing in the foyer of her apartment, still with that look in his eyes. That ungodly twinkle of shock.

Terror.

Jessica knew what he was thinking. He was thinking that if this had happened to her, then what was to stop this maniac from finding him? From killing him, and then raping and killing his daughters. Jessica knew that Captain Briar had almost reached his threshold. He was an egg with a cracking shell, and there was nothing he could really do about it. He was feeling a cosmic despair. Vague, yet pressing.

Helplessness.

Jessica didn't say anything to him for a while. She was treating her apartment like she treated all crime scenes. Recording all the details in her mind.

Everywhere were splinters of furniture, and shards of glass. Smashed mirrors and doors. Demolished walls. It appeared as though he had not taken the time to make any type of art out of it. He had come, he had smashed, and he had left. She wondered what kind of rage he had felt when he realized that she wasn't home. She wondered if he had thought about jumping out of her window, doing the world a favor by flattening himself on the asphalt below. She wondered if he had intended to rape her. Anger. Violence. Sex. These things almost always went hand in hand.

The forensics team began processing the scene. It would take many hours before they would finish combing through the debris, piece by piece, looking for clues, looking for answers, anything. She could tell that most members of the team were already thinking the same dark things Captain Briar was thinking. Was I next? My family? My place?

They went through endless amounts of unrecognizable things. A handle for a door. Screws from a dresser. Shredded curtains. There was nothing there. He had left nothing.

She again wondered how furious he was. She wondered how frightened he was.

"Detective," a voice came from her bedroom, and she and Captain Briar immediately made their way inside. Jessica stopped dead in her tracks when she saw it. Captain Briar's head swooned, and he was forced to balance himself against the wall until his equilibrium returned.

When the forensics team flipped over her mattress, they found a message for Jessica. It was crudely written in blood. Maybe his. Maybe not. Either way, it didn't concern her right then. What concerned her, was the inhuman rage that was erupting inside of her while she stared at the mattress.

"You motherfucker!" she screamed, and punched a new hole in the wall. "You piece of shit! I'm gonna kill you!"

The message on her mattress read:
Pretty like a butterfly.

CHAPTER 18

A single question blared through her mind. Coincidence?
It was a common word, meaning a striking occurrence of two
or more events at one time, apparently by mere chance. It was a
word that Jessica had never been fully comfortable with. There
were two schools of thought on the subject. The first implied that
experiencing a coincidence was obvious proof of the complete
randomness of the universe. The second, implied obvious proof
of destiny.

The truth, she believed, was that what people called
coincidence was really only retrospect. Coincidence was blind
to people until after the fact, and although it was impossible
to have knowledge of one before hand, people still acted as
though they could have, should have, and would have done
something differently. Most people couldn't bring themselves to
acknowledge the chaos, and instead resolved the issue by telling
themselves that it was all meant to happen in that way. A plan.
Destiny.

Jessica thought that the belief in pre-destined truth was
nothing more than a psychological defense mechanism, but for
the first time in her life, she could honestly say that she fully
understood the motivation. Chaos was unknown, unpredictable,
and terrifying.

There was no doubting the apparent coincidence.
If she had not found the diary, she could have died. If she had
never read that last chapter and frantically rushed to the office to
ravage through files and try to find Brian Hotz, she could have
been killed. If she would not have been ill and stayed home, she
wouldn't have read that chapter right then, she wouldn't have

been somewhere else when he kicked in her door, she could have been hurt, raped, murdered.

Modeled.

The idea that she was not in full control of her life, an idea she usually revelled in, was now making her incredibly uncomfortable. She could feel her mighty brain resisting it like the walls were closing in. She believed that the grand plan, or lack thereof, had no solution. Life was like an unfolding mathematical formula that could go anywhere, and do anything, of its own accord. It was self-sustaining. It was self-guiding. It was as alone as everyone else.

She thought about the journal again. If she were telling the truth, she thought that she was rather upset with herself for having read that chapter. Although she could have been killed, she could just as easily have killed him.

The great system of random chaos swinging either way without the slightest concern for anyone.

By the time Captain Briar was able to stand on his own two feet again, he was nowhere near Jessica's bedroom. He was standing out in the hallway, breathing heavily, with pain and fear flooding his eyes.

"Jessica," he said. "Jessica, you are in danger."

"No I'm not, Cap," she replied. "I can take care of myself."

"Goddamn it, Jessie!" he snapped, but it wasn't out of anger, it was out of a deep concern for her. "I'm sorry, but you are in danger, my girl. You can't stay here, or anywhere that is not protected."

"But,"

"No buts," he said. "Please, Jessica. As a friend, please do this. I need you to pack up some clothes, and I'll get you set up in a secure location."

"For how long?"

"For as long as it takes."

Jessica's heart sank. If there was anything she loathed, it was living in fear, and forced to do anything she didn't want to do. She hated being forced to alter her life because of someone else, but she wasn't being offered another choice.

"Fine," she finally said in the face of friendship, more than defeat. "Fine, Captain. Let's go."

"Don't you want to pack any clothes?"

"No," she replied, and walked down the hall toward the elevators, empty-handed.

He took her to a hotel, on the 23rd floor, with 2 officers patrolling her door in the hallway. She was now trapped in a fortified compound, and all she could do was scoff, and say, "Thanks a lot, Cap. I feel real safe now. Trapped like a mouse, but yeah, real safe."

She was frustrated, and angry. She had trouble believing that her life had gone from fairly normal, to completely wrapped up in this mess of psychosis. How could she have gone from being unknown, anonymous, and alone, to being recognized, stalked, and hunted?

The coincidence concept still pressed painfully against her churning mind.

"Pretty like a butterfly," she whispered. "You prick." She wondered what kind of demented butterfly image he'd had in mind when he'd written that. What parts of her body had he wanted to cut up, peel, and color? To rape her. To rip her throat out. To stab her in the face, and break everything in the place, then rearrange it all into some sickening scene around her limp, mutilated body.

It didn't scare her. This man. This art. The chaos. She then wondered if he had known that she wasn't home. Had he been watching her? Stalking her? For how long? She considered the possibility, but decided against it based on the way her apartment had been destroyed. It gave the impression of failure. The impression of an unexpected reality. It was the expression of an animalistic rage.

She thought of her sister again. She had been a brute victim of that monstrous rage. She had been ravaged and destroyed at the hands of this monster. She wondered what kind of fear she had felt in that moment. What kind of blind terror had flashed through her while staring into those soulless eyes? Eyes completely incapable of reason. The eyes of a demon.

Jessica undressed and hopped into the shower. She had always enjoyed those hotel shower heads that seemed like they pumped out more pressure than anything she could ever get in her own home. It was therapeutic, and relaxing.

"Brian Hotz," she said, standing under the hot spray of water. "When I find you, when I finally get to stare deep into your eyes, it's your soul that's going to shudder, not mine."

Her neck felt heavy while she washed her hair. Her shoulders felt small and weak. Her arms tired and beaten. Her entire body felt beaten. She was still feeling slightly ill, though the excitement had done a fantastic job at abating it for a few hours. But, with the adrenaline dissipating, the tired sickness was making its return.

She turned the water off and dried herself. She brushed her hair and rubbed lotion on her skin. She then lit a cigarette, and stared at the television for a while, trying not to think of anything.

Inevitably, before long, she was thinking about the media. In reality, she knew very little of the headlines concerning her case. She wondered what kind of information people were talking about. Wild conspiracies. Terror filled eyes. Frightened parents refusing to send their kids to school, or play at the park. The kind of fear a man like The Fleshcrafter could impose on the general public was stifling. The masses always did a fantastic job of taking anything from the media and blowing it way out of proportion. A man like the Fleshcrafter caused perfectly respectable citizens to buy guns. It caused them to overreact to anything suspicious. It caused them to flood tip lines with hundreds, thousands of unfounded, unrealistic, and completely irrational claims.

The media, in Jessica's view, was often just as guilty as the killers. They were the fear mongers these killers used to feel God-like while everyone else cowered and desperately tried to do the only thing they've ever truly known how.

Hide.

She also thought that the law enforcement agencies, those who hunted these psychos, were often trapped in an ugly catch twenty-two when trying to use the public for help. They helped the media produce fear, while simultaneously hoping that a breakthrough would come from somewhere in that mass fear.

The tips were usually unfounded, but it was, nevertheless, a successful tactic. At least, successful enough to warrant scaring the comfort right out of decent people.

She sighed heavily. She knew she wouldn't be able to sleep while her mind continually rushed through thoughts at near light speed.

She wondered about the blood the killer had used to leave her that message. Where had it come from? She highly doubted that it was his, forcing her to think about coincidences again. If he had brought the blood with him, he must have known she wouldn't be home.

Or had he?

It was impossible for her to decide. It was as big of a mystery as his identity was. Yet another unexplainable answer. Yet another question.

She sat on the hotel bed and thought that it was overly hard, and rather uncomfortable. She hated feeling like she was trapped. She hated doing anything that she had not decided to do on her own. She hated that Captain Briar seemed stuck in thoughts so ghoulish, he was very closely approaching his breaking point. She hated that he was afraid for her, and she hated knowing that he would never sleep well again until she brought the hammer down on the Fleshcrafter.

She put her cigarette out and decided to pull the diary from her coat pocket. Before she had arrived at her apartment and found it annihilated, she had been thinking about the possibility that perhaps she had jumped the gun on it all. The story had appeared parallel, but it had also been rather vague. Only a few lines had been enough to send her reeling like a maniac through files of faceless names.

Her stomach grumbled again, and she felt a sharp pain twist in her gut, and then recede. She opened the diary.

The Story Of Brian Hotz

Horrible dreams infected my mind last night. Nightmares. Ghosts. Monsters around the corners. Sometimes, I wonder about ghosts. I wonder if they were human once upon a time? I wonder if they ever loved someone else, or had children, or had to deal with mundane problems like bills, and money, and family? I wonder if they are lost?

Sometimes I wonder if I'm a ghost. Do any of us exist? Do I? Am I real? The possibility scares me more than anything else in life. The possibility that all of this is nothing but mindless flashes of electrodes, telling us what is real, instead of knowing what is.

I haven't moved the debris building from the floor of my bedroom. I haven't touched it. I haven't cleaned any of the mess. I haven't... I haven't done anything but stare at it and wonder.

Where did it come from? If I didn't build it, then who did? If I couldn't remember, did that still make it real?

When the doctor with the face of Satan had stood high above me with that emptiness in her eyes, I'd immediately been shifted back into horrible memories. Memories of the first time I had seen her face that way. The first time I had lost consciousness in her office surrounded by a colorful rainbow of pills. The first time I had lost my mind and couldn't remember anything at all. I had hurt a man. I'd hurt a woman. I had driven my car at top speed with suicide in my eyes. I wonder what she thought of it all?

I wonder how much she hates me?

When I woke up, I was completely naked in my bed. I never sleep naked. I hate my body. All these useless flaps and hunks of cellulite. This unshaped belly. This shriveled, useless penis that couldn't fill with blood if I injected it. My lost hair. My hair in places I never used to have. My oversized feet. My stubby little fingers. My face. My ugly, stupid little face.

I don't understand why, but I still haven't dressed. I've been up for hours now, uncomfortable with the way the air feels on my exposed skin, but not doing anything about it. I wonder why it feels so... Alien. So... Wrong.

I wonder if humans were meant to be naked? I wonder, why all the clothes when no other animal is in need of them? Most people see it as an intelligent advancement, but I always wonder how dumb we truly are as a species? Always hiding the natural, changing what we see fit to change, avoiding the real, hiding from truths. Taking ungodly amounts of pills, because it's the only way people like me can even glimpse the concept of inner peace. Inner peace. I wonder if there is such a thing? Could it ever be pure?

Speaking of pills, it's time for a few yellows and a red. An Advil for my headache. Opiates for the tremors.

I have God trapped inside of tiny bottles. I have world peace right here in the palm of my hand. I have nothing.

If I were to tell you the truth, it would be that most of the time, I feel more pain inside of my brain than I know how to deal with. I have more soul crushing fears and delusions than anyone could ever be comfortable with. Much less myself. I don't know what is truly happening around me at any given time anymore.

I am so scared.

I am so scared that I am finally losing it. That my mind is finally packing it in and bailing out on me. That I won't even be able to notice when I die. I will miss it all.

The Satan face doctor had asked me if I thought about suicide a lot. The truth is that I do not. Even the thought of suicide scares me. I am scared, and I cannot shake it. I avoid the thoughts, I avoid them at all costs, but deep down, I can feel it inside of me. I can feel it grinding hard against my soul, no matter how many pills I ingest. Maybe I should take some time to consider it. Find the little voice inside of me screaming,

"Just fucking do it already!"

With thoughts like these, I usually end up losing consciousness. I become trapped in its rapture. Trapped in its debilitating fear and savage inner torture. Trapped in this thing I apparently call my life.

Life. What a fucking joke.

Whenever I do think of suicide, I think that perhaps my biggest fear about it is that I may be wrong. I think about hell. I think about how hell could possibly be any worse than being alive like this. What could possibly be more torturous?

I fear that I am wrong about God. I fear that my father was always right. That suicide equals a first class ticket to the deepest pits of hell. That it would force me to face God. That I would be judged for bailing on something unbearable.

I fear that there is an afterlife, and even worse, that I will be conscious for it. I hope that death is absolute. The end. Nothing else. No more torture or awareness. Just death. But I fear the speculation too much to attempt it.

Just like I told Doctor Satan Face, I would never have the balls to do it. I never would.

I am tired of staring at this mystery building.
I get up and walk my ugly, fat, naked body to the bathroom to have a shower. I feel numb peace running through my veins, covering the panic like a blanket. Hiding it from reality.

I turn on the shower, then examine my receding hair line in the mirror. It's getting thinner by the day. I'm getting uglier by the day. Sadder, and sadder.

I look at my body in the mirror and wonder what kind of woman wouldn't mind it? There were none. There were none period. I wonder how many people feel like me? I wonder what kind of excuse God could ever give to any of us? None would ever be acceptable. Not in the face of this kind of depression.

I step into the shower and feel the water run down my body. I let it run over me while I stare at the wall and try to concentrate on that one point. That one point where there are no thoughts, no emotions, no reality. The complete absence of logic, patterns, and place.

Peace.
I lather my hands with soap and rub it on my body. Even the soap feels abrasive. It feels unnatural. I search so deep inside of me for confirmation, no matter how far away, that there is still some kind of residual lust for life left over somewhere. Some kind of will to be here, alive, and living.

Nothing.
"Jesus Christ," I mutter. "What... What the fuck am I even doing?"

I begin crying. Not a feel good cry, like those people who have never truly cried before liked to call it, but a debilitating, frustrating, annihilating cry. A dark empty, devoid of anything meaningful, or even real. So ugly, and shameful, and weak.

I wonder how I was even made aware of such an emptiness? It surely isn't normal. It can't be, or else people would be offing themselves faster than they could actually get a start in life.

I watch the walls of the shower swell in size, and pulsate away from me. My eyes feel wide open, like I can't blink even if I want to. My mouth is drier than a desert. I feel a swoon coming. The frantic panic. The monstrous fear. The shaking tremors.

I watch the water come out of the shower head in slow motion. Every drop suspended, every sound so far away. The lights dim. The sounds stop. My vision becomes dream-like. Surreal. Alien.

The only things I can see are not real. They are in my head. They are in my soul. They are haunting. I see nothing but pain and suffering. I see images of a car crash. A woman falling to the ground. A mess of pills flying upward and away from me. I see the empty.

I feel my body relax, and my eyes roll back. I feel my legs turn to rubber. I feel my vision returning, the tremors stopping, the panic receding. I feel it all dim down, and return to a comprehensible consistency. I see the walls around me come back into focus, and I am suddenly reminded that I am standing in my shower. I see the water falling on me at a regular frame rate again. I feel my heart pumping fast for no plausible reason at all.

Please kill me.

CHAPTER 19

The Story Of Brian Hotz

I'm staring out of the window, looking over the city. I see all of these people simply irking through life without the slightest clue. All of these people ignoring me, pushing me aside, hating me, repulsing me, avoiding me.

No love for this man. No love from any source at all. Not even close.

I want to love. I want to love so badly. So much, and so deeply. I want to see beauty in the world. I want to see beauty in people. I want to see beautiful women. I would kill to see a naked woman that was actually there for me. I would like to feel love no matter how threatening sex may be, no matter how disgustingly filled with killer microbes. I want to be able to look past that. I want.... I don't know what I want anymore. I doubt I ever did.

This will all end soon.

That was the end of the page. Jessica was taken back by its sheer honesty. It was different from the rest of what she had read about Brian Hotz so far. Even the handwriting was quite unlike the panic stricken hand that had insecurely penned the rest of the journal.

He was a man lost in the nightmares of his own mind. She flipped to the next page.

The Story Of Brian Hotz

This little fragmented building of mine hasn't budged. I haven't touched it. I've barely looked at it in the past day or so to be honest. I haven't done anything except my usual empty wallows. I tried going for a walk, I tried clearing my mind, but it seems the problem has embedded itself into the very fabric of my psyche. It is unclearable.

But I did go for a walk. I went around the block, and felt the choking grasp of phobias. The pollution. The rank air. The diseased oxygen. The parasite infected insects. The burning sun. The sick people. The decaying bricks. It was all too much.

Now I'm here, standing in the doorway of my bedroom, staring at this thing. I wonder if someone has broken into my apartment?

I wonder if I'm the one who finished the building?

Jessica quickly flipped to the next page.

The Story of Brian Hotz

I'm wondering how I got these cuts on my hands. Little nicks that look like paper cuts. I wonder if they're infected? I wonder if they will eventually kill me? I wonder why people always seem to die from their greatest fears? Do they attract them? Does the human mind truly have that power? The power to make reality? The power to create it, and alter it based solely on inner thoughts?

Sometimes I think so. Most times, I think there is no such thing as control. Discipline.

Sometimes I think it feels like we are all trapped in a violent whirlwind of chaos. The same madness that created the universe is still strongly evident in our behaviors. Violent. Inconsiderate. Selfish. All of these attitudes, and personalities, all carrying the same basic undertones as every other. The same chaos. The same seething randomness. The same fear.

Sometimes I wonder why I'm alive. I wonder why I try? I wonder why? I wonder why.

I fear that I am not alone. I fear that everyone shares that same emotion, no matter how badly some of them try to hide from it. We look for the break in the wall. That little crack. That massive answer. But all we ever see, is nothing.

I wonder how much power I have? Any of us have. What could I alter if I wanted to badly enough? Do I have God-like powers? Do any of us, or are we all a bunch of complete fools?

I am a fool. I have all the proof I need. It's everywhere I look. Everything about me is foolish.

I'm thinking about Doctor Satan Face. I wonder what she thinks of me? I think that she hates me. I think that she can tell that I am a fool. I think... I think...

I think that she can save me.
She can save me with her eternal beauty. She can save me with her soft soul. She can save me with her Satan face.

I think... I think I love her.

She was completely unaffected by fatigue. She was intrigued by the journal. It was a documented destruction of a man, piece by piece, play by play. One layer peeled away, giving light to the next horrid one below.

"You love her?" she whispered. "This is you, isn't it?"
She remembered all the love put into Nicole White's murder. That simplistic beauty. That horrid, ugly, misguided love. She thought of the way her body had been broken and then placed to make her look so weak, so powerless, and frightened.

The killer had raped Nicole White. There was no forensic evidence left behind, but he had done it. He had loved her so much. He was a very sick man.

She flipped the page again.

The Story Of Brian Hotz

The building has completed itself. I don't know, seems like I just woke up, and there it was, sitting idly, just waiting to be judged. Waiting to be feared. Waiting for me to wonder just how in the hell any of this is possible.

I can't remember, but there it is. Without a doubt, as concrete as anything else I can perceive.

The building has actually been complete for over a full day now. Infinitely there on my bedroom floor while I struggle and plead for some kind of release, some kind of salvation.

I don't now why, but I keep finding myself completely naked.

I hate my body. I hate this life.

She flipped to the next page:

The Story Of Brian Hotz

Something happened to me today. Something unexpected, unnatural, and unheard of. When I woke up this morning, I felt fantastic. As fantastic as I've ever known. As amazing as staring into the eyes of God himself.

I had a shower and went for a walk, without a destination, just to get out. I revel in how odd that statement feels to me. Just to get out. Just to change my mind for a bit. Just to move on to a happier illusion.

I don't know why, but I felt that having a cigarette was a good idea. I had no cigarettes, so I walked to a convenience store and went inside. I was perplexed by the complete absence of anything resembling my usual frantic bug fixations. Diseased threats. Sick hanging in the air. I felt none of it, and I could not understand why. Something was wrong.

The girl behind the counter reminded me of Doctor Satan Face. A beautiful specimen. A gorgeous female. She also smelled like heaven. She also had eyes like diamonds. She also had the face of an angel.

Her smile made me tingle all over. I felt my chest tighten, and it jolted me slightly. It wasn't fear. It wasn't panic. It was... I don't know... Happy? What's happy?

When she spoke, her voice was like music. It was calm, and filled with happiness. It was exciting, and filled with life. It was... It was so soothing.

The girl was gorgeous, and I suddenly felt incredibly nervous. Nervous, yes, but the room hadn't swelled, or spun, for some reason. Some reason.

She looked into my eyes when she spoke. I could see her lips move, I could hear words come out, but I wasn't really listening. I was enthralled.

I was bewildered when I heard my own voice come out of me like a confident womanizer. I had no idea. I had no control. It just sort of... Happened.

I still don't remember what was said, but I suddenly found myself with her number scribbled in my palm.

I... I don't know what happened.

She wondered if this was all becoming a delusion. An unintended work of fiction. Real, but only to one person, and only in his mind. Blatant lunacy. A crazy person.

She wondered if Brian Hotz knew where he was tonight. She wondered if he thought about his killings. Was he proud of them? Was he frightened by them? Did they disturb him and treat him like a tortured victim instead of an intoxicated madman? Did he, no matter how obviously insane, did he still have a conscience? No matter how evil or cruel, no matter how devastatingly grotesque, was it still in some way intact?

She associated it in her mind with the very definition of normal. What was normal? It was exactly what everything else was–an opinion. Could that be applied to someone's psyche? Only insane to us? Only haunting to suburbia? To what was, normal?

She continued reading.

The Story Of Brian Hotz

I am sitting in my bathtub, completely naked, but without water. I am shaking so hard. I'm... I am freaking out. I think it's close now. Closer than ever.

Ever.

I... I don't know what happened. I... Can't, I can't remember. Remember what?... Exactly! Goddamn it. Ah, God. Fuck you. Fuck. You. Fuck. You.

I'm beginning to feel the tiles of the shower wall squeeze my face against the other wall that I know is at least eight feet away, but not now. Right now it's trying to crush my skull against the shower. I feel pain flood my head. My vision is hazy, dream-like. My breathing is frantic, and heavily labored. My body shakes. I cry. I swallow more pills. I hold them tight in my hands. So tight. So desperate. All I want is a release. All I want is freedom. Please! Please! Goddamn it.

I swallow more yellows and try to concentrate. I try to force the walls away from me. Return the ceiling to its natural height. The floor to a smooth solid surface, instead of a black hole trying to swallow me forever. I try... I try so hard.

I... I'll have to write later. This isn't fucking helLPING

The Story Of Brian Hotz

No one should ever have to look into a mirror and wonder who he is looking at. No one should ever be able to touch their own head, or arm, or leg, and feel like it's someone else's. No one, should ever have to be me. Ever.

Last night, I was trapped in a whirlwind of panic. A monstrous, unknown menace had gripped my heart and squeezed. Nothing but the spins. Nothing but inconclusiveness.

Nothing. Always, nothing.

My mind was standing strong against the pharmaceuticals, refusing to give in to them, but I was still sent on a savage roller coaster ride of emotional torture. The memories that flew through my mind, I didn't know if they were real or not. I... I don't even know if this is real anymore.

Before that episode, I had actually thought that perhaps things were beginning to look up. I had met a girl. A woman. Was that real? I had her number scribbled on the palm of my hand. Was that real? Was she... Real?

No one should ever have to look at something after the fact and wonder if it actually happened, wonder if it was real, wonder if it was possible.

I am so, so tired. So beaten. So ugly.

I am sick of these pills, and these panics. I am sick of me, and this shitty apartment. I am sick of the fact that I have lost my job for reasons I can't explain to anyone, let alone myself. I am sick of society staring down at me all the way from their big noses. Judging me. Laughing at me. Talking about me after I'm gone. After I don't exist anymore. Who wants to be remembered that way? Who wants to live life like that? Who wants that?

I am sick of Doctor Satan Face asking me questions. I am sick of her not being able to help me. I am sick of not having anyone able to help me period. No one. Not even myself.

I am sick of the girl's face flashing through my mind, no matter how beautiful she may be. The one from the store. I know it's impossible. I know we could never be together. I know that I will screw it up. I am sick of asking why. I am sick of being so afraid. So depressed. So panicked, and destitute, and desperate.

I am sick of me. All of me.

Every pill I take brings on a whole new wave of shame. Of despair. I am sick of knowing that I personify failure in every possible way. I am sick of being the antonym of society. The black sheep. The toilet paper.

I am sick of all of it. I am sick.

I'm just sick.

I am sick.

I am sick.

I am sick of wondering why I was freaking out in a bathtub last night, swallowing pills, and grabbing at walls, trying to figure out just why I was covered in blood and no vomit.

"Blood?" Jessica said, and felt her chest tighten. The writing on the page was not over. Brian Hotz seemed to scribble about how sick he was for a while, and then, Jessica thought something odd happened.

The Story Of Brian Hotz

I keep having this dream. Her face is far away. Very far, but still staring directly at me. Her eyes are happy. Her eyes are free. Her eyes are angelic.

I do nothing but stare at her for a long time. Her supple lips. Her immaculately soft skin. Her breath against my face. I feel like God. I feel like the sun. Mighty. Powerful. Unrelenting.

This girl, this is the girl from the store. This is the girl I had said things to, but couldn't remember what. This was the girl who took a pen and wrote her number in my palm without causing me to lose my mind in a flood of imagined bacteria and soul eating worms. Quite a feat for a little girl.

Mostly, she reminds me of Doctor Satan Face. Sure, I doubted the doctor could help me, but she was a sinfully beautiful woman. The most beautiful, maybe. At least in my eyes, and with one extra bonus too; perhaps she also held the keys I needed. The direction of travel. The answer.

I stare at her naked body laid out in front of me. When was the last time I had seen a real naked woman? A stupid question when I couldn't tell you what month it is at the moment.

I can smell her. She smells like heaven. She smells like... She smells like God. She smells amazing.

I look at her perfect breasts. They feel like heaven, and suddenly, I think that if perhaps there was one gift sent directly from God for us losers down here, women like this must be it. They must be.

I hear her soft voice say that she wants me. She wants me inside of her, caressing her, holding her. I drop my body onto her, and I suddenly notice that the entire room around me is flailing and exploding. Things bounce high up in the air, and then fall back to the ground in pieces. Things whirl around us while I hold her body so tightly against mine. So closely to mine.

I pay no attention to any of it. None of it is real. None of it is happening around us. She is all I can see, and all I can feel. She is my momentary rapture.

She whispers something. She whispers, "I want you to want me. I want you to show me."

I stand back for a moment and look down at her. Gorgeous as ever. Dream-like as ever. I suddenly wonder why this dream isn't a nightmare. Why? When was the last time that had happened? Only God knows.

Maybe.

"I want you to rub me," she says, so I begin. I rub her entire body with such finesse that I am surprised by it. Her skin is unbelievably soft. Unbelievably erotic. I see her so clearly. So concisely.

Her face then begins to confuse me. She is happy. She is joyful. And then she is sad. Then she is scared. Then she is happy again. Then scared. Then happy.

I decide to look away, not wanting to ruin the moment with a rabid panic. I continue rubbing for as long as she won't show any sign that she wants me to stop. I rub and rub.

I take my finger and begin tracing lines all over her; over her face, her breasts, her legs. She rolls over, and I continue. I trace all over her back, and her butt, and her legs.

The lines I trace begin taking shape. They begin taking color. This dream is as magical as anything I have ever experienced. Slowly, she begins to squirm slightly, but doesn't pull away.

I continue.

I draw long circles, and lines stretching all over her. Some from her shoulders, and all the way down to her feet. Some very short. Some in medium lengths.

She is suddenly filled with color, and I feel happy. I feel safe. She looks tribal to me. Like an ancient Indian dancing for her Gods.

I stand back and marvel at the transformation of it all. She is gorgeous. She is ancient, and eternal in her beauty. She is constant, and happy. She does not move while I admire her. She doesn't seem to be afraid of me. She doesn't seem... She seems... She seems happy. Yes... Happy.

She looks like a painting, and it makes me smile. I wonder why I don't have more of these wonderful dreams? I wonder why my mind insists on punishing me, instead of giving me these fantastic tableaus to view?

I wonder... I wonder so much.

Her image is forever etched into my mind. That beautiful tribal girl, stuck in time forever in full colors and magical grace. A frozen angel. She looks so real. So, so clear.

For a moment, I can't see anything but her body, and her colors. It looks like her body is spreading apart, becoming a part of the very thing that had created her. The fabric. She is bursting with beauty. Immaculate. Forever.

I can't remember anymore of it after that. I think I woke up in my bathtub. Naked, and without water. Shaking, and frantically swallowing insane amounts of pharmaceuticals. Desperately trying to get a grip, and wrap my head around it all. There is only one pressing question I still really want an answer to.

If I did not cut myself, then why all the blood?

"Holy shit!" Jessica yelled out. "Are you kidding me?"

She closed the book and threw it as hard as she could against the hotel room wall, screaming at the top of her lungs in rage.

She paced the room, holding her belly. Her mind raced with what she had just read. It was, it was inexplicably disturbing.

She ran to the bathroom and puked again. She couldn't tell anymore if it was her earlier illness making a comeback, or if this was the work of Brian Hotz. Her skin crawled when she thought of it. A dream? A happy dream? A blessing?

"Son of a bitch!" she panted. "Ah, shit."

Her mind was fixated on the image of the first victim now. Her body lying face down, filled with tribal-like lines cut into her skin, colored in with charcoal. She saw the intricate mosaic of debris heading away from her in every direction. She had seen exactly what he had described in his journal... Just, not with such a demented perception. She thought of her sister. Her sister, killed by this psychotic. At the moment, she truly was not looking forward to continuing the story. She was trapped in a volcanic rage, that incredibly intense emotion she never truly had full control over. She did not want to see anymore through the eyes of this pathological monster on a bad trip.

"A bad trip?" she screamed. "You're killing and you think it's a dream, you prick!"

There was a knock on the door, and someone's voice asking if she was all right. It was one of the officers stationed in the hallway to keep her protected while she lost her mind inside the hotel room.

"I'm fine," she yelled out. "It's okay. I'm fine. Thank you."

She thought about bad trips. A person's mind whacked out on drugs and operating on some basic core of emotions like a short-circuiting computer trapped in a nightmare, but the body is left to react as though it were actually happening.

Could a total breakdown like that happen naturally? To that degree? Was that what Brian Hotz felt? Hell. Pure, horrible, personal hell. Was he really so delusional as to write something so grotesquely disturbing with such happy charm? Trapped in an illusion? Was he... Was...

She puked again. She felt so weak. Not only physically, but she felt it in the way she hated most. Personally. She tried concentrating her thoughts, but her mind was fiercely avoiding it with all kinds of ridiculous side thoughts. The story. The obscene, crazed tale of sadistic murder in a fairy tale.

She couldn't concentrate anymore. All she could do was repeat the same question, "What am I going to do? What am I going to do? What am I going to do?"

CHAPTER 20

When she woke up, she was still sick. On top of that, she was more disappointed with herself than ever. Brian Hotz had succeeded in making her feel uncomfortable. He had made her hate him with every ounce of herself. He had made her squirm like a bug.

Twice!

She wasn't going to work. She was to stay in the hotel room until she either felt better, or another victim was found. Otherwise, Captain Briar had ordered her to not leave the hotel room.

In reality, he had begged her with that ungodly fear clouding his eyes. Jessica wouldn't have gone to work anyway. She was ill. She was frustrated. She was disgusted, and she was still lonely.

Her body had taken a brute beating by whatever illness she carried. She was exhausted, and she felt... She felt as though her mind had been violated. She felt like Brian Hotz had violated her in a way far worse than anything physical he could have done. It was from the inside. From the mind out. From her core.

She couldn't get him out of her head, it was driving her insane. She decided to have something to eat, and ordered eggs from room service, but ended up only eating toast. Her stomach couldn't handle much more.

She lit a cigarette and turned on her television, flipped through the endless channels of crap.

Absolutely nothing interesting. Surprise.

She landed on a news channel discussing her case. The man speaking, identified as a psychologist, was attempting to give a psychological profile of The Fleshcrafter killer. Jessica listened casually.

"The thing about a killer like this," the psychologist was saying. "Is that he is consumed with killing. A person like this cannot stop, because it is a compulsion, and one that will never end until he is dead. Killing probably makes him feel like a supreme person. Like a God. He is probably a man with a very normal life. Perhaps even with a wife and kids. A home. But in reality, the man must kill, or he could not keep it all together. Of course, eventually, just like any other urge people overindulge in, it gets out of control, often times becoming the very thing that destroys them."

"Nope," Jessica said.

She admitted that she had initially considered such a scenario. A normal man. A normal life. Secret killings of passion. There was no doubting the passion in the crime scenes she had seen, but as far as the situation went, this Fleshcrafter beast, this Brian Hotz psycho, was a case all of his own. A new breed of killer. A new wave of savage.

There was no psychologist, or profiler, or anyone who could concisely define a man like Brian Hotz. No one could accurately deduce a description of a man so blatantly insane from crime scenes that had been so calculated, precise, and methodical. There was very little insanity in the crimes, except for the passion.

She wondered if humans often confused the two; sheer insanity for passion.

She wondered if it was possible to do something so enthrallingly sadistic and not have any real recollection of it. She wondered how all of it could then be so precise and calculated. She wondered how he could be trapped in a heavenly dream, making love to a girl smiling back at him, when in reality, he was committing a savage murder.

How?

Did human beings have that capacity? Was that even fair to anyone?

Jessica chuckled lightly.

"Fair... Ha."

She stared at the diary sitting on the hotel desk. It had

taken on a life of its own. It had become far more than just a story. More than an account. Now it was different. Now, it seemed evil. It seemed ugly, and harsh. It seemed like something that should not exist, and should not be disturbed in any way. As though simply touching it would singe your fingers.

She quietly hoped that Brian Hotz would be consumed by his own insanity, and end it all, but she already knew the truth.

Everywhere she looked for him, it was already obvious. Brian Hotz was already consumed with insanity. He was so far inside of it all that there was no hope for him to ever return to civilized life. It was too late. Too wrong.

She stared at the book, wondering how much he'd written before doing what? Giving the journal to Nicole White? Hiding it himself for her to find? How had she come into possession of it?

She didn't want to read those ugly pages anymore. She didn't want to see the disturbed scribbles churning out a story so unbelievably wild that it was hard to believe that any of it was real, no matter how opaque the reality of it seemed to be.

Jessica took in a deep breath, knowing what had to be done. She had to finish it. She had to keep going despite her personal feelings. She swallowed hard, and opened the book.

The Story Of Brian Hotz

This coffee tastes empty. Flavorless. It feels ugly.
I wonder about the girl I met. The one from the dream. She had wanted me to call her. Had that happened? What had I done with the number?

I feel like shit.
Lately, it seems like I'm having more and more trouble defining if dreams are dreams, or if life is a dream, or even, what reality means. What does it mean? Where is it? How is it even possible? I don't know anymore. I don't know. I think I may be losing my grip on things, but I can never tell for sure. Even worse, I can't even realize it until well after the fact.

Is that hell? Torture that you didn't see coming, didn't feel overtaking you, didn't feel it possessing you until you suddenly find yourself looking around the room and wondering what the hell just happened?

Goddamn. I'm at a loss. I'm so scared. I'm so, so scared. I think about the blood and I still can't understand what happened. There isn't a scratch on my entire disgusting body. Not one. When I woke up in my bathtub, I looked like I had just skinned an animal. An animal! In a city?

I hate blood. It makes me queasy. It makes me dizzy, and uncomfortable, and weak. It makes me puke.

I don't think I will tell Doctor Satan Face about this right now. I think it's weird enough for the moment. Our "relationship". She is so beautiful. I know, I've said that a lot, but it seems like it's the only thing I am sure of these days.

She wouldn't understand. How could she? I couldn't. She couldn't.

I am wondering if maybe she feels bad for me? I hate it when people feel bad for me... but with her, it's different. I think I would like that. I think I like her a lot.

Who knows? I do not.
I know pills. I know fear. That's about all I know. Suffering. Pain. Madness.

I hurt all the time.
I think my appointment with Doctor Satan Face is tomorrow. I don't know what to say. I don't know how she will react, or if she could ever understand. Worse, I don't know if what is being said is actually happening. I don't know.

I think... I think I may give her this journal. I think I want her to read it. Maybe she could somehow understand me. Maybe she could help me. Many, many maybes.

I think it would help our little "relationship", seeing as right now it's more like a stunning angel with a complete lunatic addicted to pills and panic. Addicted to fear. Aren't all humans addicted to it? Fear. Who knows? I do not.

Yeah... I think I will give it to her. I think that would be nice.

So, good doctor. I suppose I should say that I apologize for anything that may offend you in this text, but please understand, I have nowhere else to go. I have no direction to turn in, or face, or even understand. I am being more honest with myself right now than I have since I was a little boy.

I need help.

You cannot understand how completely embarrassing and frightening those words are to me. You have no idea. But the real truth is that I still somewhat know that something is seriously wrong. It is an extremely rare occurrence lately, but it still does happen.

What will happen if I simply continue to let it overtake me? What then? When I no longer have the conscious ability to even realize that something is wrong. That I am odd. That I am a freak. That I am alive.

What happens when you lose any and all concepts of mundanity? What then?

Do you see my fear, doctor? Right now, I am terrified that by the time you get to read this, it will be too late. I will already have slipped into some weird dimension of constant imaginations. Lost in the subconscious. Lost in never ending dreams.

What then, doctor?

Please. I am so desperate. I need some help. I need some help. I need some fucking help.

Goddamn it I hate that.

I am feeling rather lucid for the moment. Aware, for who knows how long? I won't even notice it happening. But it is the truth.

Please doctor. Please. Do everything you can. And doctor. I... I think I love you.

I love you so much.

CHAPTER 21

Jessica read the last page of the journal ten times over. It made her heart quiver. It made her brain stop everything and really take notice.

"You did love her, you cruel son of a bitch," she said. "It was all there. All that love. I bet you loved all of them, didn't you?"

It made Jessica's blood boil with rage. It made her want to put a bullet into Brian Hotz's severely demented brain. She was afraid, though not in the common sense. She was afraid of the book.

The book itself contained undeniable evidence of psychosis; of delusions, and personal suffering. That book meant that this killer was not ever going to see justice for anything he had done. Nothing. This man, because of that book alone, would undoubtably spend endless years drugged on better dope than he had ever used, and spend his time staring deeply into pictures, playing inside of those particular worlds. He would never go to prison. He would spend the rest of his life talking to walls, oozing with nonsense.

Jessica wasn't sure what to do about it. The book. That book only meant trouble. She knew it was her fault. She also knew that it was far too late to do anything to fix it.

It was what it was.

Reality shifted.

She still could not understand why the killer hadn't taken it when it had been in plain sight on her night stand. Why hadn't he taken it from Nicole White's office? He had been there after he killed her sister, but for what? Was he there for some other cryptic reason? Had he not recognized it? Could that be? Pouring your heart into something and then never recognizing it again? Something that personal?

She couldn't tell Captain Briar about it, and she also couldn't reference any of it for the case without arousing suspicion. Everything about Brian Hotz was psychotic. Things you simply couldn't just blurt out and not expect anyone to question.

It was what it was.
Impossible.

She wondered what she should do with it. Keeping it was a grave danger. Destroying it was... Well, it was... She stopped and thought about it. She wondered why she felt some type of attachment to it. Had she truly been so powerfully drawn into the wild and fanatical ride that was the unfinished story of Brian Hotz? A meaningless name. A nobody. A ghost.

She shook her head. She hated it. The way he had crept inside of her brain. He infected her without them ever having met. It was yet another one of those things. An innocence lost. Knowledge that could not be unlearned.

She decided to simply leave the book for the moment and tried to focus on something else. She ordered chicken soup from the hotel restaurant and then curled up in her bed again. She still thought it was a hard mattress, but she was slowly getting used to it. She turned on the television and found the movie menu. After scrolling through every possible selection, she decided to watch Sacha Baron Cohen's Borat. That was her kind of comedy. Society's hypocrisy thrown right back into its face. It always made Jessica feel better knowing that she was not the only one who happened to view society in such a realistic way. All of the illusions peeled away. The truth, and nothing but.

She laughed, and it felt good. It felt like going outside and taking a break from something. Moving away from the doom clouds and seeing some sunshine for a little while.

She continued to bounce through a variety of movies in all kinds of genres for the rest of the day. Changing moods. Thinking about nice stories. Escaping reality. Or at least, distorting it.

She watched many different stories and many different people throughout the day, and never once did she take another moment to think about Brian Hotz.

She had forbidden herself from it, and it had been the best decision she could have made all day.

She fell asleep with the clearest mind since before she had ever heard of the killer they had named, The Fleshcrafter.

CHAPTER 22

She slept through the night and woke up in sweat soaked sheets. As soon as she opened her eyes, she knew she felt much better. She sat up and stretched. Her mind was clear, and familiar. Unbothered. Unshakable.

Despite feeling better, she still wasn't going to work. She had fiercely fought against it in the beginning, but she was now realizing that taking time off was probably the best thing she could have done for herself. Even the hotel room helped. Away from everything common. Relaxation. Peace.

She spent the afternoon eating and watching more hotel menu movies. She felt in control of herself again. She felt like she would soon be ready to return to work and begin with a fresh mind. A clear vision. A specific point to look at.

Her only real fear was that this killer might not be captured using standard investigative tactics. There was nothing standard about the man. The way his brain processed information was nothing like what was considered normal. There was no healthy monotony, no routine, no patterns of logical behavior. Brian Hotz was a complete victim of his own mind. Shattered from the inside, with the outside left to react.

And then what?

She wondered how he chose his victims. Were they all random hallucinations of insanity? Were they social vagabonds that happened to be unfortunate enough to have made it through all the crazy and catch Brian Hotz's eye? He seemed obsessed with pretty women. He seemed obsessed with Nicole White. He had never used her real name. Aside from referring to her as Doctor Satan Face, the only other name he had used in the journal was

Dr. Miller. Was doctor Miller real, or was the name made up? Was it all an unbelievable coincidence?

She shuddered at the thought of coincidence again. What was his real name? Given that her real name was so far away from what he had used, she wondered how far away his name was. Brian Hotz, from what?

An impossible guess.

But there was another factor weighing heavily on Jessica's mind. She thought about how he had met the first victim. She wondered if it was possible. Brian Hotz had seemed like a man who couldn't have produced a social skill to save his worthless little life. Could he somehow have managed to actually talk to the girl with enough confidence to get her phone number? Was that possible? A man who couldn't even talk to himself without losing his mind, could he have somehow found some shred of confidence big enough to actually pull it off?

He had said that he couldn't remember. She wondered about it. She thought about various mental illnesses that could perhaps explain it in some way. Multiple personalities was something that had always piqued her curiosity, but somehow, Brian Hotz was different. He didn't seem to only lapse into other people, but was front and center for the ride without ever even realizing that he was not controlling anything. He was watching, and what he was seeing was so far away from reality, that it was plainly haunting. It was a joke, in the most disheartening sense of the word.

It was foul.

How had he met her sister? She wondered if he had approached her like some silver tongued devil with the charm of Don Juan DeMarco. Could that be? Some subconscious part of him coming into total control, and in total ignorance of the reality around it? Completely unaware of anything that is Brian Hotz. Could he have infatuated her somehow? Was he truly as ugly and repulsive as he insisted he was?

There were too many fables. Too many possibilities. Of course, because of the diary, Jessica knew Brian Hotz better than anyone else. She knew his inner thoughts and actions. She knew all kinds of sick and demented things about the man, yet, she still knew nothing about him. She knew nothing about his plans. The book had ended far too abruptly for her to fully understand his thought process in regard to his murders. What had he seen with the other girls? What had he seen with her sister?

She feared that the original man would be completely regressed into the subconscious by the time she would get to him, leaving behind only a conscienceless monster who knew nothing but spewing terror.

She doubted that he was even still aware that something was seriously wrong with him. She doubted that he even realized that he had killed anyone. He had described himself as a foul, weak, scared little pill popping fiend, trying his best to hide from everything, avoiding confrontation with the determinism of a cheetah taking down its prey. The Brian Hotz from the beginning of the book wouldn't have been able to swat a fly to death out of pure terror, how could he possibly have gotten to the point of not only killing another human being, but mutilating them with such grotesque and malicious intent?

How could that be?

He also stated that he had never shown any artistic talent in his life. Could talent, no matter how disturbingly foul, lie deep inside of someone without them ever being aware of it? Jessica herself possessed many talents. They seemed completely natural to her. She had taught herself to play the piano when she was a young girl. With enough practice, she was able to see all the patterns and play virtually anything she put a small effort into. It seemed built into her. Hard wired. Could the same be possible for Brian Hotz? A special talent for killing that he wasn't even aware of?

It could be, but she saw people mistake hate for passion almost every day.

The thoughts were running circles around her. She hated how no matter what the subject was, if she thought about it long enough, it always came back to the same lost questions. Coincidence? Destiny? Meaning?

All of it forever empty. All of it unfounded for everyone.

***

Jessica skimmed the pages of the diary quickly. She was letting the pages flutter at a steady speed in front of her. She was trying an old trick she knew her brain liked. It was her attempt to, "Step back and look at it from somewhere else", as her father had always told her. A sentence that used to send her into a blind rage of annoyance as a teenager, but as she matured, she realized that her father had been right all along. She had never told him so. She would fan through the pages quickly, hoping that maybe a single word, a single page, anything might jump out and hit her square on the nose. Jessica already knew that more often than not, that tiny revealing detail was exactly what had been missing in order to piece it all together. Even if it seemed to mean nothing at the time. Eventually... Somehow... It happened.

Connect the cosmic dots.
There was nothing jumping out at her yet, but Jessica's experience with this strategy had proven time and again that answers were hardly ever apparent at face value. She knew that perhaps a few hours later, or perhaps even days, or weeks, while she was watching television, or having a shower, all of a sudden, there it was. The magical glimpse of understanding. The answer to all of her questions. The missing link.

She put the book down and lit a cigarette. She stared out of the grand window in her hotel room. The street below her buzzed with activity; so many lives, so many opinions.

She was thinking about work. She thought that she would return in the morning. She'd had enough of the nonsense; trapped in a room like some frightened animal while a killer was out there slinging terror across the face of her city. She wasn't afraid of him, and she wasn't afraid of death.

It was what it was.
Inevitable.

CHAPTER 23

Jessica hung up. She had been talking to Captain Briar while driving to work, enjoying the sunrise a little extra this morning. She thought that perhaps a few days locked inside of a room was something she should make a point of doing more often. She felt so clear, so... Like herself.

The hotel was closer to work than her apartment. About half way, she figured. She liked her apartment. She wondered how long before she could return there.

Home was a feeling that only existed to you. Home was synonymous with safe. Safe was synonymous with every possible human action at all times.

The conversation she'd just had with Captain Briar, was to let him know that she was reporting for work, and he in turn informed her that the blood found on her mattress, the one spelling out "Pretty as a butterfly", belonged to an unknown. No past victims. Leaning toward a future one.

Jessica had already guessed that. She had guessed that there were probably twice as many victims as she knew about by now. She guessed that his murder rate would accelerate, as it seemed to have done from the beginning. She didn't want to guess how many more macabre art plateaus she would have to stare at before she could catch him.

She pulled into her parking spot, walked inside the building, and immediately noticed some of her co-workers staring oddly as she walked toward Captain Briar's office to report for duty. They were sympathetic, and some even fearful. She felt bad for most of these people. Brian Hotz had succeeded in creeping into their souls as well. She smiled, nonetheless, and greeted those who met her eyes.

She knocked on the door and heard him invite her inside. "Jessie!" Captain Briar exclaimed with happy eyes. "How are you, my girl? Are you well rested?"

"I am," she replied. "Thank you..." She hesitated. "For ordering me to take some time off, I mean. It was exactly what I needed. You always know what's best."

Captain Briar smiled big. His friendliness, and genuine goodness was instantly apparent to friends and foes alike.

"I've seen many things over the course of my career, Jessie, and although I may not know exactly how to solve certain cases, or where to turn next, I can always recognize when one of mine needs a break to recharge. Aside from other things happening at the moment, the old adage still stands true no matter what. Never kill yourself at the expense of someone else, right?"

"Right," she said.

Captain Briar held his bright smile.

"So, I suppose you would like to know where we stand now?" he said. "All of the files have been sorted and documented. If you would like information from any of them, they are still in the conference room, as well as on here." He handed her a memory stick. "They're all in there. Every name, every diagnosis."

Jessica grabbed the memory stick in her hand. "Thanks Captain," she said.

"You're welcome, but Jessie... That's not all."

"What is it?"

"It's nothing really. It's just, I got a call from Commissioner Dean yesterday. They're now seriously pushing to get you off of this case. It's mostly due to your apartment being destroyed."

"But..."

"Don't worry. I stood up for you. I also made the point extremely clear to them that this was out of your control altogether, and whether they took you off of the case or not, it would most likely..." He trailed off and swallowed hard for a moment. "I'm sorry, but I told them that either way, this case would likely end with you, seeing as you are obviously not the only one obsessed with this killer, but he seems to now be obsessed with you. You are an unbeatably intelligent girl, and without you, this case would probably take five times as long to solve."

"And what did he say?"

"He told me to keep doing what we were for now. Surveillance for you, on the job baby-sitting by me, and to catch this sick bastard as quickly as possible."

She smiled while thinking about it.

"Thanks, Cap," she said. "I always appreciate you standing up for me."

"I only give credit where it is due, my girl."

"Aside from that, well, we are still pretty much exactly where we have been. Staring at a giant wall and inspecting it for cracks. There are very little so far."

"Yeah..." She said. "But ah... But, how are you doing, Captain? Personally, I mean."

He stared at her in silence. Jessica hated watching his eyes cloud over with fear. Helplessness.

"I'm fine, Jessie," he said.

"Captain, I can tell. I just want to make sure you're all right, just like you want to make sure that I'm okay."

"I'm fine," he said again, placing a gentle hand on her shoulder. "I just think that we need to catch him quickly. I think that without him off of the streets, no one is safe. I think... I think I may be getting too old for this case."

"You're not that old yet, Captain." She smiled.

"Well, I suppose not. But I do feel it." He returned her smile. "So I guess that's it for the moment. If you need anything else, you come and see me, of course. And yes, the rules are still in place, you do not go anywhere without my presence. Sorry, kiddo."

"I know, it's out of your hands," she said. "I'll be in my office going through these names." She walked away, waving the memory stick through the air.

"He has to be in there somewhere," he said.

"He is," she replied. "And I'm going to crucify him for it."

"Do what you do," he said. "It hasn't failed you yet."

***

She spent the morning going through meaningless names. None of the descriptions fit her savage killer. None of it meant anything to her. She wondered if perhaps he had been cunning enough to steal his own file while he had been in Nicole White's office. But why the file and not the journal? Why not the journal while he was in her apartment? She again wondered if perhaps the writer was a different person. A novelist of some sort. She liked that idea, but it didn't feel rational. The descriptions were in that diary. The confessions, no matter how blatantly ridiculous they may have been, were there. The book that gave her an insight into the killer. The book that could guarantee him an insanity plea, and tear her case against him to pieces.

For lunch, Captain Briar took her to a Chinese Buffet just down the street from their office, where they threw around ideas, but lunch ultimately ended as fruitlessly as it had begun.

In the afternoon, Jessica spent long hours in the conference room physically going through files again. She had never been a fan of computers. The files were real. They had character, and some of them happened to jump out at her for whatever reason. The human emotion showing through. The handwriting. The scribbled thoughts.

There were so many names. So many lives all neatly paraphrased within a few pages. She took notes. She felt even more helpless with every one she pulled out.

By the end of the afternoon, she was still left with nothing. It was what it was.

She bid Captain Briar goodbye, and left for her hotel. On her way, she let all of the names and descriptions flash aimlessly through her mind. Letting it do all the work. All she could do was wait until it was done computing the countless bits of information.

When she pulled into a spot, shifting the car into park, her phone rang.

"Hello?"

"Jessie," Captain Briar's tiny voice blared through the speaker. "Jess, come back. We just got a new one."

"I'll be there in five minutes."

She raced through traffic and made it back to her parking spot, finding Captain Briar already standing there, waiting for her.

"Are you all right?" she asked.

"I'm fine," he said. "Let's go. This one is fresh, apparently. No more than twenty minutes they're guessing."

"Really?" she said. "Jesus, are we getting closer to him? Then again, what difference does it make if we're twenty minutes behind him, or twenty days? We're still behind and can't reach him either way."

"We'll get him," he answered. "We're close, Detective. We are really close. I can feel it."

She wondered if he could. Had all of that experience given him some kind of edge that she didn't yet possess? Maybe, but she didn't fully believe it.

"Maybe," she said.

"You don't think so? You don't think he may be feeling the pressure? He obviously knows we're on to him, he tried attacking you."

She said nothing, but Captain Briar's stare was obviously asking for a reply. At the very least out of politeness.

"He wasn't attacking me," she finally said.

She watched his face sag like someone had shot him in the belly. His eyes flashing confusion, and wonder.

"What?" he said.

"He..." She hesitated again. "Captain, I don't think he was trying to hurt me."

He let out a belching laugh, but immediately realized that she wasn't kidding. He abruptly caught his breath and shuffled in his seat with hot embarrassment flushing his face.

"I'm sorry, Jessie." he said. "I didn't mean to..."

"He loves me," she cut him off.

Suddenly, the vehicle was void of human sounds. A deafening silence. The kind that is more painful, and nervous than anything else. The kind that makes you hold your breath. His face was fixated on her now. An absolute, totalitarian attention.

"I..." She tried speaking again. "I... Don't know. I just...

I get the feeling that he is not doing any of this out of hate. Somehow, someway... It's out of love. Desperation."

Captain Briar sat back against his seat and stared out the window. Jessica knew that he couldn't possibly be expected to wrap his head around such a blasphemous notion without first having read the journal. He was obviously transfixed with deep thoughts. Inner conflicts filled with more irrationality, fear, panic, and wonder.

He finally looked at her again.
"What makes you think something like that?" he asked.

"Nicole White," she replied plainly. "He loved her. I could tell, just by the way he placed her. The way the room was set. It was... It was, I don't know... Considerate?"

"He cut her goddamn heart out!" he said, not believing it.
"Yeah," she said. "But it was love, Captain. I don't know, maybe she refused him, or made him feel inferior somehow, but he did love her. Cutting out her heart was a display of love in the context of a sick delusion."

"What about the others?" he asked.
"I suspect the same," she said. "He seems to be searching for something. Searching for... I don't know... Something. He liked the others a lot, but Nicole White, he loved her. Maybe he thinks he sees it in certain women. All of the victims. My sister, even with me, now. He... He's desperate, Captain. He is so desperate for something."

"Don't say that," he said timidly. "I don't want to hear that some psychotic surgeon is out there slaying women like it's as regular as painting on a canvas, and now he's in love with you. Please."

"I'm sorry, Captain. We're almost there anyway."
She could see the deep seeded concern in his eyes. It was a personal concern, for her, for his friend, for his young protege he had taken under his wing. Captain Briar was a man who contained a wealth of care inside of him. He would have felt deep concern, and sorrow, and pain for anyone in trouble, whether he knew them personally or not. He believed that humans were mostly good. He believed that good was as present as evil. Jessica tended to agree with him. For the most part, people were

good, and decent. But on the flip side, she could also see the
rapid decline of it all. Her generation was not one of help, or of
love, or kindness. It was one of selfishness, of debauched ideas
for the future. Her generation was the one that would finally
tip the scales and change the world, only, that change seemed
grossly misunderstood by the masses.

She hoped that she was wrong.

"It's right here on the left," Captain Briar said, and when she
turned the corner, they suddenly found themselves speechless.

The scene was incredible. Far more public and hard hitting
than any case, or crime scene, Jessica had ever been to. The
crime had taken place in a condo building. She and Captain Briar
could see the building, but the crowd pouring into the street was
what had rendered both of them without words.

"What the hell is going on?" Jessica asked.

"I don't know. They didn't say anything. We just got the call and
responded. Just park up here."

She parked her car, and attempted to infiltrate the crowd,
heading toward the building's entrance.

"Police!" she yelled with her badge out. "Excuse me,
coming through, police, excuse me."

The closer she got to the building, the denser the crowd
was. Captain Briar had started out in front of her, but was now a
few bodies away, beside her, and pushing through the mass in the
same fashion.

When she reached the edge of the crowd, she could see
that the area in front of the building had been cordoned off with
police tape. She could see the officers keeping guard on the
perimeter, and regularly having to answer, "No. I am sorry, I do
not know what happened. It's an on-going police investigation.
Step back, please."

She pushed herself through the last of the bodies and
flashed her badge at the perimeter guard. There were police lights
everywhere, bouncing off of everything. Dusk was beginning
to overtake the city. The air was moist but still warm. More and
more people were cramming themselves into the crowd around
the condo building, all looking for the same thing they were
always looking for.

Some kind of answer.

Jessica noticed an officer walking toward her as soon as she and Captain Briar had crossed the tape. She knew the officer, his name was Derek Smith, and they had been in the academy together when she had first joined, but that had been about as far as their acquaintanceship had gone.

"Hello Detective. Captain," he said plainly. "Long time no see. How have you been?"

"I've been good," she replied. "How about yourself?"

"All is good," he said, and then hesitated. "Well... In my life anyway. Not so good here."

"What happened?"

"A woman, murdered and mutilated, and..."

"Mutilated how?" she asked quickly.

He stared at her. She could tell that he was trying to act unbothered by the crime at hand. She could tell he was being as fake as all the other men she had ever spoken to, melting in nervousness around her.

"It's your guy," he answered. "But he threw her out of the window."

"Out of the window?" Captain Briar questioned.

"Landed on the roof of a car," he replied.

Jessica said nothing while the officer and the Captain spoke.

"Out of the window?" She wondered. That wasn't his style. He liked the tableaus. He liked the outlandish displays and evil theatrics. Why would he have thrown her out?

"Did anyone see it?" she asked.

"They're interviewing now," the officer answered. "A lady called it in. She was walking her dog, but I'm not sure if she saw it happen, or if she happened to pass by and notice the body.

"Okay," she replied. "Thank you, Officer Smith."

"Hey, no problem, Detective. Anytime. The car is just over there by the entrance to the building."

"Thank you," Captain Briar said.

"You're welcome, Captain."

They walked slowly toward the vehicle, and Jessica immediately let her brain absorb the complex scene. This scene was one of deductions. See the scene, delete the crowd, delete the traffic, delete everything that is happening at the moment, and try to find what has happened; what details were already there before all of these people filled the streets like a flood.

When she reached the car, she stopped, and scanned around it. She could see nothing. She turned and quickly scanned the crowd around her. There were so many people. So many blurred faces, and insignificant bodies, forming a uniform wall.

She didn't know why, but she couldn't help but momentarily glance at them.

"Focus!" she said to herself.

The car itself looked as though a meteorite had made a direct hit from a billion light years away. It was obliterated, and smashed down to the height of perhaps a bicycle. Every window had been blown out. The passenger doors were bent, mangled by the blunt force. The roof of the car was nearly touching the inside floorboards, effectively enveloping the woman's body like a final cocoon. Her final metallic tomb.

The crowd was loud. She was trying to block them out, but everytime she lapsed and heard them again, she felt compelled to stand there, and stare back. Stare through them, and around them. All of those faces. All of those questions.

It suddenly dawned on her.

"Are you still here?" she whispered to herself. "Are you watching me? Is that why you threw this poor woman through a window?... For me?"

She couldn't see anything of particular importance, and returned her attention to the vehicle tomb.

"Can I get a step stool or something?" she asked a patrolling officer.

"No problem, Detective," he answered. "Be right back." He returned quickly with a small step ladder. She unfolded its legs and stepped up.

"Real nice, you bastard," she said.

There was no doubt about it, her killer was responsible. There was no doubt about the savage bludgeoning. There was no doubt about the amount of sheer pain and fear this woman had felt. She had been crushed and thrown out like a piece of trash.

Inches of blood had collected on the bottom of the
vehicle's roof, slowly leaking onto the asphalt below. The fall
had done that, and despite all of the blood, Jessica could see the
intricate lines cut into her face. Her throat punctured like the
others. The artistic value of the cuts ever present.

She could see the bright colors that had been pressed into
her skin after the cuts. The sick model. The mangled beauty.

She lifted her head and scanned the crowd again.
"What's it like upstairs?" she asked Captain Briar.

"It's destroyed. Same psycho. Same sadness," he replied
with a crackling voice.

"You doing all right, Cap? I'm starting to get worried
about you,."

"Don't worry about me. Just worry about catching him."
"Well..." She said. "There isn't much here. I'm having trouble
seeing her whole body. I'm not sure what she's meant to be yet.
It's an odd design. I'll have to inspect her once they get her out,
but get it photographed anyway, please. Just in case."

"No problem," he said. "I'll arrange it now with the
forensics team."

Captain Briar was off to speak with the team and explain
Jessica's instructions, and she once again found herself transfixed
with the crowd.

"Okay, why am I looking?" she asked herself. "What's
there? Why do I keep staring?"

She scanned the crowd incessantly now. Face after face.
Looking past the giggles and the laughter. The crying and the
fear. The pressing faces to see closer, better. It was human nature
at its most obvious. Always get there first, see first, be first, and
then, if you are first, blow the bridge behind you, and to hell with
everyone else.

She couldn't see anything important, but she could feel her
mind trying to tell her something that she was not yet aware of.

"Okay," Captain Briar said. "They've assured us your
pictures... What are you looking at?"

"I'm not sure," she said. "I... I don't know... Something.
There's something."

"Something?"

"Never mind," she said. "Let's go have a good look at the apartm..."

She stopped dead in her tracks. She saw him. She knew she had. Not directly, not yet, anyway, but like a bolt of lightning, she had characteristics stuck in her mind. She had seen him in there, but where?

"Hang on!" she said urgently to Captain Briar. "Don't speak, just for a minute."

Captain Briar remained in silent wonder.
She incessantly scanned the crowd. She could feel him. She could still see his eyes in her mind. She could feel his eyes staring at her from somewhere, and suddenly, she found herself overwhelmed with a feeling of grotesqueness.

"You did throw her out for me, didn't you?" she whispered to herself. "Didn't you? You're trying to bait me."

The crowd seemed mostly unaware of Jessica staring back at them. Most were busy coming up with wild rumors and myths to explain the exciting event. This was what many people lived as "truth". That was the foundation of most hard held beliefs. Big, unfounded, dramatic, wishful guesses. But Jessica wasn't interested in their guesses, she was still scanning people with the concentration of a laser beam.

She could see no one in particular standing out to her. She guessed that there must have been at least one hundred and fifty people, all closely knit together like a veritable wall of curiosity.

She decided to continue with the investigation, but the instant she turned to enter the building, she stopped dead in her tracks again.

There he was!
Right there in the crowd, to the right of where she had concentrated her scanning. She was staring deep into his empty eyes amidst a sea of cackling faces. She knew it was him. She could tell by the way he seemed absolutely perplexed that she had been able to find him despite the mass of bodies around him. He was amazed.

Immediately, she saw him begin to push people away from him, trying to escape.

"Stop!" she screamed, and in a split second she lunged into

the crowd with her gun in hand, determined to bring him down. It was instant pandemonium. Confusion spread through the crowd like a shotgun blast. There was sudden panic. There was sudden fear. There was sudden hope.

"Move!" she screamed. "Move! Move! Move!"
She violently pushed her way through people. She thought she could still see him forcing his way out ahead of her. She thought that he was going to get away with all of the confusion constantly blocking her way.

"Move! Get out of the way! Stop him! Stop that man!" she screamed.

It was hopeless. No one would help. No one would have time to register what she was saying before it was too late.

"Shit!"
She pushed even harder and finally made it to the other side, only to find herself standing on the sidewalk opposite the crime scene, her gun in hand, her lungs out of breath, and absolutely nothing to run after.

He was gone.
"Motherfucker!" she panted. "I'm going to get you now! You shouldn't have pushed your luck, you idiot!"

Her hands were numb with adrenaline. The crowd barely noticed her anymore. Out of sight, out of mind. She could hear Captain Briar calling after her, trying to get through the crowd himself. She didn't answer him right away. She was allowing her brain a moment to remember his face. Remember those eyes. Remember his surprise.

"I'm over here, Captain," she finally yelled back, but she wasn't sure if he had heard her over the crowd's incessant banter. She was about to call out to him again, when she felt something tugging at her shirt. With the speed of lightning, she turned and pointed her gun directly into the face of a young boy.

"Oh, my God!" she screamed. "I'm so sorry, kid. Are you okay? Are you all right?"

He nodded yes, and smiled at her. She smiled back, and he handed her an envelope.

"What's this?" she asked.
"I don't know. A man said it was yours. He gave me a whole five

bucks to bring it to you, look!"

She took the envelope from his hand, amazed.

"Thank you. Hey, you want to switch me bills?" She searched her pocket and found a ten dollar bill. "Here, I'll give you ten bucks for that five."

His eyes grew big and his face brightened up.

"Wow! Thanks, lady!"

"No problem," she said. "Thank you. Hey, do you remember what the man looked like?"

"Um... He looked... He looked normal." He shrugged.

"Huh, all right. Thanks, little guy."

She stuffed the envelope into her pocket and turned to find Captain Briar. She found him exhausted and out of breath, mostly from panic, as he was emerging from the crowd.

"Good God, Jessica! What are you doing?" he demanded.

"He was here," she said. "Right over there. Just standing there, watching me."

"How do you know?"

"I saw him," she answered. "I saw his face drop in shock when I finally pegged him against the board. He was here... I... I lost him through the crowd."

"Do you have a direction?"

She sighed heavily. "No direction. We need to get cars patrolling the streets. He's not far, but, he does look rather normal. His face anyway. I... I don't know."

Captain Briar was suddenly scanning the street, just as Jessica had been doing only moments before.

"Do you think he's still watching?" he asked.

Jessica took a deep breath and looked around.

"You can bet on it," she said.

CHAPTER 24

I am guessing you want an ending to that worthless drivel you've been reading lately. A conclusion? Huh? Do you want to know how your sister died? How I took her into my arms like the angel that she was. How she loved me. How she took me.

Do you think I am mean, my pretty little Butterfly? Do you hate me?

Of course, I know what you are thinking right now. You are wondering why my tone has suddenly changed to this wonderful, confident prose, instead of the usual mindless lunacy you have become accustomed to reading from me.

Let's just say I've learned a few things about myself. I am also guessing that you are wondering why I didn't take it. Why didn't I take my diary back from her office? Why didn't I take it from your apartment? Fear not, my pretty Butterfly, they are only logical guesses. It may have confused you, but now you understand, don't you? You know me. You know who, and what I am. Perhaps like a wife knows her husband. Do you know me, Butterfly? Do you really? I am sure you think you do, seeing as you are some kind of big shot detective around these parts, but the real truth of the matter is, I don't even know myself. Not fully, anyway. Not yet.

Does anyone ever know themselves? Are we constantly changing? Does such a thing as identity even exist?

Usually, I would be shoving pills down my throat after daring to ask myself such perplexing questions, but it seems I no longer want them. The pills, I mean.

Plus... Something happened to my shrink. Anyhow, it doesn't matter anymore, does it? Any of it. Does it?

Do you think it does, Butterfly? Do you think that you know what will happen next? That you will somehow be able to intercept me? Do you think that you are smarter than I am? Do you think you can beat me?

Perhaps you do. Perhaps you don't.
Either way, I hope you are not relying on that dreadful journal to catch me. It's ancient history, no matter how recently I may, or may not have jotted down that insecure insanity. I do not pay much attention to time anymore. I am much more comfortable now. I am focussed.

And all you have is a stupid book, and no usable name. Thank God, that even through my manic insecurities, I was still smart enough to at least attempt non-identification. How embarrassing would that have been?

Did you like my stupid little book, Butterfly? Did it make you understand anything at all? Did it give you some type of ulterior insight into my mind? Did it consume you, Butterfly? My book? Me?

Well, my pretty little Butterfly, let me tell you a little something about books that I am sure you will find interesting–perhaps even agree with.

You see, we humans are a stupid species. The stupidest, in fact. The most dangerous, and most disgusting. We humans are an embarrassing parasite. Imagine observing us from a distance. We spread like wildfire, and reproduce, and rape our host. We demolish things until they fit our artificial needs, and to hell with anything else, it is none of our concern so long as we are content.

For that particular moment.
And we stupid humans do a lot of stupid things in our lives, in our history, and that is the real infection at hand here. The stupid ideas. The stupid ideas that are passed down from one generation to the next, and the next. Ideas that are forever altered and changed by every hand. Stupid, dynamic, ideas. And then we stupid humans read books, books like you've read, and even books that are thousands of years old. Thousands of years old, Butterfly! And here is the problem with we stupid humans. We idiots of the universe.

We love to think that we are so much more intelligent and

important than will ever be truthful. We just love to think that we are important in this unimaginably vast universe of ours. We are complete and utter fools, and the only real truth about our existence, is that we are hopelessly addicted to grandeur. We are completely blind, and yet, we act like arrogant sightseers combing through the streets of some ancient city like we own the place. Hell, we built it! It says so in some of those thousand year old stories we read and accept as absolute truth. These are our lands now!

So here is my question, Butterfly.
Isn't that backward? If people, if anyone had the answers thousands of years ago, then what? Have we been going backward since then? Are we getting dumber as time goes on?

Before anyone knew of science, of molecules, of space, or of physics. Before people knew the earth was round, and the sun would rise either way, no matter how many hearts you sacrificed to the skies, or how many witches you burnt. Before medical advancements, pills, surgeries, and technology. Before telescopes, and endoscopes, and videoscopes. Before entertainment, and vehicles, and telephones, and electricity, and society, and worldwide information shared in a split second. Way, way before all of that, and whatever incredible future knowledge that may lie ahead of us... People had an answer? They were found? They had no other questions about what, who, and why they were?

Some insist that they were much richer spiritually than we are now, and perhaps they are correct, perhaps they simply had wilder imaginations, or wilder superstitions, but whatever the defending argument may be, as I look around, it seems to be taken quite literally to me.

I do not see a difference in our stupid human brains between the literal and the spiritual. Our belief in a rich spiritual past quite obviously molds our lives, in turn defeating the very definition of what is spiritual. It is exactly as everything else out there that we could ever ponder.

It makes no goddamn sense whatsoever.
A fact that, in turn, leads every single conscious being to ask the same questions. Why? Why? Why am I here?

Does anyone actually know what reality even is?
The nightmares that have plagued my life, the fears, the panic, the pills, the ridicule, the inferiority, the pain, the confusion, the shattering of my soul and everything that makes up me... Was that real?

You goddamn right it's real. It's as real as tasting food. As real as an orgasm. As real as life. As real as real.

Do you see the problem, Butterfly?
Reality is a situation that has no definition. It lacks substance. It lacks answers and reasons. It seems to lack direction and goes against every grain of sense our brains know how to operate with, and yet, there it is. All around us. All the time. It is the same for everyone, and yet completely different.

I often wonder if you've ever felt pain, Butterfly. Real pain, I mean. Suffering of the kind you never thought imaginable. Hopelessness of the kind that makes you want to jump out of a window and squash the machine that so faithfully contains that stupid brain of yours and all of its impossible conundrums against the black pavement. All the fear, and the panic, and the psychosis, all of it just left to dry and evaporate under the sun, which, once again, we do not really understand.

Do you know what it's like to try everything you could possibly come across and still come up empty? Do you know what empty feels like? Most people do not, Butterfly. Most people's empty is synonymous with boredom. Have you ever felt the kind of empty that makes you want to rip your own skin off? Do you know what it is like to desperately want to leave your flesh prison, but there is no escape? No drug, no action, no hope will ever set you free from your stupid human brain.

Do you ever wonder if it's all a big joke, Butterfly? Stuck on our little bubble in the universe, in the middle of nowhere, and with nothing from the outside. A pure fluke of chaos. A statistic.

A reality.
Our stupid brains like to make us think that we are so important, don't they? They have a way of making us feel like we have a right to be here on earth. To modify it, and alter it, and destroy it. Our stupid brains are really good at making us think all kinds of ridiculous, unfounded, and purely offensive follies. They are

really good at thinking that we are the best that we will ever be. That we can beat God. That we can be better. That we can all be kind and loving. That we will survive forever. That we can understand anything at all.

But anything of nothing, is still nothing.
Who the hell really knows anything anyway? The search for answers in all possible directions all end up at the exact same conclusion, don't they? Whether it's science, or religion, or drugs, or murder, it all ends with the exact same words.

"It's right as far as we can tell. We don't know for sure, it's what we believe."

What cruel, stupid brains we have. Tunnel visioned into ignorance.

But I suppose there is nothing anyone can do about it, is there, Butterfly? When you know nothing, then there is presumably nothing to know, quite as much as there is presumably something to know. Our stupid brains don't like those possibilities. Luckily, there are plenty of distractions.

I have been thinking on my past. My meaningless, substanceless, ridiculous little adventure I dared call a life. My stupid series of insignificant little actions that have brought you, and I, and everyone to this point in time.

I think of all the pills I have taken, of all the nightmares that have infected my stupid little brain, of all the questions, and the blackness, and the voids. I often find myself wondering why. Why was I made like this? Our stupid brains like to make us think that we have some type of cryptic purpose here. Is this my purpose? Was I set up to fail? Why couldn't I have been a movie star, or a rock star? Why couldn't I have been born a female, or better looking, or successful at anything? Why is it that our stupid brains insist on defining something that isn't there?

Are there reasons? I do not know for sure, but I highly doubt their existence. In fact, I hope for that, because if there is a God like my childhood priest so stringently forced onto me, and this was my purpose, to be me and to live in this fashion... Then there will be hell to pay!

I do not want a caring God like the one incessantly preached to me on street corners by shabby lunatics. Nor do I want the vindictive, hateful, and punishing God my parents used to forcefully drive deep into my skull. I want nothing to do with God. I want him to leave me alone. I want the fear to subside. The fear of uncertainty. The unknown. God.

I don't know, my pretty little Butterfly. I do not know anything, and neither do you, or anyone else. We are all fools.

Now, I know, Butterfly, you are wondering what any of this has to do with anything. How is any of it relevant? Well, it's me. I am giving you insight into me and my stupid brain. I want you to see things through my eyes. I want you to feel my pain, and my sadness, and my suffering, and that ugly, empty void of darkness that forever hovers inside of me like a thick fog. I want you to understand me, Butterfly. I want you to know me.

I want you to see how I spent days naked, shaking, frightened in the bottom of bathtubs, and hiding under beds like a goddamn child. I want you to see how I took all of those pills, all of those safeties, in search of artificial peace. I want you to see the women I have loved, and I want to be released from this hopeless pit of emptiness.

Above all, I think it's important for you to know, Butterfly. I think you can understand. I think... Well, let's not get ahead of ourselves.

I remember the first time I sat in the tub, covered in blood, frantically trying to remember what I had done. I was so terrified. So–ill. I remember wondering where the little building of broken knickknacks on the floor of my bedroom had come from. I wondered why I kept taking so many pills when none of them did anything real. I wondered... Why I couldn't tell what was real! I remember thinking that Doctor Satan Face could save me somehow. I decided to give her my journal, the same stupid book you've been reading, thinking you're a step ahead of me. I wondered if she could understand me, if she could free me.

I remember thinking that I loved her, and that she loved me, and that she was only lacking that realization. I remember her face when I gave her my journal. She scratched her forehead and stared at the floor. I remember wondering how insane she thought I was, hopelessly lost in my own world. I remember how she smelled, and how beautiful she was. Not quite as beautiful as you are, Butterfly, but not far behind.

I remember how she asked me to leave. Her voice was stern, and her face was like stone, but I couldn't remember what I'd done wrong. Had I done anything? Was it real?

I remember her eyes, tinged with fear, her breath labored–fierce. I remember my rage, and my shame, and my emotional pain.

My embarrassment!

I went home that night and sat on a regular wooden chair. I stared out the window for hours, into the blackness of night, and the only thoughts running incessantly through my stupid human brain were of the woman from the store. The one I'd met while going for a walk. The one who had written her number in my palm. The one I had made cosmic love to.

Cosmic love. I invented that myself, Butterfly.

Sitting there, I remembered all of the colors, and the smiles. The lines, and the developing tableau. I remembered wrapping my arms around her and feeling her breath against my cheek. I remembered that room swirling around us and smashing to the ground, but it was not evil, or even angry, it was–it was meant to be–somehow.

Do you see what our stupid brains do, Butterfly? They contradict themselves while still caught up in the same thought. How can that be considered advanced? How can it be real?

Was the blood real?

I remember wondering about that for days, maybe even weeks, I can't be sure. I wondered where it had come from. How had I been covered with it? Had I even met the girl? Had I even gotten her number? Had I called?

Inevitably, I was once again plunged into horrid darkness, impossible inner torture. I was back to my old self. Back to being the panic stricken idiot, prancing around with offensive amounts of pills in his pockets, and uncertainty dancing in his eyes.

Any shred of safety, of happiness, or of reality, was absolutely abolished. A bumbling, pill popping fool, being eaten from the inside by his own demons.

Then one day, something uncertain happened. One moment I was curled up in my bed, naked, and scared, and crying, pleading with the air around me to just give me a break, and suddenly, it did, and I found myself dressed in jogging sweats and walking down the sidewalk in confident strides. I remember my amazement, but I could not remember anything in between. How had I gone from my bed to there? Had I gotten dressed?

I didn't know.

The only thing I could do was look around with amazed eyes, and simply enjoy the ride. Cars passed by me as I walked on the sidewalk, but they seemed so distant, so... Surreal, I believe is the word. Yeah, what isn't surreal, Butterfly? I felt elated. I felt powerful.

It's an odd thing to feel powerful, isn't it? Our stupid human brains love nothing more than to have the power to control things, and other people. To cause harm without the slightest reproach of consequence. To demean, and ridicule, and believe that we are better than everyone else. Stronger, faster, smarter, richer. Power is the real drug. Power is the eternal addiction. Our undying lust for it is proof of what primitive fools our stupid brains make us out to be.

In my daze, I crossed streets effortlessly with no real direction in mind, and eventually found myself in a park, where children chased after dogs, and dogs after children, and smiles filled the air around me. I was smiling, too, although I didn't know why.

I remember staring at the playing children, and the over-excited dogs, and the happy parents, and I then realized that I was sitting on a bench, next to a woman more beautiful than I would ever have the balls to approach. I hadn't jogged a single step in my life. I had never made a woman like her smile. Not ever. But she was smiling at me then; she was happy to talk to me, to sit next to me.

The details after that are sketchy. All I get are indefinable flashes of memories, but I can still see her face pressed so closely to mine. I can feel her breath, and I remember that I couldn't even think about what, or how, or why any of it was happening. I simply accepted it, and let the feelings plunge me into an odd rapture. An absolute peace of the kind no amount of pills could ever achieve.

Her eyes are still so vividly defined in my mind. She looked into my soul. I still wonder what she saw. What did anyone see?

I felt passion wash through me, filling me with confidence. I remember her perfect body sprawled in front of me. I could see her so clearly, and yet, she was completely blinding. She looked like a swan. So serene and docile. So beautiful and pure. So powerful and distinct.

So real.

I remember rubbing her body. Her skin was incredibly soft, like... Like feathers. I don't remember her showing any emotion toward what was happening. She was very still. Very quiet. Very focussed. I stared into her eyes and ignored the room around us spinning and crashing into itself. The splinters. The violence that seemed so completely natural. The primitive.

I stared deeply into her eyes, and do you know what I saw, Butterfly? Do you know what was apparent in that moment of pure human experience? Do you know what's in our eyes, we humans, with our stupid punishing brains?

I saw nothing.

There was nothing at all, and at first, it truly was a violent shock to my mind. How could it be? How could something evolve and grow into a person, a personality with fears, and hopes, and dreams, and love, and hate, and when it was all said and done, there was nothing left behind? Not even a void? Just nothing?

It's a difficult concept to digest, Butterfly. It is extremely difficult to accept.

The nothing.

But, once again, after the internal pain subsided to a tolerable level, and after I stopped wondering what had happened and stopped fearing the answer, I suddenly understood something so basic, and universal, that it was a farce to think that it had never crossed my mind before. A truth, I suppose. The truth, that everything dies.

The personalities, the feelings, the hopes and dreams, the questions and fears, the planets, and stars, and galaxies–all of it– dies.

Absolute entropy.

The realization was as depressing as anything could be. What's the point if it's all for nothing? That was my question. That is everyone's question, isn't it? I thought about it for a long time, feeling my heart sink while I tried to gather enough courage to face it, until a new answer came to me. It had been right in front of me the whole time, but our stupid tunnel visioned brains often refuse to look any further than what we initially see.

The answer, was that none of my questions even mattered. Not to the universe, and not to anything beyond myself. My feelings, my thoughts, my beliefs, are the things that make up who I am, but nothing more. Without me, none of these things exist, and none of them matter to anyone, not anywhere– but that's okay. For the first time ever, I was able to see the incredible, yet subtle beauty of the meaningless. I am here, alive, aware, and that means something to me. I, we, have these things in the face of an absolute void of nothingness. How incredible is that? Statistically, it is damn near impossible that we are even here, how can any of us deny that kind of meaning, that kind of beauty?

The truth is, Butterfly, that you, and I, and this entire situation, will mean absolutely nothing within a hundred years from now. No one will remember. No one will bother. No one will care. I have realized that no one here gets out alive. No one, and no thing. Everything dies, and is returned to our completely indifferent, completely irrational, yet completely real universe.

It is stunningly beautiful.

Thus, welcome to the new revelations, my pretty little Butterfly. If none of it matters, then what do I have to fear? What do any of us have to fear aside from losing our selfish, careless, and savage awareness our stupid brains are programmed with? It is all we have. It is all we truly fear to lose. I now realize that people are not actually afraid of death like they so stringently claim to be. What they are, is afraid of losing the awareness. Their thoughts. Their consciousness. Their fears.

What they are afraid of, is that big nothing I was just describing. We are terrified of nothing. It is far too absolute for our stupid little brains to accept. Anything is better than nothing, isn't that right, detective Butterfly?

Knowing this philosophy now, I am afraid that I no longer feel fear like I used to. I do not think that I truly fear anything anymore. How could I when I know that there is an expiry date stamped on each one of our foreheads? No matter what happens, no matter how evil, or crude, or happy, or sad... Eventually, none of it will matter. It is the only true meaning in my life now. That fascinating, completely perplexing, temporary beauty.

But I am rambling on now. I still have interesting things to tell you, Butterfly.

You see, I soon found myself face to face with yet another beautiful girl, except this time, I was slightly more aware of what was happening, though I could not control any of it. Not the conversation. Not the movements. Not myself.

I met this woman in a movie theater. Can you believe that? A movie theater! A place crawling with filth, and bugs, and organ eating sloths wafting through the place. I couldn't remember how I had gotten there, or why, but I was enjoying the feeling. The feeling of being, of existing, of occupying a notch on the space-time continuum, no matter how insignificant the future may be.

When I spoke to her, the words flew out of me like a planned dissertation, but I couldn't remember having practiced anything. I was possessed. I loved the sound of my voice. I loved the confidence in it. The humor. The normalcy. It was all very, surreal, once again.

Of course, my pretty little Butterfly, you must understand that at that point in time, I had no knowledge of you. I also had no knowledge of your sister. Would it have made a difference if I had known? Well, I am in no position to answer such questions.

As I stood before her, I considered the possibility that none of it was real. That perhaps I was simply lying in bed, or in a coma, or dead already, and everything was simply happening to me, and to me alone. There were no women. There were no fears. But once again, when it doesn't matter, why think about it? It is as real as I can qualify it, and that is all that matters.

I spoke to the woman, the unknown sister, your sister, for a long time. She was as beautiful as an angel. Her eyes were like sparkling diamonds. Her lips were supple, and friendly. Her body was immaculate. She had perfect teeth. She had a soul melting laugh. But she was sad on the inside. She wasn't conveying it so openly, or purposefully, but I could see it in her eyes; she was hurting from a deep cut in her past. A dull pain ever present, regardless of her current mood.

Our stupid human brains at work again.

I don't know what we talked about. I don't really remember anything else aside from watching her lips move as she spoke; and then I remember being above her, naked, and confused. She was demanding me. Commanding me. She whispered sweet things. Things of love, and of life. Things I had never heard before.

I remember her eyes focussed intensely on mine, but I was having trouble seeing her whole body. She was so bright, so pure. She sparkled and shimmered as though she were made of eternal diamonds. She was angelic, and loving, and kind. I loved her. I loved her so much in that moment. I caressed her in my arms, and when I did, the room began spinning, and splitting, and exploding all around us, but I was focussed solely on her eyes. I wanted to see her soul. I wanted to see her as the angel I knew she was.

I couldn't see my hands through the pure white light emanating from her angelic body, but I could feel them feeling her. I could feel her skin rubbing against my palms. I could feel her warmth, and suddenly, something I can only describe as silent noise came over me. It was overbearingly quiet.

I could see things flying all around us in my peripheral vision. Tiny glimpses of chaos through the bright white light, but none of it mattered. I still only wanted to see her soul. I put my face directly against hers, and stared. I wanted inside of her. I wanted her to show me. I wanted her to save me.

I then remember the light growing in both intensity and heat. It was unbearable, and I could hear screaming from a distance. I could hear panic, but none of it registered. The light simply continued to grow whiter, and brighter, until I couldn't see anything, and I thought my eyeballs had been burned out of my skull.

I wanted to see her eyes. I wanted to see her nothing. But

when the light finally dissipated, I had no idea how much time had passed, if any. I didn't know anything. I looked around quickly and realized that I was sitting on my living room couch. I looked down, and I was completely nude, my body distorted by the glare of the television. I stared at my hands, they were stained with blood, and a very rude awakening occurred. I'd been jolted from the arms of an angel, and brutally awoken in my own home with a thousand yard stare, and a million questions. How could I be in two places at once? It was impossible, yet how could I ever claim anything different?

Our stupid brains hate reality.

It was all too violent, and the knowledge was all too new for me to wrap my head around. I was, after all, still covered in blood. I remember wondering if it was new blood, or the same from last time. Had there been a last time? Had I met another girl? Was I–actually–home?

Frantically, I stood from my couch, but the room responded by swelling fifteen sizes and bending back on itself. I closed my eyes, desperate to get a grip, but when I opened them again, I was in Doctor Satan Face's office, except it was dark out, and there was no one else there. I had no idea how I had gotten there. I remember wondering if I had been home. Was there blood on my hands? Was that possible?

In her office, I felt like a spectator, a fly on the wall. I felt detached from my body, and out of my mind! I remember digging through the files, and taking my own.

You do not know who I am, Butterfly. You do not know me! Not yet.

I then felt a stunning panic race up my spine, and I fell to my knees, gasping for air. The room lit up, just like it had with the sister, your sister, and I found myself mumbling nonsense to empty walls. I remember grabbing my temples and screaming as loud as I could, trying to stop the pain. When the light began fading, I heard something confusing. It was my name being called. I was, I was hearing her.

"Brian? Brian, are you all right?"

And suddenly, I was dumbfounded! I was staring into Doctor Satan Face's eyes, but I was no longer in her office, I was in her home. I was crying, and losing my mind while she desperately attempted to calm me. At that moment, I remember thinking that she hated me. I knew she thought I was a disgusting little fiend. I could hear it in her voice. She hated me. She was repulsed by me. She was afraid of me.

I felt control because of her fear.

Her eyes hated the sight of me. They angered me. I loved her. Of all the people who could possibly have understood me, there she was, belittling me with stares, and expressions of horror. Was I still full of blood? I don't remember. But I do remember the kind of claustrophobic choking I was feeling.

I remember feeling like I wanted to kiss her. I wanted her to hold me, and tell me everything was going to be all right. I wanted her to save me and take me away from myself. I wanted her to help me. Nothing about her was helping!

I remember imagining ripping her fucking heart out of her chest like she had done to me. She had betrayed me. I had given myself to her. I'd given her my journal so she could understand, but I doubted that she had ever even read a single page. I was furious!

I remember the empty in her eyes, the fear. She felt fear like I have felt it my entire life. She felt the crushing, choking, all encompassing horror squirm awfully throughout her body. She felt the nothing. She feared the nothing with her stupid human brain.

I then only remember watching her sleep. For how long, I could never tell you, Butterfly. I don't know. I just sat there. I watched her. I watched her suffer. I watched her pay for it. I watched justice unfold. I watched the walls begin cracking open, bursting into my face. I remember the blinding explosion, the deafening silence, and the darkness overtaking the place, overtaking us. It drowned us, and became absolute, until there was nothing left. I had no body. I had no fear. I had nothing. I was trapped in my own nothing.

I can't remember anything else after that. I don't know how long it was before I was back home, sitting in my tub, and shaking again. The only thing I do remember, are the flashes in my mind. Flashes of your face, my pretty little Butterfly. Flashes that told me that we suddenly had a connection to each other. They told me that you knew who I was, and that I had to reach you, Butterfly.

I have a hunch that you know something that most people do not. You know something that I do not.

You have answers.

While lying in my tub, shaking, and trying to wipe the blood off my body, I remember how the room imploded on itself with me inside. I remember screaming, pleading, crying. I felt panic engulf my heart, seize my lungs, and I was desperate to get out of there. I remember abruptly standing from the tub, wide eyed and dizzy, dashing for the door, when I noticed that I was standing in a subway car, underground, surrounded by staring strangers.

I couldn't understand, couldn't remember. How had it happened? I avoided the stares and stared at the floor, but next to me, a woman stood, smiling. I didn't know her. I didn't know anyone, but she seemed to be there with me. How could that be? I remember staring at her face, but the only thing I could think of was the sister, your sister. If she was the angel, what does that make you?

I remember riding the train with this girl, fascinated by the sheer lucidity of it all. I followed her home, holding hands. I remember that. I remember that it felt so empty, so distant.

I followed her home, and she was laughing. She was happy, though I couldn't say why. And then I was over her, just like I remembered being with the others. High above her, and staring intently into her eyes, I remember trying to see life, trying to see anything, and still, I found nothing. But my reaction this time was drastically different. I fell into a rage so savage, so ungodly, so terrified, that I thought I had ripped a hole in the very fabric of space and time. Her body exploded in a fantastic blast, and I remember seeing the sister, the angel, you. I remembered you.

Sister.

And I suddenly hated her! I hated her guts! I wanted to rip her to shreds. I wanted to squash her with my bare hands; crush her under the pressure of my ungodly rage like a fucking cockroach! The room swelled, and swirled, and crashed all around us, and then a flash of bright light caused me to blink. It couldn't have been more than a blink, but when I opened my eyes again, I felt myself crash through a door, and I was standing in a strange room filled with things that were not mine, except for a single book. That was mine. The rest was yours, wasn't it, Butterfly? Please, understand, I did not intend to destroy your home, if that is what has actually happened. I only really remember glimpses. Only a spinning room exploding around me.

Although, thinking about it now, it was quite unfortunate you happened to be out, Butterfly. Perhaps we can catch up at a later date.

But for now, here we are, and I am tired of the emptiness. Even though everything may seem meaningless, and will cease to exist forever, it does not need to be empty, does it? Wholeness can still be found in the meaningless, can it not? Of course it can. Reality is a feeling. Reality is real to each individual. Reality has meaning amongst a vast sea of nothingness. Somehow. It is the great mystery.

And now, it seems I am also fairly knowledgeable about you, my pretty little Butterfly. I know who you are. You have a very special gift, don't you?

I know that you have made a fine career catching psychotics on power trips. Control trips. Chasing that eternal, all encompassing addiction to power.

I know that you have caught some of the most elusive and cunning of all criminals. You have solved cases that were deemed closed for lack of evidence, or direction. But you figured them out with that not so stupid human brain of yours, didn't you? I am wondering if it is easy for you? I am wondering if you ever have to try? I am wondering if you know me on a level that is beyond what anyone else can? On a cosmic level. On a primitive, absolute level. A universal understanding.

Can your human brain do that, Butterfly? Imagine if it could.

I already know that you are convinced that you will end me. You will find me, and end me. You will outsmart me. You will out do me. The only real problem, Butterfly, seems to be a total lack of control. Am I doing these things? Am I really, or am

I simply watching them happen?

Either way, we both know that this story is far from over. I am looking for my freedom. I am looking for my place in time that was so savagely robbed from me. I am looking for my innocence, and my decency, and my normalcy. I am looking for my reality.

I am still only looking for safety, Butterfly.
Do you feel safe? Do you? Do you think that I don't know where you are, or what you are doing? Do you think that I do not see you out there? Do you think that I do not know who you are?

Do you think that this is almost over?
I suppose only time will tell, as they say. This is only the beginning. This search of mine. This answer I must find. This vengeance that needs to be justified. I will never stop until it's done. I will never stop losing myself in savage dreams. I will never get a grip on any of it. I will simply continue to watch. I will be watching you, Butterfly. I will be following you. I will always be in the back of your mind from this day forward.

Of course, by the time you read this letter, you will have just returned from investigating a brand new crime scene. You will think that it is uncharacteristic of me. You will think that this needs to end immediately. You will think many things. But if your stupid human brain isn't so stupid after all, then all things will surely fall into place, and you will be holding this letter in your hands, slowly beginning to understand.

If you are reading this letter, then I am assuming one of two things. The first is that I am dead, and you have ended it all before we could get to know each other any better. A shame. The second, is that my vague plan for the night has been successful. Either way, I suspect that you were absolutely correct in your assumption, my pretty little Butterfly.

I did throw her out of the window for you. For this. For us. I killed her for you. To see you concentrated on your silly work, always, as beautiful as a butterfly in the cool night air.

We will soon see each other again.
Sweet dreams.

CHAPTER 25

The letter had shifted gears on her. Her mind refused to accept it. She hated fucking butterflies.

She sat on the edge of the bed for a long time with the letter still clutched in her hand, staring at the floor, breathing calmly. Her eyes were unwandering, but her thoughts were infected with ominous emotions she couldn't quite define.

She was disturbed, and she hated every second of it. In time, she shredded the letter and flushed it down the toilet. She let herself fall onto the hard hotel mattress and closed her eyes.

She didn't want to think about it, or butterflies, or Brian Hotz, or her case. With her skin crawling, she shuffled uncomfortably under the blankets, settled on her side, and passively wondered if anything could have disturbed her more than what she had just read. Could anything be more grotesque, or repulsive?

She was hard pressed to find anything worse, but she didn't waste much time with it. In minutes, fatigue overtook her and whisked her away to a land of dreams.

***

Sitting in his living room chair, Captain Briar nursed a drink and thought about The Fleshcrafter. He wouldn't admit it to Jessica, but ever since they had come across the first victim's body, he'd been spending long nights lying awake in bed, counting the plaster lines in the ceiling. Every time he closed his eyes, he was haunted by ghoulish nightmares, waking him in the grips of terror. Every day, he dreaded the approaching dusk, and tried his best to keep sleep at bay, but he could only do so for so long. Inevitably, the nightmares would come, and panic would rush through his heart.

He had a gulp of whiskey and thought about Jessica. Over the years, he'd taken care of her as if she was his own daughter. Though he would never admit to it, deep down, he often felt bad for her. He felt bad that she had no parents, and he felt it ten fold now that her sister had been erased from the world. But indirect guilt was not his motivation for caring about Jessica, she was a person on her own terms, strong, and passionate. From the day they met, they shared a strong connection together. He admired her passion, her intelligence, and was often reminded of himself at her age. Hungry. Driven.

He had always been there for her, and she for him. They shared a mutual, fundamental confidence in each other's qualities, and talents, and as a detective team, they were a force to be reckoned with.

But things had changed. The killer they were now chasing was something he couldn't properly explain. He had spent more than half of his life hunting psychotics, but this person was unheard of. This killer was obscene, terrible. He committed acts that left anyone with a decent mind gasping in repulsion; in a deep, sobering sadness.

Worst of all, this killer scared him. He was terrified of him. Whenever he thought about the woman's tongue, or Jessica's annihilated apartment, he felt an uncomfortable pressure build up in his chest, cutting off his air. Every murder scene they visited, he was left dizzy and leaning up against walls.

He felt an intense urge to protect Jessica, but he couldn't see a solution. What could he do? They had nothing to work with, no suspects to grill. Jessica's safety was out of his hands, and it was heartbreaking.

He was worried ill, but the source of his concern wasn't solely rooted in the killer; Jessica's passion was what truly scared him. He knew she would never hesitate, never think twice, before throwing herself in the thick of the action, rabid to catch her killer.

He had another drink of whisky and thought about the

crime scene he and Jessica had just investigated. When she had lunged into the crowd without explanation, his heart had walloped painfully in his chest.

She was an incredibly talented and capable detective, but her passion trumped everything else when she was in full predator mode. Captain Briar feared that this killer, as sick and demented as he was, would succeed in using her passion against her. He feared that she would jump into an impossible situation, foaming at the mouth to get the upper hand, but never realize until it was too late that she'd walked into a trap.

What could he do?

He'd struggled with the case from the beginning, but he knew that Jessica was in her element with it. A real challenge; the only thing she truly lived for.

For him, The Fleshcrafter case was nothing but emotional torture, forcing him to ponder on early retirement, to wonder if he was getting too old for his job, or if he was out of touch with the modern world, unable to understand all of the forces at work.

The dreams that infected his sleep were filled with the horrors he had seen in those rooms. Broken bodies, grotesque art. It felt like proof that he no longer understood the world. This killer, he had no idea about this man. This man had shaken his very foundation and left everything he believed in fiercely challenged.

He often found himself wondering about the victims. Wondering about their families and their friends. Who were they? What did they stand for? What dreams had they aspired for the future? He felt bad for them. He was angry for them.

In all of his years as a law enforcement officer, he'd never come across anything, much less anyone, that had shaken his never ending quest for justice. If there were any absolutes the good Captain knew, it was decency. He prided himself on always doing the right thing, and strove to be as fair as he could be in any situation. But now, sitting in his favorite living room chair, nursing a drink, he realized that he had no idea of what to do next, no direction to take. He couldn't see how to bring this case to an end without having to sacrifice something, or someone. Fear. Unease. He felt helpless, and frustrated. He had long sip of his whisky and sighed. He was tired, but he knew that he wouldn't fall asleep quite yet. He didn't want to close his eyes and drift away to a nightmarish world filled with colorful ghosts and mangled bodies; filled with debauchery, and indecency, and an absolute disrespect for human life.

In all, his main belief was that Jessica would eventually catch her killer. She would figure him out, and whittle him down until he was pushed into a corner, slashing back like a rabid animal. But it hardly made him feel any better. Despite having unwavering confidence in his top detective, he wondered at what cost her success would come.

Captain Briar thought about retirement. He wondered if he could do it under the circumstances. He wondered how he would feel if he retired because of the actions of another man. He thought it was weak. He thought he was being weak. He thought that he was being beaten into submission by this strange monster. Everything he loved in life suddenly felt vulnerable. Threatened.

His family. He loved his family more than anything else in the world. He could see no purer joy in the world than a family in harmony. He had loved his wife for over three decades, and he still loved her as much as when they had first wed. He loved his children. He loved his grandchildren, and his home, and his life. He loved it all, and it was always at the forefront of every action he ever executed.

"What about my family?" he would ask himself first. He finished his drink and immediately poured himself another. He had never been much of a drinking man, save for occasions and holidays, but this was beyond all of that. He sat back into his favorite chair and stared at the wall before him. He felt alone, and frustrated. He stared for a long time, allowing his mind to flood with fragmented thoughts and ideas. He leaned his head against the back of his chair, his eyes heavy, his mind tired.

His final thought before falling asleep was:
I think I love my family too much to keep doing this work.

CHAPTER 26

Captain Briar had asked her if she'd gotten a good look at the killer's face in the crowd, but she hadn't known how to answer him right then. In her mind, she had a picture perfect portrait of the man. Playing over the events, she could still see the way his features had dropped in surprise when he realized that he'd been pinpointed against all odds. She could see the way his mouth had hung open awkwardly, and the way his arms had flown up in alarm to push people out of his way. She could remember it all with unwavering precision, but she'd been unable to describe him to Captain Briar at the time because something sinister had crept inside of her.

It was his eyes. When she'd locked on to them, she was shocked by how cold and empty they were. Throughout her career, she'd stood face to face with many psychotics who carried cold, calculated, and evil eyes, but none had matched what she'd seen in The Fleshcrafter. His stare carried something different. It announced something terrible about the man, but she was unable to identify exactly what it was. It was something empty, something haunting.

That feeling was now dominating her dreams, filling her mind with ominous undertones, and fragmented images of murdered art. But these were not the only images working through her unconscious mind. For unexplained reasons, her infallible memory was busy churning through the lists of names she'd spent days diligently pouring over. Something bothered her about the names of those who'd been court ordered to see Nicole White. Something was missing.

There was a name missing—somewhere. Her mind had

recorded it on some lists, but not on others. And just like a beam of light slashing through a dark room, it came to her, and jolted her body out of bed. She screamed the name straight through her dreams and into reality.

"Clinton Fisher!"

And no sooner had she finished speaking the name, did her hotel room door come crashing down in giant splinters. Out of pure surprise, she collapsed to the ground. She was frantic, and desperately trying to decipher what was happening.

"Hello, my pretty little Butterfly."

His voice sounded exactly like she had expected it would. Ugly. Harsh, and depraved.

"Fuck you!" Jessica hissed, and feverishly clawed at the floor, trying to decide what to do next, where to go. He stood there for a moment, staring at her. She could hear him breathing while her brain concocted too many plans of attack to handle at once. She couldn't concentrate.

Initially, she thought it wasn't real; she thought she was still caught in some distant dream. But those possibilities disappeared once he came at her like a phantom through the dark.

It was no dream.

"I know you've been thinking about me, Butterfly. Let me get a good look at you," he said, and violently grabbed her by the throat.

Jessica's eyes grew wide, but they were not filled with fear. She hoped with every ounce of herself that he could see that. She was not afraid of him. She was angry; filled with an irritated, justified, and hate fueled rage.

He picked her up clear off the floor and powerfully shoved her across the room. She hit a lamp, and smashed it into the wall, before landing in a chair and flipping it over.

"Because I've been thinking about you, my pretty little Butterfly. I've been thinking that I need you. I've been thinking that you know me. Do you know me, Butterfly?"

"Fuck you!" she hissed again, and searched frantically through the darkness for some kind of weapon. Her gun was nowhere near her; it was in the night stand drawer, and she knew that the possibility of making it passed him and getting to it was more of a wish than anything real.

He came at her again, like a vampire from a dark corner, and punched her in the face.

"You are so beautiful," he said, and kicked her in the ribs. "You know so much, don't you?" He kicked her again. "Do you love me, Butterfly? Are you ready to be released from that ugly cocoon of yours?"

Her body was electrified with pain, but she was strong enough to keep her focus.

"Answer me!" he screamed, and pulled her by the hair until she stood up, only to throw her into the wall again.

She was frantic, but still, she was not afraid.

"Answer me!" he screamed at her again.

She started laughing, which caused him to take a step back for a moment, perplexed. She laughed, and said,

"You can't break me, Clinton Fisher. You're never going to get to me, and you're never going to get away with this. You're a sad, little, insignificant man, and I will stare deep inside your eyes and watch your nothing take you."

He cocked his head to the side when she said it. She wondered if it was phasing him, reciting his own stupid words right back to him. He slapped her mightily again.

"Bitch!" he screamed. "You fucking bitch! You're a leech like the rest of those whores. I thought you were different, Butterfly. You're... You're ruining it! You're ruining it, you fucking..."

He came at her again with his boot cocked, ready to deliver another shot to her ribs. She took the pain without so much as a yelp.

"Now you're going to die for it too," he said, and viciously grabbed hold of her hair, trying to pull her back to her feet.

She struggled against him. She was physically strong, just not directly out of bed, and without any understanding of the situation at hand. He was strong. He was brutal, and savage.

He violently yanked on her hair, pulling her up, but at the last second, she grabbed a pen from the ground, stood up, and screamed.

"You're never going to beat me! I'm better than you!"

He was about to throw her again, but before he could, she spun around and stabbed him in the chest with the pen.

The pandemonium was instant.

"Argh! You whore!" he screamed in anguish.

When he let go of her hair, she kicked him in the crotch, and then landed her knee into his face as he went down.

"You're gonna die, you little bitch!" He was furious now.
"Fuck you!" she screamed. "You're the only one dying tonight."

She ran to the night stand for her gun, but he seemed to know what she was going for. She fumbled with it for half a second, and already he was getting back to his feet, trying to attack her again. She got the gun out of its holster and pointed it directly at him. He tried grabbing for it in a struggle, but without hesitation, she pulled the trigger and hoped for a hit.

The bang was deafening. His eyes grew wide, but she stared back with a face of stone.

"Fuck!" he screamed, and backhanded her so hard she banged her head against the wall behind her. When she looked back, he was already halfway out the door.

"Oh no you don't!" she snarled, and pounced after him. Panicked, he ran down the hallway, but she was already on attack behind him like a predator. She took a single moment at the door to gasp in horror. The two officers assigned to protect her had had their throats slashed open right there in the hallway. It was savage. She felt rage bubbling inside of her more intensely than ever. She was going to kill Clinton Fisher.

He was already at the door leading to the stairs, and crashed through it with a loud bang. She ran after him at full tilt. When she got to the door, she hesitated for a moment, more out of training than any actual fear. She kicked it open, but there was no one there. She stopped on the landing for a moment, listening to see if he had gone up, or down.

"Down!" she said to herself, and began vaulting steps on her way down. She could taste nothing but blood. Her throat was unbearably dry, and her head was pounding with rage.

She heard another door crash below her, but she couldn't see it yet. She tried going faster, jumping from one landing to the next.

"No. No. No. No!" she said, and began feeling a mute fear taking over her anger. He was about to elude her once again.

She got to the last door at the bottom of the stairs and plowed through it with her gun gripped tightly in her hands. She was standing in a parking garage. It was vast, and filled with cars and obstructions. It was the worst possible place for her to try and find him.

"Shit!" she panted, trying to regain her breath. "You fucking asshole!"

She stared intently in between the cars and pillars, hoping for a break, a slight movement from a hiding body. She had already decided that if she found him, she would open fire without hesitation. It was for the greater good.

She couldn't see anything moving.

"Son of a bitch!" she said. "Shit!"

She shook her head in disappointment, but knew that she should leave the parkade. It was too risky. She already knew his real name. She needed to call Captain Briar immediately. She needed to hit the streets and hunt him down like a worthless little animal. A pest. A disease. A virus.

She ran back up the stairs and barged into the main floor lobby of the hotel, screaming like a crazy person, and interrupting the nonchalant conversation going on between the two clerks behind the reception desk.

"Call the police!" she screamed at them. "There's an emergency! Two cops are dead on the 15th floor! I've been attacked! Please..." She fell into a lobby chair and panted, trying to regain her composure. "Please! Call the cops. The guy is still here somewhere."

Their faces were dangerously excited, suddenly menaced by her words. He is still here somewhere.

The man behind the counter frantically jabbed at numbers on the telephone, and his voice crackled when he spoke to the dispatcher, demanding help. They were both terrified.

Jessica buried her swollen face into her hands and tried to catch her breath. She could feel huge goose eggs growing on her skull, and fresh blood all over her cheeks and lips. Her ribs felt even worse. Clinton Fisher had kicked her with all of his might, and every blow had been more debilitating than the last. She was in pain, but the adrenaline rushing through her was doing a fantastic job of masking it all.

Despite all of her pain, and all of her frustration, she could only truly feel one thing.

Disappointment.

Disappointment in herself. She was pissed off, furious that she had let him slither away before she could get the upper hand on the situation.

Her mind rushed through the details with incredible speed. She could hear his voice so clearly, his screams so pitch perfect. When she had landed the pen into his chest, she'd hoped that he would drop dead in front of her, but she'd had no such luck. She had stabbed him. She had shot him. She had ridiculed him. And still, somehow, he had gotten away.

She felt more pain with that thought than with any other. No matter what had happened, or what she had done... The bottom line was unfaltering. He had gotten away.

At least, she was quick to take solace in knowing that he now had nowhere to go. This psycho, he wouldn't be able to prowl the streets without attracting attention. And now, armed with his name, they would be kicking down his door in no time at all.

"You should have killed me, you moron," she whispered. "Now you're screwed. Now you're gonna pay for it."

She watched the first police cruiser come to a screeching halt, followed by two officers coming through the doors and into the lobby with their guns drawn.

"Jesus! Are you all right?" One of them asked Jessica. "Fifteenth floor," she said. "Two cops down."

The officer immediately reported the situation into his radio.

"Dispatch... Send me an ambulance, and back-up. We've got two officers down. I repeat, two officers down. Requesting immediate assistance."

"Please stand by, back up has been dispatched. ETA one minute," a tiny voice came back through the radio.

"Do you have any identification?" he asked Jessica.

"I'm Detective Jessica Sanders," she replied. "I'm here under surveillance, protection from a serial killer. He showed up. He killed them. He tried to kill me."

He seemed confused for a moment. "The... The Fleshcrafter?" He asked timidly.

Jessica nodded her head.

"Yes," she said. "The big scary Fleshcrafter."

Two other police cars screeched to a halt and more officers poured into the lobby.

"Fifteenth floor!" One of them yelled, and a group of them made their way upstairs to investigate the situation.

Paramedics soon followed and rushed upstairs. Then a new bunch came in to tend to Jessica. They checked her out. She seemed fine, but she would still have to get to the hospital for x-rays of her ribs. They cleaned up her face and bandaged her wounds, and no sooner had they finished, did Jessica realize that Captain Briar was already standing in the lobby, staring at her with the most disgusted look she had ever seen on his face.

"It's okay, Captain," she said, but he offered nothing in return except a disgruntled shake of his head and an absent stare.

"Captain?" she said. "Captain, I'm fine. This won't last much longer."

"You were almost murdered, Jessie," he mumbled.

"Captain..." she said. "I know his real name."

His face dropped in confusion. Wonder.

"What?"

"His name," she said. "It's Clinton Fisher. He was one of the court ordered clients of Nicole White. I... I don't know. It just came to me in a dream. His name is not consistent throughout all the lists. We can crush him, Captain. We can beat him now."

She could tell that he was lost in horrified thoughts. More irrational thoughts of what could have been, but were not.

"Captain," she began again. "It's okay. This is a huge break. We have him pushed into a corner. He can't do much either, I shot him."

"You did?"

"I shot him, and I stabbed him in the chest with a pen. He can't do much now, Captain. We need to patrol the hospitals, and especially the ones close to here. We need to patrol the streets. He can't be far away, and it's going to be real hard for him to be inconspicuous right now."

Captain Briar immediately got on his phone and demanded the patrols. To the hospitals. To the streets. To every corner of the city. The man with a crude stab wound and a gunshot wound was out there. He was hurt very badly. He must be found immediately.

He hung up his phone and absently stared at Jessica again. "I have to go upstairs," he said.

"I'll come with you."

"No," he replied sternly. "Jessie, you need to go to the hospital and get checked out. Don't worry, none of us are going to bed now."

"But..."

"Jessica," He interrupted curtly. "Get to the hospital and get checked out. Then you call me, and I promise you, we will work together for as long as it takes to catch this bastard. Go make sure you're okay, and then we'll get him."

Jessica hated it. She wanted to be on the streets, on the front lines with sweaty palms and dilated pupils, searching back alleys, and hospitals, and medical clinics–but listening to her captain was the only offered option.

It was what it was.

Just like the killer getting away from her in those incredibly tense moments.

Reality.

CHAPTER 27

"That's him," Jessica said sullenly, feeling a cold chill race up her spine. "That's the son of a bitch."

"Okay, get it out there, guys."

She was staring at a passport photo of him; his cold eyes were as haunting as she remembered them. Clinton Fisher. Brian Hotz. The Fleshcrafter. His face was on the computer screen before her, and all around her, dozens of bodies crammed into a huddle, asking her urgent questions about her case.

These bodies, most of them, anyway, worked for the FBI. They had been sent no more than two hours ago to take charge of her investigation. They'd come as a result of Captain Briar's demand from Commissioner Dean for immediate assistance.

"There is no excuse!" he had urged. "It is unacceptable, and we must use any and all resources available to help end this lunacy, immediately! Please, sir! This is the second time he almost got to her. This was pure luck."

It was too much for the Captain.

In the room with Jessica and the agents, he sat silently behind them, without expression, focussing his attention on Jessica, and hoping that she was okay. He could tell that she was exhausted. He could tell that she was enraged.

This was Jessica's kryptonite. Being beaten.

"Did he say anything else to you?" Agent McKay, the lead investigator asked Jessica.

"No," she answered plainly. "Just what I already told you."

The results of her x-rays had revealed evidence of four cracked ribs. The doctor had been amazed, given the sheer amount of bruising her body had sustained.

"A very lucky girl," he had said.

Real lucky.

The nurses had bandaged her face and torso while the doctor recommended at least one week away from work; she was in bad shape.

But there had been no question about it, Jessica was going directly back to work. Beaten, broken, even lying on her death bed, if she was still breathing, she was going back to work.

Barely six hours later, she was surrounded by FBI agents, and staring at a picture of the same man she had chased through a curious crowd at a crime scene. The same killer who had just beaten her to a pulp. She sat, and quietly answered endless amounts of questions. Her case was no longer an investigation, it had officially become a manhunt. This killer, this Clinton Fisher, his time was limited. The FBI team was making hurried phone calls and sending hundreds of emails to the media, getting his face plastered in as many newscasts, newspapers, hospitals, and internet sites as possible. They had given the media all of the details. He had been stabbed in the upper chest, and shot in the mid section or upper thigh, and would be walking with a painful limp.

Jessica didn't necessarily like the fact that they were single-handedly causing mass pandemonium through the media, but there was little she could do about any of it. It was all out of her hands. She was now a victim. She was now related to this case as much as any other victim involved in her investigation. She had now been beaten.

"What about this? Have you ever seen this before?" Agent McKay asked, dangling Brian Hotz's diary in front of her. He was a kind man, but took his job very seriously. He was being professional, and trying to understand things wilder than he had ever heard in his life.

"I... I don't know," she answered. "What is it?"

"Looks like a diary to me."

"I don't know what it is. I've never seen it before."

"Do you think it was his?"

"Maybe," she said. "I don't know... I do have reasons to believe that he is in love with me. Maybe he wanted me to understand him somehow. I don't know. I don't know what's in it."

"Well, we'll find out soon enough," he said, and handed the book over to another agent. "So... I'm sorry, one more time. You were sleeping, you didn't hear anything out in the hallway until your door was kicked in, and then?"

She sighed and went through it again. She hated repeating herself. She wasn't worried about the book. She had destroyed the letter in disgust and flushed it down the toilet. They would undoubtably find her prints all over the cover, but how could she be expected to remember the exact details of such a traumatic event? She was sleeping when he attacked. She was startled, and confused. For all she knew, he had knocked her clean off her feat with the book.

She wondered if that was cowardice of her, or if it really mattered either way?

It was what it was.
Meaningless.

The killer was still out there.
With the adrenaline now almost completely dissipated from her system, she was beginning to feel the pain of the beating she had taken. Every breath felt like she was being stabbed in the side of her chest. Every word felt like her face was splitting open a little more. She was exhausted, and she could barely think clearly anymore.

Agent McKay's phone suddenly rang. He pulled it out of his pocket and stared at it for a moment, then jumped to action.

"All right people," he raised his voice above the room. "We've got an address."

"Where?" Jessica asked.

"About ten blocks away. On one forty ninth and fiftieth."

"I'm coming!" she demanded.

"Sorry, Detective, but you are in no shape for a raid. No offense, but we need you safe. We'll update you as soon as we can," he said. "All right, come on people, let's get this son of a bitch."

And just like that, Jessica was left in that big room, on her cold seat, bloodied, and swollen, and filled with festering emotions. She stared at the absent face of Clinton Fisher on the computer screen. From behind her, Captain Briar gently placed his hand on her shoulder.

"How are you doing, Jessie? Do you need anything?"

"I'm fine," she sniffled. "I just want to nail this asshole so badly."

"I know, I know," he said. "But this is the FBI. This thing is now officially being handled their way. We are only here to assist."

"It's bullshit," he scoffed.

"Is it? Christ almighty, you escaped death tonight by a stroke of pure chance. What if he had carried a gun, or had a key to your room? What if... What if..."

"I don't worry about what ifs, Captain," she cut him off. "I'm sorry, but nothing you're saying has happened. I could be dead, but I am not. I am alive. I am sore, but I am alive. The danger has passed already."

He stared at her swollen face and could not for the life of him shake the terror from his soul.

"I am sorry, Jessica," he said. "But this needs to end. It needs to end immediately, before anyone else is hurt. You do not have to do everything yourself, my poor girl. I know you like to do things your way, but this is different. This needs to be resolved, and at any cost. I hope you can understand."

"I do," she said, reluctantly. "I'm just tired. I'm... I'm so pissed off. Not... Not at you... It's at myself."

Captain Briar said nothing and rubbed her shoulder reassuringly.

"You did your absolute best, and that is all that matters," he said. "This will all be over soon, I promise. With any luck, they'll blast the bastard out of bed in about five minutes."

She took a deep breath and stared at the floor. She was so tired. She wanted to crawl into a hole and shut down for a while. A pain induced hibernation.

"Listen," Captain Briar continued. "Let's go down to Anna's. We'll get ourselves some coffee and breakfast, and we'll try and forget all about this for a little while, huh? We'll talk about everything but work. They'll only update us after they are done processing what they have anyway. We may as well go and enjoy this fine morning in the face of helpless anticipations. Call it a little celebration of your survival."

She stared at him, trying to smile. He smiled back at her with warm eyes. He was trying his best to comfort her in the face of unending personal and professional disappointments.

"You don't want to talk about the case?"

"No," he said. "I want to talk about you. I want to talk about me. I want to talk about the weather, and our dreams, and our goals, and our thoughts on everything except for this very horrible case. Deal?"

"Deal," she agreed. "I could use some food. And some rest, too, I suppose."

"We'll come back in better shape to receive their information," Captain Briar said, and Jessica smiled again. If there was ever a quality she could somehow inherit from her Captain, she would chose his ability for eternal optimism. He was always concentrating on the future, never the past.

She laboriously stood up from her hard steel chair and smiled again with furrowed eyebrows.

"What is it?" Captain Briar asked.

"Well..." she said. "At least I half killed him. How's that for optimism?"

"It's very good indeed," he said with a chuckle. "Everything is still very good indeed."

CHAPTER 28

The sun shone brightly above the usual morning rush hour mishmash. They sat and sipped on freshly poured coffee, scanning the menu.

"They make a mean ham omelette here," Captain Briar said. "Worth every penny."

Jessica smiled, but her face hurt too much to sustain it. She didn't care about the endless stream of pedestrian vagabonds giving her strange looks. It wasn't everyday, after all, that a person walked into their favorite coffee shop and saw an otherwise beautiful woman sitting there with a face beaten to a pulp like nothing was wrong.

Jessica liked their waitress. She was a young girl, giddy, and was doing her best to pretend like there was nothing wrong with Jessica's face.

"I think I'll just go for regular bacon and eggs," Jessica said.

"Yeah? Well, it's unanimous then," Captain Briar said. "Ham omelette it is for me."

The waitress took their orders with a warm smile and disappeared into the kitchen.

"So I was thinking about taking a vacation this year," Captain Briar said.

"Where to?" she asked.

"I'm not sure. Maybe the Caribbean. I've always wanted to visit Jamaica. I think it would be nice for Melissa and I. We haven't had a true holiday in a long time, what with all those new grandchildren and everything."

"I think that's a good idea," Jessica replied, thinking about her Captain's recent troubles with his own mind in the face of atrocities they weren't supposed to talk about now. "It would do you guys some good to get away. See a new country. Swim in the ocean. Spend some quality time together."

"Yeah," he replied. "I think we will. We used to be quite adventurous in our younger days, of course, but life always has a way of keeping you closer and closer to home as your age gets to higher numbers."

"I suppose so," she answered. "Your family keeps getting bigger every year."

"That, plus Melissa has problems leaving for extended periods of time without seeing her grandchildren. It's as though she has lived her entire life just to get to this very moment; to enjoy her grandchildren with her own children. It's very beautiful if you ask me."

Jessica smiled and nodded silently. His family was getting bigger and bigger. Hers had already whittled down to nothing by the ripe young age of twenty nine.

"Why don't you get away for a little while?" he asked her. "Me?" she said. "Well, I don't know. I've never really given it any thought. Where would I go by myself? A resort?"

"Perhaps a backpacking trip," he suggested.
"Like living out of hostels in foreign countries and stuff?"

"Well, not necessarily on those terms, but yes, that's the idea."

She liked that idea. She had never thought of backpacking another country before. She was always so focussed on her career, catching all kinds of disturbed individuals prowling through her city's streets. She had never considered what kind of experience might be waiting for her out there in the great big world.

"I think I might," she said. "I mean, I'll think about it. I've always wanted to go to Australia, or maybe Thailand. Ha, who knows? We'll see I suppose."

Captain Briar held her gaze for a moment. He was hoping that she would give it honest consideration. He figured she was young enough, and still without the endless responsibilities most young parents her age were faced with. She was free to go, and do as she pleased.

"It might do you some good to see the world. Get out of this foul place and visit some distant city without ever even thinking about the killers there. None of it is of your concern. You are a free agent in the world."

"Yeah," she replied. "I think you may be right, Captain. Maybe... Maybe after everything that has happened, I should just go for a while. Forget about my life, and just let the winds take me wherever they please. You are a smart man, Captain."

"Nah," he said. "I hide behind the cloak of experience. Ha! Ha! I'm just as big a fool as the next guy when it comes to the unknown. But I do know life. I better by my age. I'm an old man, you know?"

"Ha! Ha!" Jessica giggled. "You are kind of old," she teased. "But that doesn't make it a bad thing, does it? Being old? Having lived?"

"Well... I suppose not. It's a bad thing when I first wake up in the morning, I'll tell you that much. Ha! Ha! Ha!"

They laughed, and then feel into a moment of silence. Jessica looked around the room, watching people swarm in for coffees and breakfasts to go. The modern rituals of life. The superficial. The fake.

"To be honest, kiddo," Captain Briar began again. "I am thinking of... Well, I'm thinking of..." He stopped and sighed heavily while Jessica waited patiently for him to compose himself. "I'm sorry. Even I'm still trying to come to terms with it. What I am trying to tell you, is that I think I may retire after this case."

Jessica was surprised even though she had fully expected it. In all of his years of experience, nothing had ever come close to shaking him, but in a single sideswiping event, the man's very foundation had been obliterated.

"Really?" she replied.

He smiled, mostly out of embarrassment. It felt and sounded weak to the poor old Captain. It sounded like he was giving up and running away.

"Yeah," he replied shyly. "I think so. I think I've done all that I can do in this line of work. I don't think I understand the world anymore. Your generation is unlike anything any of us could have expected. There is no decency left. There is no consideration for others. Hell, some days I'm hard pressed to find any kindness around me at all. I... I think that if I don't understand, then how could I possibly be effective in my career? I don't think that I can be."

Jessica felt bad for Captain Briar. It wasn't his fault. He was feeling disconnected, and inadequate, and incapable.

Human.

"Captain," Jessica said. "Your experience is unfaltering, and it is priceless out there on those streets. I get what you are saying, about how different my generation is compared to the generations before it, but you are not out of touch. Humans are still the same, regardless of the changing landscape. Your generation fought for freedom. My generation fights for reasons even they do not understand. Yours was a generation of repression. Mine is one of expression, which is often a worse thing. When everyone is free to express themselves in any way they please, egos swell, and what's to stop anyone from developing a need to express themselves in ways that we have seen lately, but are not allowed to talk about right now because of our deal?"

Captain Briar chuckled.

"But really," she continued. "Everyone seems to think that my generation is generation me, and generation now, and they are proud of it, but they ignore the one major side-effect to it all."

"And what's that?" he asked.

"Psychological loss," she said. "When everyone is free to do, and be anything they please, they often forget about just being themselves. My generation is one of loss. It is one of hope so big that no one can truly define, or even act on. It is irrational, and it has been sugarcoated and improperly named. My generation, is generation lost. There is no real problem with people's expressions of freedom or individuality, the real problem, is in people not realizing that they cannot be rock stars, and movie stars, and revered gods all at once. We're all here for a finite amount of time. The problem is psychological, and human, and despite the landscape changing from one generation to the next, it has always been the exact same problem. People think much too highly of themselves, and all of it is in the hope of garnering superficial attention."

Captain Briar smiled and sipped on his coffee.

"My girl," he said. "How do you see things so clearly?"

"I don't know," she said.

"That's what makes you so great at what you do, Jessica. I give you a single thought that I cannot really define, and you give me a dissertation that is dead on in a matter of seconds. You truly have an amazing gift."

"Ha, thanks, Cap," she replied. "But it's not my fault."

"That's why it's so special," he said.

The waitress came hustling to their table with hot plates of steaming food. She was very friendly and made Captain Briar think of what Jessica had just told him.

"And there you go," the spicy waitress said. "You guys need anything else? More coffee or anything?"

"I think we're all right for now, thank you very much." Captain Briar said.

"All right then, enjoy," she said, and immediately moved on to tend to other tables.

Jessica was hungry. She was exhausted, and beaten, and frustrated

"Looks good," she said.

"I can always count on this place. It has never failed me." Captain Briar replied.

They fell into momentary silence while they both began picking at their food. Jessica was just about to speak again when Captain Briar's phone rang and he quickly answered.

His face contorted while he listened, flushed with confusion, and disappointment. All he ever said was, "Uh huh... Uh huh... Okay... Anything else?" When the call was over, he put his phone away with a brute disturbance on his face. He silently stared at her for a long time, almost like he was looking right through her.

"What is it? Is everything okay?"

"That was the FBI," he said, as though suddenly being snapped out of deep thought. "They ah... They raided his place."

"And?"

"And..." He hesitated.

"Was he there?" she asked urgently.

"He wasn't home," he replied. "He... Jesus Christ, Jessica, they said the entire place is destroyed, just like the crime scenes. Everything is broken and shattered. They found some kind of building in his bedroom built out of debris from his apartment. They said they found huge amounts of blood in the bathtub, on the walls, and the floors–everywhere."

"We have to get over there!" she declared.

"Wait," Captain Briar said. "There's more."

"What?"

"Jessica... They... They found some type of shrine in there."

"A shrine?"

"Your shrine," he said.

"My shrine?"

"Apparently," he answered. "There's a wall filled with pictures of you, clipped from newspapers, and internet sites. Jesus, Jessie... We have to stop this. You are in great danger here."

"Captain, please, I can end..."

Captain Briar's phone rang again.

"I'm sorry, Jessica, just let me grab this."

He answered the phone, and his face instantly returned to a featureless mask of confusion.

"Thank you," was all he said in response to the voice coming from his phone, and hung up.

"What is it?" she asked.

"Um... They ah... They found a body," he answered.

"What? Where?"

"A woman with her throat punctured like the others," he said. "She's been horribly mutilated, and probably tortured. He... He stuffed her in the bottom of his storage room. Jesus Christ... What are we going to do?"

"I need to see her," Jessica said, determined again. "Was she cut like the others?"

"They couldn't really tell,"

"Why not?"

"She's decomposed," he said. "They... They won't know how long she's been dead for some time."

Jessica stared directly into Captain Briar's face. He was terrified again. His nerves shot. He was much less eager to see the disaster than she was.

"Jessica... You have to stay hidden. This isn't a game anymore. This is real. He is actively trying to kill you. I mean, Christ, he's already killed two officers, and damn near murdered you. We have to let the FBI do what it is that they do. They will catch him. They will put an end to it all. And they can also offer better protection for you, which, I'm sorry, Jessie, but I have already agreed for them to arrange. I know you may hate it, but it's for your own good. Never kill yourself at the cost of another person, right?... Right?... Jessica?"

She was staring out the window like a cat stalking an unsuspecting bird.

"What is it?" Captain Briar asked, and he too began scanning the direction she was so focussed on. "Jessica? What are you looking at?"

"He's right there," she said, stunned.
"What?" Captain Briar stood up in a panic. "Where?"

"Sit down!" she demanded. "You'll attract attention. He has no idea I'm here. He's right there, on the other side of the street. See that guy with the ratty trench coat hobbling through the crowd?"

"Son of a bitch!" Captain Briar said. "Are you sure that's him?"

"Oh, I'm sure," she replied. "I could pick that bastard out from a concert crowd. That's him."

"I need to call the FBI back... Jessica!" he screamed after her as she whizzed passed him in a flash. "Goddamn it, Jessica! Don't! Stay here! Stay here!"

She was gone and running across the street like a cheetah with her prey in sight. She was going in for the kill.

"Fuck!" Captain Briar said, and ran after her while simultaneously trying to call the FBI back. Agent McKay answered on the other end.

"We've got him!" Captain Briar urged. "Get a team back down here, just down the street from the precinct, a little restaurant called Anna's, he's right across the street. Please,

please hurry. Detective Sanders is already after him and I can't stop her now. We need back up immediately!"

The agent said that they would be there in two minutes flat. Captain Briar hung up and ran even faster. He could see the back of Jessica's head bobbing in and out of the crowded sidewalk in front of him. He wanted to scream after her, but he could also see that far ahead, the man in the ratty trench coat was still unaware of Jessica's approaching attack.

Suddenly, he heard her voice rip through the busy street like thunder.

"Freeze, asshole!" Immediately, the trench coat frantically escaped inside the nearest building as Jessica shot two rounds at him. She missed.

The building was a huge warehouse that served as the base of operation for over thirty transportation companies. It was very loud, and dirty. It stunk like grease and dust, and from all directions, busy bodies hummed and rushed.

"Shit," Jessica said. She knew that it wasn't a great situation. There was too much noise and movement to be able to hone in on where he might be hiding; where he might be waiting for her.

It wasn't long before Captain Briar came crashing through the door behind her, completely out of breath. Jessica instantly spun around and pointed her gun, then lifted it.

"He's in here, Captain... Somewhere."
"Jessica, leave now! That's an order, goddamn it! The FBI is coming. Just go. There is no reason to kill yourself. They will handle it."

"Fuck the FBI," she said. "I've got him. If I leave, he'll get away again. He is not getting away from me again. Not again!"

"Jessica, please..."

"There!" she yelled, and pounced after him again. The trench coat was running away from her through crowds of forklifts and workers looking about themselves in confusion. The dangers were far from being solely at the hands of her killer. She dodged slow moving pallets and flying forklifts rounding blind corners, never daring to take her eyes off of him.

Captain Briar had started running after her, but lost her in a few seconds behind loads of freight being moved around. He turned and ran back outside, where he found dozens of official government vehicles scattered across the street and sidewalk. Frantic pedestrians were pointing and yelling about having heard gunshots.

Captain Briar waved, and an entire army of drawn guns approached him with fascinating speed.

"Where is he?" Agent McKay asked.

"In there!" Captain Briar urged. "Please, Detective Sanders is after him alone in that goddamned mess. He's going to kill her the first chance he gets, and who knows how many others in the process."

"We got it!" the agent answered. "Move in, guys."

The team of agents swarmed the building like angry wasps looking for an intruder. Captain Briar could hear them from outside yelling for everyone to stop and immediately evacuate the building. He couldn't stand it. He couldn't just leave her in there by herself. Not his own adopted daughter. Not Jessica.

He ran down the sidewalk, heading for the other side of the building as fast as he could, his gun still ready and cocked tightly in his hand.

His heart was racing so fast, he thought it was about to rip right through his rib cage. He ran with burning legs, fueled purely by a sickening fear.

Jessica still hadn't heard the agents. She was completely focussed, getting closer to him with every step. He was having even more difficulty getting around the frantic movements of the warehouse than she was, mostly due to the injuries he'd sustained at her hands. She didn't think he had another escape in him. He wouldn't last much longer. She would. She couldn't even feel a thing except for a numb tingling in her limbs.

The killer bumped into the back of a forklift and screamed in agony, but he continued moving as quickly as he could. He was desperate, and he could see a wall coming up in front of him. He darted for it with everything he had. Jessica swerved around a yelling man, and bounced off a flying pallet. She was so close. So close.

She saw sunlight appear ahead, and arrived just in time

to see him smash through a door. She jumped over a bundle of pipes, but missed her landing and fell to the filthy floor.

"Shit!" she screamed, but was instantly back to her feet, smashing through the door with her gun drawn and her finger on the trigger.

The door flew open violently, and she tripped right over him. The trench coat man, The Fleshcrafter, he was hunched over on the ground as if suffering in intense pain. Jessica lifted her gun and shot him in the back without a moment's hesitation.

His body tensed like he was being electrocuted, and then limped over to the side, and Jessica... Jessica couldn't breathe.

"What... What the hell?" she snorted. "What the fuck? No. No. No. No. No."

She rushed to the ground, pushed the killer's body over, and cradled Captain Briar's head in her arms.

"What? What are you doing here? What the... Ah, God, no! God, no! Huh huh huh huh huh! You motherfucker!"

She was overwhelmed with a type of rage that could not properly be expressed with words. It was delusional. It was... It was blind.

She stood up and kicked the killer in the ribs. "You like that?! Do you like it, you piece of shit?!"

She couldn't breathe. She couldn't focus. Was he breathing? Was... Was he breathing?

She bent over and shoved the killer on his back. His eyes were open. He wasn't completely aware, but he wasn't quite unconscious either. Not yet. He was still alive.

"You son of a bitch!" she snarled. "You ruined everything in my life for me! Everything! And for what? Huh? What goddamn it?!"

His breath was heavily labored and gurgled with blood. He was dying.

Jessica crouched, leaned over, and held her face inches away from his.

"Now I want to see your nothing!" she hissed. "Show me, you monster!"

She felt her forearm press down on his throat. She felt his muscles tighten, and his body stiffen, but it wasn't enough to stop her from putting the brunt of her weight against his Adam's apple. She heard him trying to gurgle sickeningly. See did nothing but stare into his eyes.

"I promised you, didn't I?" she whispered. "Now show me."

She lost sight of everything else around her. She was enveloped in his darkness, in his empty eyes. She watched as his heart took its final pump, and his body attempted a final twitch. She watched it leave.

Life. Whatever it was.

She watched his eyes go out gradually like lanterns with dried wicks. There wasn't even darkness anymore. There wasn't a sense of personality, or consciousness. There was exactly what Clinton Fisher had said there was.

There was nothing.

Savage.

She fell back to the ground, crying. She cried harder than she had ever done in her life. Harder than over the loss of her parents, or her own sister. She cried in the blood covered dirt while the team of agents swarmed around her and checked the bodies for pulses. She already knew–they were both dead.

Captain Briar had been stabbed in the chest, in the heart. An instant kill. Clinton Fisher, she had killed–personally. He was gone forever.

They were gone forever.

The agents hounded her with fast questions, and tried grabbing at her flailing arms, but Jessica squirmed like a child throwing a fit.

"No! Leave me alone! Leave me alone, huh huh huh huh." She couldn't even hear what anyone was saying. She felt like she was trapped inside a cocoon. In shock. Far away. Distant. Unreal.

Brian Hotz.

She sat and cried, and stared at the ground while paramedics carrying red planks and yellow medic bags took the bodies away.

Once she began to calm down and breathe normally, she allowed the medics to have a look at her. Physically, she was fine. No serious trauma, but she was in a state of shock, and needed proper rest.

She was brought to a hotel fully rented by visiting federal

agents. She hadn't slept a wink. She hadn't even tried. All she could do was cry.

She had a hot shower and tried to calm herself. Every time she thought of Captain Briar, another piece of her soul was cruelly devastated by reality, but she couldn't think of anything else.

She couldn't accept it. At any moment, her phone would ring, and it would be Captain Briar's eternally friendly voice telling her that she was needed at such and such an address, for such and such a crime.

It wasn't real. He was at home with his family. Relaxing, and telling stories to his grandchildren, making their eyes grow big with love, and happiness, and security.

It wasn't real.

She eventually turned off the water, dried herself, and crawled into bed. She stared at the TV, but didn't care what was on. She closed her eyes, and right before drifting off to a land of less pain and less awareness, she had one thought left in her mind.

She would never have thought that one day she would be wishing that the Fleshcrafter was not dead. That her Captain would call her with another victim. That he would be terrified far beyond reason. That he would be worried, and losing confidence in his work. Anything. Anything, but what was... Well... Was.

"It's all my fault," she whispered. "I'm so sorry, Captain. I'm so, so fucking stupid."

She took a final deep breath, and escaped to somewhere no one will ever be able to truly explain.

CHAPTER 29

The FBI agents told Jessica that Captain Briar had gone to the other side of the building in an effort to intercept the killer. Judging by the way he had pleaded for their help on the sidewalk, they assumed he had been quite frantic, and unfocussed.

The best they could come up with was logical speculation. He had come around the building, gun in hand, but was probably surprised when the killer crashed through the door and knocked into him. In a panic, the killer stabbed him in the chest. Death was instant.

She still couldn't believe it. How could it have happened? What was she supposed to do? She felt helpless, and miserably lost. The only thing she wished for was the ability to turn back time. She wished that she could go back and listen to her Captain for once, and take his guidance to heart.

She couldn't rationalize, or deny any of it. He had died because of her own young naivety. Her young, stupidly massive ego. She thought that she should have been the one who had died, not him. Not such a great man as Captain Briar.

The guilt was unbearable. It was so ugly, and concentrated. Ahead of her, she could only see years worth of asking empty walls for forgiveness, knowing that no one could hear her, or reverse the harsh reality of it in any way.

After the agents had escorted her from the terrible scene, Jessica spent three days in a hotel room, wallowing in emotional pain. Torture. The events were no one's fault but her own, and the thought of it was enough to make her rabidly nauseous.

"His poor family!"

She must have said it a million times, yet each time was no less painful than the last.

"His poor, ripped off family."

Too much guilt.

She tried keeping busy, keeping her mind occupied with other dilemmas not so ominous, or depleting, but it did nothing to help. She couldn't get the faces of Captain Briar's wife, and kids, and grandkids out of her troubled mind. She could see them so vividly devastated, so ugly with unrelenting pain.

She thought of his grandchildren. Because of her actions, those kids would have to grow up without their loving grandfather, without his wisdom, and advice. They would see no more of his smiling face filling a room with love, with safety. No more of his eyes beaming with satisfaction, and happiness. No more of his knowing the difference between what was worth it in life, and what was not.

No more of anything.

When she attended the funeral, a mere four days after his death, she felt like a lance had pierced her heart. Something inside of her had ruptured. Something had died.

Captain Briar's wife, Melissa, had tried reassuring Jessica that the death was not her fault. She told her that sometimes things just happened, that it was all part of God's plan, and that although they had no way of seeing it, there was a reason somewhere.

Jessica refused all of it.

There were no reasons. There was no plan. She had fucked up, and he had paid for it, that was the end of the story.

It was all so absolute. It was all so hard.

After the funeral, she took an indefinite leave of absence from work, and headed on a ten hour road trip to a cabin she rented for a month. The cabin was set on the shore of a calm and beautiful lake, and sufficiently far enough from everything familiar.

It was peaceful, hidden, and alone.

Having played through the events for the millionth time in her mind, she was now staring out the window of her cabin at the thick fog hovering over the lake. The sun was slowly dissipating the fog and exposing a thing of beauty beneath. A thing many people called God. A thing that caused many people to see something of meaning, some type of connection, no matter how indefinable.

Jessica raised her hand and rubbed the back of her neck. Her entire body was sore. It was sore from being beaten by a monster. It was sore from the loss of her entire family. It was sore from thinking about what she had done to Captain Briar's family–what she had done to the Captain himself. It was unforgivable.

She watched as a flock of ducks landed in the water. They were so free and unbothered by anything aside from casual hunger. No family. No rat race to live in. No depression.

Nothing but bliss, ignorance, and food.

She watched as they played with one another, and chased after food. She wished that she could be a duck. She wished that she could be anything else but herself.

She wondered what she was going to do.

She rubbed the back of her neck again, cocked it sideways, and felt it crack. The skin felt irritated. It felt as angry as she was.

She watched the ducks splash away, and soon found herself thinking about Brian Hotz, or Clinton Fisher, or the Fleshcrafter. The savage monster son of a bitch who had taken everything from her. The one who had caused her unshakable mind to crumble and fall in shame, and anger, and a debilitating confusion she had never before known.

His real name had been exactly what she had guessed it was, Clinton Fisher, and as far as his diary was concerned, every word of it had been true... To a certain extent.

She was angry with herself over the fact that she never did get the opportunity to actually speak to him about any of it. She had secretly hoped that he would emerge as a bumbling fool, completely unable to keep in touch with the reality around him. A psychological assessment of the kind most psychology students would only dream of. A deranged, disillusioned, and dangerous man still operating out there in society under the same rules as the rest of us, and getting away with it. Any student would have loved to interview someone so batshit crazy. So evil.

Clinton Fisher had not only been dangerously insane, and purely evil, he had also been astonishingly intelligent. Even in pure insanity, it seemed, intelligence could still prevail.

The Fleshcrafter had been the most difficult offender she had ever chased down. She also knew that in over 30 years of experience, Captain Briar had shared the exact same opinion. The killer had been cunning, and skillfully evasive, but those hadn't been the reasons for her difficulty in apprehending him. The difficulty had come from the fear he evoked in her, and in Captain Briar, and in the rest of the residents of the city. It was a doom so pervasive, and psychologically imminent, it caused purely irrational reactions in an attempt to fight against it. It was the most basic of all human emotions, and despite her training, and her beliefs, she hadn't been immune from it in any way. She had fought fire with fire, taken a tooth for a tooth, an eye for an eye. An idea of justice.

Foolish.

She had killed him in cold blood. She had shot him, and then cut off the air struggling laboriously through his windpipe. She had watched his nothing take him away.

It had disturbed her more than anything she had ever seen in her life. Not the murder, she had seen plenty of murder, it was the nothing. The void. The black. The non-existence.

It was all so unbearable. So... Empty.

She stretched out her arms and rubbed the back of her neck again. She was so angry, and frustrated.

Whenever she closed her eyes, she could see his eyes cloud over horribly all over again. She could see Captain Briar's limp head cradled in her arms, his eyes already blank, already dead. She could feel the pressure building up in her chest again, chocking out her lungs, forcing tears from her eyes.

She allowed tiny tears to stream down her cheeks. From the open window, she could smell fresh air coming into the cabin. There was no air like that in a city. It smelled so pure, so clean, and even a little alien.

She wondered about what she could ever do to make it up to Captain Briar's family. Was there anything? There wasn't. There was nothing for her to do but stare at the lake from her cabin, and cry, and try to stop thinking about it, and then cry some more when it was wholly apparent that she never would stop playing it through her mind. Not now. Not ever.

She would never come to terms with it, never accept it as something that had just happened and couldn't have been helped. She would never escape the fact that it was her fault. She was alone, lonely, and scared.

She was scared.

She noticed the ducks moving on farther across the lake. The fog was almost completely lifted from the water, as though an incoming doom had suddenly decided to retreat and wait for another day before unleashing its wrath.

She felt like that fog; like she was dissipating, and disappearing into thin air. She felt a dark, threatening doom, not only hovering above her head, but breaching inside of her too. It was infecting her and spreading like a ravenous virus. She felt defeated, and lost. She felt what Brian Hotz, or Clinton Fisher, had felt for all those years.

Worthlessness.

She now understood his ugly diary, and found herself surprised to be agreeing with him. No one should ever be aware of such a debilitating emptiness. No one should be tortured by their own mind, reeling with horrors both real and imagined.

To be human is often unbearable.

Choking on her tears, she wished she had never read Clinton Fisher's words. It angered her that the same person who had written them was also responsible for ripping all sense of family away from her. He had destroyed her life; he had destroyed her.

She rubbed her neck again. It was really starting to irritate her. It was starting to piss her off, even though she knew it wasn't the true cause of all of her hate, and anger, and loathing. All of that was directed at herself. She had failed. She had failed more grossly than ever, and she hated herself for it.

She hated herself so much.

It was causing her to seriously ponder the human condition. What did it all mean? It was an awareness that was universal, and yet alien at the same time. It was happiness, and sadness, and kindness, and malice in unbalanced amounts. And in the end, when all things settled down and consciousness was set free into the universe, what was left was as... Nothing. No effect. No meaning. It was all gone.

Over the course of her career, she had seen a lot of murder, and hate, and evil, and plainly grotesque examples of conscious destruction. And in her personal life, she had seen love, and happiness, and kindness, and caring for others, even between complete strangers. She had seen both sides of the fence. She had seen the faithful pray, the atheists scoff, the kind help, the evil murder, the happy smile, and the saddened cry. She had seen it, and experienced it all. From the seeming light hearted zeal of pure bliss, to the dark, ominous empty of complete depression. She had covered the complete spectrum of the human condition more than once in her young age, and it all still seemed to boil down to a single truth in the end.

What did any of it matter?

Whether your life was filled with good luck, or bad, or you've suffered, or prospered, or made tons of money, or lived in poverty, or were happy, or sad, or depressed, or eccentric–what difference did any of it make?

She had seen enough of the good and the bad in life to be able to have an answer about what the human condition truly meant–but she did not. Not now. Not ever.

It just didn't seem to matter either way.

She sighed and shook her head. Brian Hotz had been correct, there was no answer to anything, not in any direction, and not for anyone. It was all just a big joke.

Fucking hilarious.

We were all born the same, shared the same universal emotions, and we all died the same. That was the true extent of everyone's knowledge. Anything beyond that was imagination, and nothing but.

She remembered a story her father had told her when she was a little girl.

He'd said, "There are a lot of bad people in the world, and there are just as many good people, but there is something you always need to remember in life. Even good people sometimes do bad things, sometimes even by accident, but regardless of if they are good or bad, if they break the law, they all end up in prison. And prison is a very bad place where everyone has to live together, and eat to together, and even shower together. And here's what I always want you to remember, sweetie, because it is very important. I want you to remember that when all of those people, the good, the bad, the unfortunate, the rich, the poor, the healthy, the sick, when they are all crammed into a small room to shower with no clothes on... What's the difference?"

She remembered staring at him for a long time after that. It had been a dramatic story for a little girl, but he understood then what she did now. Without the dramatic, nobody ever listens. His message had been clear, and she had never forgotten it.

"Don't ever think you are better than anyone," he had said. "You are better than no one, and no one is better than you. On some basic level, we are all exactly the same. If you ever do feel superior to anyone, I want you to put yourself into those showers. Imagine yourself pressed up naked against hundreds of other naked people, and have an imaginary look around. What difference does your social status make to anything of value?"

Thinking about her father, she suddenly burst into a fit of tears. She felt as though her soul was being torn to shreds. She felt her body convulse, and her bruised ribs rattling inside of her chest in sheer pain. She felt like her head was swollen, and her heart was about to rip out of her chest. She felt like she was about to collapse and cease to exist forever, and no one alive would ever know the difference. She no longer knew anyone alive.

Her neck was on fire while she cried. It was bothering her more than anything now. It was irritating, and frustrating, and making her feel like she wanted to destroy the entire cabin with her bare hands, and then set it on fire.

Her body trembled uncontrollably.
She reached up and rubbed the back of her neck one last time, and finally decided to lift the noose back over her head, and carefully step down from the creaky chair. She fell to the floor in a gasping fit of tears, her body convulsing violently.

"Fuck!" she screamed as loud as she could. "Fuck you! Fuck you!"

She felt tears pour out of her, but they were no longer solely tears of sadness, they were now part of a grander rush of emotions. Happiness, sadness, guilt, pride, shame, hate, fear, confusion, love, pain...

Human.

They were the tears of the human condition. She realized that in a world filled with so many seeming absolutes, it seemed holistically impossible to find a point to it all, but even worse, it seemed holistically impossible to ever deny one either.

None of it ever changed. Ever. It was the same for the first humans as it was today. Her answers regarding the meaning of life had always been correct. It was that all of it, the emotions, the universe, the people, the pain, the happiness, the confusion, all of it just... Was.

It just was, and that was the end of the story. No other explanation was ever offered or needed, because where would the point be with all of the answers in hand?

She cried, sprawled out on the floor, feeling every emotion possible rip through her at the same time. She cried, and cried, and punched at the floor, and then cried some more.

She stared at the folded note on the table. That note was supposed to be her suicide note. It was meant to be her final words to a very cruel, and very unforgiving reality. She grabbed it and opened it, shaking her head in despair.

"You idiot!" she cursed herself.

On the page were two simple words that explained everything she had been feeling to anyone interested. She stared at it for a long time, still panting, and letting the tears wash down the sides of her face.

All the note said was:

"Fuck it."

CHAPTER 30

"I would like to thank everyone for coming today, as it is a rather special day for myself, as well as for a very dear friend of mine. I know these things are usually formal, but I would like to speak to you about the recent events in my life that have caused me to be standing before you today."

Jessica was the guest of honor. She was delivering a speech to a packed house of colleagues, superiors, and media hounds about the current state of affairs in her city. She was being honored with a medal for her bravery and talent in her respected field, but Jessica was there for one purpose alone. She was there to honor her best friend, her mentor, and her honorary father, Captain Briar.

"As you are all aware, our city has recently been host to one of the most prolific, dangerous, and disturbing serial killer our nation has ever known. We have been through incredible hardships, and many families in this city have lost loved ones... Including myself. But I am very pleased to announce to all of you here, and at home, and across the country, that this killer's reign has been put to an end."

The crowd applauded loudly, and the camera flashes momentarily blinded her vision.

"I would like to take this opportunity to truly honor the real hero behind all of this. The one who made all of this possible with his sheer determinism, hope, and honest belief in the goodness of mankind, is my dearly beloved friend, mentor, and personal hero, Captain Briar."

The crowd erupted in another fit of approving claps.

"Captain Briar was a man of many facets. He was a kind, intelligent, faithful, and hopelessly dedicated officer, leader, husband, father, and grandfather. Without Captain Briar, without his direction and his taking me under his wing from my very first day as a detective, I cannot presume that I, or the department, would have been able to efficiently track down such a killer and put an end to his savage killing spree. Everyone in this room has something to thank Captain Briar for, whether directly or indirectly. The man was a staple of decency, moral integrity, and leadership for the entire department, as well as for anyone who has had the privilege of knowing him personally."

The crowd applauded once again.

"I am honored to be here today, and I accept this medal on behalf of the city for catching the Fleshcrafter killer, but I cannot in good conscience do so without first making it very clear, that I am in no way the only one responsible in this case. This was a team effort, stretching all the way to the FBI's assistance in the matter. From the forensics teams, to the people answering the telephones and collecting tips, and all the way to each and every individual who calls this great city home, I thank you, and I accept this medal on your behalf. Thank you."

She received a standing ovation while photographers flashed their cameras, and reporters tried their best to gesture their rabid enthusiasm for an interview.

"Thank you very much. Thank you, Captain," she said, and shook hands with her superiors. Commissioner Dean congratulated Jessica and placed a platinum medallion around her neck. She flinched on the inside when the cloth of the necklace touched the back of her neck. The earlier incident in the cabin had left her with a keen sense of timid serenity. She had never attempted something so stupid in her life. She had never quite succeeded in honestly scaring herself quite so blatantly, and yet, she felt like she had learned something arcane.

After nearly killing herself, after crying sprawled out on the floor, staring at the stupidest suicide note she had ever heard of, something drastic happened inside of her. She spent hours on the floor with that note clutched tightly in her hands, her body convulsing in shame, in pain. She'd felt so vulnerable, and lost.

Eventually, she was able to compose herself. She grabbed the rope, and the note, and even the creaky cabin chair, and dumped them all into the fire pit outside and set them ablaze. She watched the flames, and suddenly found herself comparing her situation with the basic principles of nature. Through destruction comes new creations. She had felt the destruction, and the pain, and the chaos, and through it all, somehow, she had managed to feel a type of hope that she had never needed to find in herself before.

She'd spent the rest of that afternoon smoking cigarettes and taking long walks along the beach. She sat at the edge of a dock, not too far away from where the flock of ducks had landed, and let her feet dangle in the cool water.

Nature. It was so beautiful. It was so complex, and strong, and everlasting. For all intents and purposes, it was a miracle that something, or some force, had the ability to set off the chain reactions necessary to create such beauty.

Her cabin was tucked in between a long line of similar structures surrounding the lake, all housing a variety of young families, and retired couples, and visitors from everywhere, and yet, it was nothing like being in a city at all. There was an air of relaxation surrounding the place. A sense of vacation and worry free fun. It felt like when she was a little girl, chasing after her sister along the beach, camping with her now defunct family.

She thought she felt peaceful.

That evening, she ordered a grilled chicken sandwich from the very friendly waitress in the lodge's restaurant. Only smiling faces surrounded her there, and she savored the kindness, the side of humans she rarely got to see.

Once finished with her dinner, she chatted with a few of the locals, and then retired for a cigarette on the restaurant's veranda overlooking the lake. She'd felt so much better by then, accepting that she could do nothing about the past.

The moment she lit her cigarette, a man came around the corner of the veranda, puffing on his own cigarette, and sat on a chair across from her.

"Beautiful isn't it?" he said.

"So beautiful," she replied. "I've never been here before. The lake is gorgeous. The forest is peaceful. Even the people around here are... Well, they're relaxing... If that makes any sense."

He smiled.

"I know what you mean," he said. "This place has never changed much, which is a good thing. It should stay the way it is. Some places are just special, you know?"

"Yeah," she said. "I know exactly what you mean. This will probably be the most meaningful place in my life."

He stared at her kind of strangely.

"I'm sorry, I'm a total weirdo; but this place is special to me now."

She wasn't about to get into details with a complete stranger, but she had felt like there was something different about this man. He wasn't the same type of bumbling idiot she was used to meeting in the city. He was well built from hard work, and strong. His eyes radiated with an innate intelligence. They radiated happiness. She liked his big, genuine smile. For all intents and purposes, she thought that he was beautiful man.

They spent almost three hours talking on that veranda. There was no need to hurry. No need to get anywhere or do anything. They simply sat and enjoyed a simple conversation about each other.

She walked away thinking that she'd never quite felt that way before. Something was different. She hadn't thrown herself at him, or even given out strong overtones that she might like him. It had all been so simple; so clear and enjoyable.

The man's name was Jeremy Blaine, and he worked in the boat repair and tackle shop not too far away from her cabin. He was a mechanic, and spent his spare time restoring boats, solely for the love of it. He told her that if she ever did feel the compulsion to get out on the lake and do some fishing, that she should come and see him at the shop, and he would gladly take her out and show her the "hot spots", as he called them.

She hadn't been able to stop smiling around him. He had been kind, and genuine, and honest, and she went to see Jeremy Blaine only two days after they had met on the veranda, and went fishing with him in the late afternoon. Consequently, she spent every remaining day of her holiday with him. By the end of the month, she thought that maybe, somehow, she felt love.

It was very odd for her, feeling love for someone else. He hadn't been just some fling she'd had while at the lake, someone she would easily forget about the instant she left there; no, it was the beginning of love. She liked how close she felt to Jeremy Blaine. She liked how close he felt to her. She liked that she could talk to him about anything, at any time, and he would never judge her, or mock her, or even not listen to her. Jeremy Blaine listened. Jeremy Blaine was interested in Jessica as much as she was in him.

After a full month, she returned to the city, but promised Jeremy that it would not be long before they were together again. And almost like clock work, everything seemingly fell into place in the order that she needed.

Jessica never returned to her apartment. It had been destroyed, and it felt like going backward. Instead, she stayed in a hotel room, reorganized herself at work, and tried to adjust to not having Captain Briar around.

Only a few days into it, she suddenly had the overwhelming compulsion to begin looking into buying a house. She'd never wanted a house before, but for reasons unexplained, she felt like she should buy one and perhaps settle down, cement some roots in her life.

With pure luck, as much as she hated that word, the first house she liked from the real estate websites was situated about a block away from Captain Briar's house. She smiled when she saw it.

She bought the house and settled in in less than two months. Captain Briar's family was elated, and she became very good friends with his wife, Melissa, and his kids, and his grand kids. She regularly took the grand kids out to play at the local park, and spent time going through pictures of the Captain with his wife, and children. Jessica was instantly accepted as a family member. She loved them, and they loved her. They became as close as any other family could ever dream of being.

Another month or so after Jessica was settled in, Jeremy said that he wanted to see her more often. The next step was clear to her.

"Why don't you move in with me?" she asked him. "I've got this beautiful house here, and this beautiful family that has adopted me into theirs, and everything is going well, and... And I love you. I'm pretty sure I love you, and you mean everything to me, and I would really like it if this thing could be allowed to develop and take us wherever it goes."

There was little hesitation in his decision.

"You know, I love you too," he said. "Let's do it."

And just like that, her life was drastically altered, and for some reason, she never could deny the feeling that Captain Briar somehow had a hand in it all.

Somehow.

And now, she was standing before a room filled with people there to honor her work, and the work of Captain Briar. She was receiving a medal, and a promotion, and she vowed to make Captain Briar proud. Before every decision she would ever make over the course of her career, she promised to always ask the same question first.

"What would Captain Briar do?"

She stood on stage and stared at Jeremy. He was sitting with Captain Briar's family, her family, and there was nothing else that mattered to her.

In that cabin, Jessica learned the most important lesson of her life. It was that although some things may never be understood, and at times life may seem like nothing but hurdles that cause you to question why you are even alive, the one thing you can never do, is give up.

She thought Captain Briar would like that philosophy. It was a simple extension of her old one.

It is what it is.

Just keep going.

THE END.